THE WHITE ROSE MURDERS

THE WHITE ROSE MURDERS

Being the first journal of Sir Roger Shallot
concerning certain wicked conspiracies
and horrible murders perpetrated
in the reign of King Henry VIII

Michael Clynes

St. Martin's Press
New York

THE WHITE ROSE MURDERS. Copyright © 1991 by Michael Clynes.
All rights reserved. Printed in the United States of
America. No part of this book may be used or reproduced
in any manner whatsoever without written permission
except in the case of brief quotations embodied in critical
articles or reviews. For information, address St. Martin's
Press, 175 Fifth Avenue, New York, N.Y. 10010.

Library of Congress Cataloging-in-Publication Data

Clynes, Michael.
The white rose murders / Michael Clynes.
p.   cm.
ISBN 0-312-08920-1
1. Great Britain—History—Henry VIII, 1509–1547—Fiction.
2. Detectives—England—Fiction.   I. Title.
PR6053.L93W48   1993
823'.914—dc20   92-43889   CIP

First published in Great Britain by Headline Book Publishing PLC.

First U.S. Edition: March 1993
10 9 8 7 6 5 4 3 2

Foreword

In 1485 Richard III, the last Yorkist King, was killed at
Bosworth by Henry Tudor. Twenty-four years later the
Tudor's son, Henry VIII, began his reign: hailed as the
'golden boy', he promised to be a dazzling King but soon
the dark clouds of conspiracy, treason and murder were
visible. The bloodletting prophesied by seers and
magicians was about to begin, and the world was now
ready for Roger Shallot.

To my father, Michael

Historical Personages Mentioned in this Text

Richard III – The last Yorkist king, called the Usurper or Pretender. He was defeated by Henry Tudor at Market Bosworth in August 1485. He was the wearer of the White Rose, his personal emblem being *Le Blanc Sanglier* – the White Boar.

The Princes in the Tower – Nephews of Richard III, allegedly murdered by their uncle in 1484.

Henry Tudor – The Welshman. The victor of Bosworth, founder of the Tudor dynasty and father of Henry VIII and Margaret of Scotland. He died in 1509.

Henry VIII – Bluff King Hal or the Great Killer, he had six wives and a string of mistresses. He is the Mouldwarp or the Dark One as prophesied by Merlin.

Catherine of Aragon – A Spanish princess, Henry VIII's first wife and mother of Mary Tudor.

Anne Boleyn – Daughter of Sir Thomas Boleyn: 'A truly wicked man'. Second wife of Henry VIII and mother of Elizabeth Tudor.

Mary Boleyn – Anne's sister, nicknamed the English Mare at the French court, she had so many lovers.

Bessie Blount – One of the more dazzling of Henry VIII's mistresses.

Margaret Tudor – Henry VIII's sister, married to King James IV of Scotland and later to Gavin Douglas, Earl of Angus: 'Trouble in petticoats'.

Mary Tudor – Daughter of Catherine of Aragon and Henry VIII, nicknamed Bloody Mary because of her persecution of Protestants.

Elizabeth I – Queen of England, daughter of Henry VIII

and Anne Boleyn, nicknamed the Virgin Queen though Shallot claims to have had a son by her.

Catherine Howard − Henry VIII's fourth wife. Executed for her extra-marital affairs.

Francis I, King of France − Brilliant, dazzling and sex mad.

Will Shakespeare − English playwright.

Ben Jonson − English playwright.

Christopher Marlowe − English playwright and spy killed in a tavern brawl.

James IV of Scotland − First husband of Margaret Tudor.

Suleiman the Magnificent − Turkish Emperor.

Thomas Wolsey − Son of an Ipswich butcher, he went to Oxford and embarked upon a brilliant career. He became Cardinal, Archbishop and First Minister of Henry VIII.

Mary, Queen of Scots − Granddaughter of Margaret Tudor and mother of James I of England and Scotland.

Darnley − Husband of Mary, Queen of Scots.

Bothwell − Lover of Mary, Queen of Scots.

Thomas More − Humanist, scholar. Minister of Henry VIII, later executed for opposing Henry's divorce from Catherine of Aragon.

Edward VI − Son of Henry VIII and Jane Seymour, a sickly boy who died young.

The Earl of Surrey − One of the Howard clan. He fought for Richard III, was pardoned and proved to be Henry VIII's most capable general.

Prologue

Murder raps on my door every night. When the sky is dark and a hunter's moon hides behind the clouds, Murder sweeps up to this great manor house to kill my sleep and plunder my dreams with ghosts spat out by Hell and images of bloody and horrible death. Oh, yes, I hear them coming in the darkness outside as the wind rises to moan through the trees. I hear the clip-clop of spectral hooves on the pebble-strewn path in front of the manor door. I lie awake waiting for them and, at the first ghostly moon, I rise and stare through the mullioned glass at men and women from my past whose souls have long since slipped into the darkness of eternity.

They gather under my window like some ghastly chorus, grey shapes still displaying horrible wounds; the hideous faces of those I have worked with, played with, wenched with, dined with − as well as those I have killed. (May I say, always in fair fight.) The moon slips between the clouds and bathes their blue-white faces in a silver light. They stare up, black-mouthed and hollow-eyed, stridently baying at me, asking why I do not join them. I always smile and wave down at them so their howling increases. They slide through the walls and up the great, oak-panelled staircase along the wainscoted gallery and into my chamber to stand, an army of silent witnesses, around my bed. Hell has cast them out to bring me back. I just stare, each face a memory, a part of my life.

My chaplain, the vicar of the manor church, says I eat too much and drink too deeply of the rich claret but what does he know, the silly fart? I have seen them, he hasn't.

Doesn't he believe in demons, sorcerers, ghosts and ghouls? I do. I have lived too long a life with the bastards to reject them. A fool once told me about Murder, a little dwarf woman, who dressed in yellow buckram and burgundy-coloured shoes with silver buckles. She was the jester at Queen Mary's court. You know — pale-faced, red-haired Mary, who married Philip of Spain and thought he would give her a baby. Her belly grew big though no child was there. Poor, bloody Mary, who liked to put the Protestants in iron baskets and turn them to spluttering fat above roaring fires at Smithfield next to the meat shambles. Anyway, this jester, God knows I forget her name, she claimed the sky turned red at night because of the blood spilt upon the earth since the time of Cain, the first murderer. Another man, a holy vicar (a rare thing indeed!), once wondered whether the souls of murdered men and women hung for all eternity between heaven and earth. Do they, he wondered, float in some vast, endless, purple-coloured limbo, like the fireflies or will-o'-wisps do above the marshes and swamps down near the river?

Oh, yes, I often think of Murder as I lie between my gold-embroidered, silken sheets with the warm, plump body of Fat Margot the laundress lying hot beside me. She shares my bed to keep the juices running though, of course, the vicar objects.

'You are past your ninetieth summer!' he wails. 'Turn to God, give up the lusts of the flesh!'

I notice his lips appear more thick and red whenever he drools on about the lusts of the flesh. (Have you ever observed that? Most of the snivel-nosed bastards can tell you more about the lusts of the flesh than I could.) Nevertheless, I keep my vicar in line. A good rap across the knuckles with my stick soon diverts his thoughts from the rich, creamy plumpness of Margot's tits. Moreover, I know the Bible as well as he.

'Haven't you read the Scriptures?' I bawl. 'Even the great King David had a handmaid to sleep with him to keep his body warm at night. And that was Jerusalem which is a damned sight warmer than bloody Surrey!'

Oh, yes, the vicar is right on one thing: I am well past ninety. Sir Roger Shallot, Lord of Burpham Manor near Guildford, Surrey, master of its meadows, pastures, granges and barns. I own chests and coffers stuffed with gold, silver and costly fabrics; plump fallow deer run in my lush woods; clear streams feed my stew ponds stocked full of silver carp and tench. My manor has opulent chambers, the walls lined with polished, open wainscoting, carved in the neat linen folds after the French fashion. Above them, my servants have hung velvet drapes from the looms of Bruges, Ghent and Lille. My floors are of burnished pine wood and covered with woollen rugs from Turkey or the weavers of Lancashire.

I am Roger Shallot, Justice of the Peace, Commissioner of Array, Knight of the Garter (there's a good story behind that) and member of the Golden Fleece of Burgundy. I hold medals from the Pope (though I have hidden these); gems from the spider queen, Catherine de Medici. (By the way, Catherine was a born poisoner but a most accomplished lover.) I hold pure brown leather purses full of clinking gold given to me by the present Queen's father, Bluff King Hal. Bluff King Hal! A fat, piggy-eyed, murdering tub of lard! Do you know, he wasn't very good in bed? Oh, he often boasted about his exploits between the sheets but Anne Boleyn once confided in me, with deep sighs and loving whispers, how with some men, even kings, there is an eternity between what they say and what they can do – but that's another story! Oh, you know, she was a witch? Anne Boleyn, I mean. She had an extra teat with which she fed her familiar, and six, not five fingers on her right hand. She tried to cover it with a long, laced cuff and started a new style in fashion. God rest her, she died bravely.

Oh, yes, I hold all these honours. Even Hal's daughter, red-haired, cat-eyed Elizabeth, travels from Hampton Court to seek my advice. A strange one, Elizabeth! Her hair has all gone now but she wears the best red wig London can sell. It's a pity about her teeth; her mother's were a beautiful white, very strong if I remember correctly. Now, I am speaking truthfully (you wouldn't think it, looking at Elizabeth's white, narrow face; she doesn't smile now, lest the paint crack), she was a bonny girl and a great ruler – though no more a virgin than I am. We both know that! When she visits me, we sit in my private chamber downstairs, laugh about the past and wonder about our bastard son. Oh, a marvellous bonny girl, Elizabeth . . . those strong, white legs! A great rider but, as I have said before, that's another story.

Now where was I? Murder, that's what I was talking about before my chaplain, the vicar who is writing my memoirs down, distracted me by picking his nose and asking stupid questions. I was talking about the undead, those stained with the blood of others. How they visit me every night, stand round my bed and mock my titles and the riches I have amassed because they know the truth.

'Old Shallot!' they taunt. 'A liar, a thief and a coward!'

The latter really hurts. What's wrong in running? I have had to many a time. I thank the good Lord that I was born with the quickest wits and fastest legs in Christendom. But that's in the past. In my chamber I have a portrait of me when I was thirty. It's painted by Holbein and I recommend it as a fair likeness. I often stare at it: the hooded eyes, one with a slight cast in it (I told Holbein what I thought of him for that!) and the black, glossy hair falling in ringlets to my shoulders. My face is sallow but my lips are free and full, and my eyes, though severe, are ringed with laughter lines and there is a dimple in both cheek and chin. God knows I look as holy as a monk but you've heard of the old adage: 'Don't judge a horse by its looks'? I recommend it to you as one of the great eternal truths. I am the biggest sinner who ever prayed in church and I confess to having a personal acquaintance with each of the seven deadly sins except one – murder!

I have killed no woman or child and those who have died at my hands probably deserved an even more horrible fate. Indeed, these are the spectres who come to haunt me after the chimes of midnight.

Last night I recognised some of the men and women from my past. This morning their faces are still fresh in my mind as I sit at the centre of my maze and bellow for the vicar to bring his writing tray. One face, however, is always missing. Well, one in particular: Benjamin, my master, nephew of the great Cardinal Wolsey, one of my few friends. Benjamin with his long, kindly face, sharp quill nose and innocent sea grey eyes. Of course, he never comes. I suppose he is walking with the angels, still asking his innocent bloody questions. Oh, but I miss him! His eyes still mock me down the years: he was kind, generous, and could see the image of Christ in even the most blood-soaked soul.

I am of the old faith, you know. Secretly I miss the Mass, the priest offering the bread and wine, the smell of incense. I have a secret chapel built into the thick walls of my great hall and keep a blackened statue there which I rescued from Walsingham when the soldiers of Protector Somerset vandalised the chapel. I took the statue and every day, when I can, I light a candle in front of it for the soul of my dead master. However, let me concentrate on the dreams which come when the night is silent, except for the screech of the bat and the ghostly wafting of the feathered owl.

My chaplain is ready. There he sits on his quilted stool, his little warm bum protected by a cushion, quill in hand, ready to shudder with delicious horror at my shocking past. He tut-tuts as I drink my wine. One glass a day, that's what the little sod of a doctor ordered, but it's not yet noon and time for the Angelus bell and I have already downed six full cups of blood red claret. But what do doctors know? No physician can ever be successful. If he was, his patients would never die. I have known many a hearty fellow who thoroughly enjoyed life and the most robust health until he fell into the hands of physicians with their secret chants, newtskin medicine, horoscope charts and urine jars. Last week the mealy-mouthed hypocrite who proclaims he looks after my health came scuttling in to examine my urine so I filled the jar full of cat's piss. The idiot stood there, holding the jar against the light, before solemnly declaring that I should eat more fish and drink less claret. Good Lord, I nearly died laughing! Mind you, doctors are not all bad. If you want a real bastard, hire a lawyer. One of these imps of Satan came up from the Middle Temple offering to write out an inventory of my goods so I could make a will. 'After all,' he commented, looking slyly at me, 'you have so many offspring.' I asked the bastard what he meant? He replied with a knowing leer how many of the young men and women in the surrounding villages bear more than a passing resemblance to my goodself. My little fart of a chaplain nods, but I am not ashamed. I have, in many ways, been a true father to my people. Anyway, back to the lawyer! I soon wiped the grin off his silly face when I asked him if he was a good runner. 'Swift as a hare,' he declared.

I hope he was. I gave him five minutes' start and loosed my dogs on him.

Ah, yes, my memoirs . . . If I don't start soon the chaplain will claim he feels faint from hunger. So you want to hear about Murder? So you shall. Bloody, horrible deaths. Murder by the garrotte, by the knife, by poison. Murder at the fullness of noon when the devil walks, or in the dark when that sombre angel spreads his eternal black wings. Murder in palaces, Murder in rat-infested hovels, in open country and in crowded market places. Murder in dungeons, assassination in church. Oh, Lord, I have seen the days! I have seen judicial Murder: those who have died at the hangman's hands, strung up, cut down half-alive, thrown on the butcher's block and their steaming bodies hacked open. The heart, entrails and the genitals slashed and plucked out and the rest,

God's creation, quartered and thrown like cold meat into refuse baskets. I have seen women boiled alive in great black vats, and others tied in chains and burnt above roaring fires at Smithfield.

The chaplain leans forward. 'Tell them about the maze,' he whispers.

'What do you mean?' I ask.

'Well,' he squeaks, 'tell them why you dictate your memoirs in the centre of a maze.'

I'd like to tell him to mind his own bloody business but it's a fair comment. You see, at Burpham I have laid out the manor gardens like those I saw at Fontainebleau when I served as fat Henry's spy at the court of the lecherous Francis I. Now mazes have become very popular, although they weren't meant to be: you see, years ago, people took a vow to go on a crusade but, because of lack of money or time, some never reached Outremer. So Holy Mother Church decreed that they could be released from their vows if they travelled a number of times round a subtly devised maze. Of course, what was planned as a penance soon became the fashion. Francis I loved mazes. He used to take his young maidens in there and only release them if they succumbed to his lustful embraces. When the bastard found out I was a spy, I was led into the centre of the maze, hunting dogs were put in and the entrances sealed. You can imagine old Shallot had to use both his wits and legs! (However, that's another story.)

Anyway, I like my maze: it protects me from the importunate pleadings of my brood of children, legion of relatives and all the other hangers-on. Oh, yes, there's another reason — during my days at the court of Europe I became the sworn enemy of certain secret societies. I may have grown old but I still guard against the soft footfall of the assassin so I feel safe in my maze. No one can get near me and no one can eavesdrop. And if the weather changes and I cannot smell the perfume of the roses or listen to the liquid song of the thrush, I shelter in my secret chamber. After all, my memoirs are meant for posterity, not for the listening ear of some secret spy.

But don't worry, I'll confess all to you. I am going to give you your fill of Murder, but I must get it right. Go back down the years to tell my tale. Trust me, I really will try to tell the truth . . .

Chapter 1

I was born, so I tell my family — the offspring of my five wives — at a time of terror when the great Sweating Sickness swept into London, moving from the hovels of Southwark to the glories of Westminster Hall. All were culled: the great and the good, the noble and the bad, the high and the low. That was in the summer of 1502 when the Great Killer's father, Henry VII, reigned: lean-faced, pinch-mouthed Henry Tudor, the victor of Bosworth, had seven years left to live. I could tell you a few stories about him — oh, yes. He killed Richard the Usurper at Bosworth and had his torn, hacked body thrown into a horse trough at Leicester before marching on to London and marrying the Usurper's niece, Elizabeth of York. I once asked the present Queen, God bless her duckies, who killed the princes in the Tower? Was it their uncle, the Usurper Richard, or her grandfather Henry Tudor when he found them alive in the Tower? She shook her head and raised one bony finger to her lips.

'There are rooms in the Tower, Roger,' Queen Elizabeth whispered, 'which now have no doors or windows. They are bricked up, removed from all plans and maps. Men say that in one of these rooms lie the corpses of the two young princes.'

(I wondered if she believed she was telling the truth for I once met one of the princes, alive! But that's another story.)

Well, back to the beginning. I was born near St Botolph's Wharf which stands close to the river at the end of a rat-infested maze of alleyways. The first sound

I heard, and one which always takes me back, was the constant cawing of the ever-hungry gulls as they plundered the evil-smelling lay stalls near the black glassy Thames. My first memory was the fear of the Sweating Sickness. Beggars huddled in doorways; lepers, their heads covered by white sacks, heard of his approach and forgot their miseries. The traders in greasy aprons and dirty leggings shuddered and prayed that the sickness would pass them by. Their masters and self-styled betters thought they were safe as they sat at table, guzzling delicacy after delicacy – venison and turbot cooked in cream, washed down by black Neapolitan wine in jewel-encrusted goblets – but no one was safe.

The Sweating Sickness took my father; at least, that's what my mother said. Someone else claimed his weaving trade collapsed and he ran away to be a soldier in the Low Countries. Perhaps the sight of me frightened him! I was the ugliest of children and, remembering my fair-haired mother, must have owed my looks to Father. You see, I was born a month late, my head covered in bumps, one of my eyes slightly askew from the rough handling of the midwife's instruments. Oh, Lord, I was so ugly! People came up to my cot ready to smile and chuckle, they took one look and walked away mumbling condolences to my poor parents. As I grew older and learnt to stagger about, free of my swaddling clothes, the loud-mouthed traders along the wharves used to call out to my mother:

'Here, Mistress, here! A cup of wine for yourself and some fruit for your monkey!'

Well, when Father went, Mother moved on, back to her own family in the rich but boring town of Ipswich. She assumed widow's weeds though I often wondered if my father did flee, swift as a greyhound from the slips as Master Shakespeare would put it. (Oh, yes, I have patronised Will and given him what assistance I could in the writing and the staging of his plays.) Anyway, when I was seven, Mother became friendly with a local vintner and married him in the parish church – a lovely day.

Mother wore a gown of russet over a kirtle of fine worsted and I, in silk-satins, carried the bridal cup before her with a sprig of rosemary in it. I was later very sick after stealing some wine and gnawing voraciously at the almond-packed bridal cake.

My step-father was a kindly man – he must have been to tolerate me. He sent me off to the local grammar school where I learnt Maths, Astronomy, Latin, Greek, and read the *Chronicles* of Fabyan, as well as being lashed, nipped, pinched, caned and strapped along with the other boys. Nevertheless, I was good at my studies and, after Mass on Sundays, the master would give my mother such a glowing report that I would be rewarded with a silver plate of comfits. I would sit and solemnly eat these whilst plotting fresh mischief against my teacher.

One student who was not drawn into these pranks and feats of malice was my future master, Benjamin Daunbey: quiet, studious and bookish to a fault. One day I and the other imps of Hell turned against him, placing a pitcher upon a door and crowing with delight when its contents, rich brown horse's piss, soaked him to the skin. He wiped his face and came over to me.

'Did you enjoy that, Roger?' he asked softly. 'Did you really? Does it give you pleasure to see pain in the eyes of others?'

He was not angry. His eyes were curious: clear, child-like in their innocence. I just stammered and turned away. The master came in, cloak billowing like bat wings around him. He seized Benjamin by the nape of the neck, roaring at him while he got his switch of birch down, ready to give the unfortunate a severe lashing. Benjamin did not utter a word but went like a lamb to the slaughter. I felt sorry then, and didn't know why. My motto has always been: 'Do unto yourself what should be done to your neighbour.' I have rarely been brave and always believed that volunteers never live to pay day. Perhaps it was the meek way Benjamin walked, the cowardly silence of my comrades . . .

11

I stepped forward.

'Master,' I declared, 'Benjamin Daunbey is not to blame!'

'Then who is?' the beast roared back.

I licked my lips nervously and held out my hand.

'He is!' I said, turning to the smallest of my coven. 'He placed the pitcher over the door!'

Benjamin was saved, someone else got a beating, and I congratulated myself on my own innate cunning. Well, I went from bad to worse. At night I would not go to bed. In the morning I would not get up. I did not wash my hands or study my hornbook; instead I ran wild. My mother, sickening from a strange humour, just gazed speechlessly at me, hollow-eyed, whilst my step-father's hands beat the air like the wings of some tired, feckless bird. I mocked their advice like the arrogant young fool I was. My backside became hardened to the master's cane and I began to play truant in the fields and apple-laden orchards outside the town. Once the master cornered me, asking where I had been.

'Master,' I replied, 'I have been milking the ducks.'

He grabbed me by the ear but I hit him hard under the chin and ran off like a whippet. I didn't go home – well, not to see my parents. I stole some money, packed a linen cloth full of food, and it was down to London where the streets are paved with gold. London I loved with its narrow alleyways, teeming Cheapside, many taverns, and, of course, well-stocked brothels. I will skirt over my many adventures but, eventually, I joined the household of old Mother Nightbird who ran one of the costliest brothels near the Bishop of Winchester's inn at Stewside close to the bridge in Southwark. I found out more about women in a month than some men would in a dozen lifetimes. I became a bully-boy, one of the roaring lads who drank deeply, and paraded the streets in a shirt of fine cambric linen, multi-coloured hose, high-stepping riding boots and a monstrous codpiece. I swaggered about, armed with hammer and dirk which I prayed I would never use.

I fell in with bad company, one especially, a lank-haired, cunning-eyed weasel of a man called Jack Hogg. We took to breaking into houses, taking the costly silks and precious objects back to Mother Nightbird who would always find a seller. Naturally, it was not long before we were caught. Two nights in Newgate and up before the Justices at the Guildhall. We were condemned to hang but the principal justice of the bench recognised me. I knew a little abut him and made it obvious that if his sexual exploits were not to be part of my last confession, I should be given a second chance. Hogg died, swinging at Elms. I was given the opportunity of either joining him or enlisting in the King's Army now being gathered in the fields north of Cripplegate to march against the Scots.

Strange, isn't it, that even then the great mysteries of Flodden Field came south, like a mist, and changed my life? I didn't know it then. All I knew was that while King Henry VIII was in France, James IV of Scotland had sent his herald RougeCroix south with an insulting challenge to battle. Henry's Queen, the sallow-faced, lanky Catherine of Aragon, pining for her husband and longing to provide him with a lusty heir, accepted the challenge and sent insolent-eyed Surrey north with a huge army. Now old Surrey was a bastard. He drank so much the gout stopped him walking and he rode like a farmer in a cart, his orders being taken by outriders and scouts. A vicious man, Surrey, but a good general. You know, as a young man, he and his father Jack, the 'Jockey of Norfolk', fought for the Usurper Richard at Bosworth. Old Norfolk was killed and Surrey taken prisoner before Henry Tudor.

'You fought against your King!' the Welshman shouted.

Surrey pointed to a fence post.

'If Parliament crowned that fence King, I'd fight for it!' he bellowed back.

The Tudor prince seemed to relish this. Surrey went

13

to the Tower for while but was soon released because of his qualities as a general. He kept good discipline on that march to Flodden: he built a huge cart which carried a thirty-foot-high gallows, loudly declaring that if anyone committed a breach of camp discipline he would dance at the end of it.

Anyway I went north to meet my destiny. The dust of our great baggage train, stirred up by wheels, feet and hooves, hung above our forest of lances, almost obscuring the late summer's sun which struck bright sparks from halberd, sword and shield. In the front, old Surrey in his cart, his yellow hair now white, his ageing body held straight in its cuirass of steel. Behind him, my goodself among the bowmen in deerskin jacket and iron helmet.

Most of us were pressed men: gaol birds, night hawks, roaring boys. I have never seen so many evil-looking villains together in one place. We were armed with white bows six feet long, cunningly made from yew, ash or elm and strung with hemp, flax or silk. We had deep quivers full of cloth-yard arrows of oak, tipped with burnished steel and ringed with feathers of goose and swan. During the day the air was thick with the hum of flies and sour with the stench of marching men. At night we froze or shivered in our rough bothies of hay and wood and we cursed the Scots, Surrey and our hard-mouthed captains who urged us on.

We reached the Scottish Marches and crossed into a land rich in fish, wildfowl, deer, dark woods and great flocks of sheep grazing on bottle-green pastures which ringed shimmering lochs. (I won't keep you long.) Old Surrey met James at Flodden Field on Thursday, 8 September. We deployed our cavalry, massed in squadrons of shining helms and hauberks. I remember the creaking harness of our great war horses, the bannered lances and emblazoned shields. James, of course, wanted a set piece battle but Surrey's reply was sharp and caustic.

'I have brought you to the ring, dance if you can!'

The bloody dance began on Friday morning with the

Scots massing on Flodden Ridge. All day we stood to arms. I was terrified. We saw thick smoke as the Scots burnt their camp refuse and a stormy wind blew the smoke down on us. James used this haze as a screen to launch his attack two hours before sunset. First, a steady flow of lowered spears down the slope which soon became a landslide of barefoot men across the rain-soaked grass. Thankfully, I was on the wings for the centre became a bloody slaughter house. The Scottish squadrons floundered in the marshy ground, mowed down by arrows which dropped upon them like rattling rain until the grassy slope became russet and strewn with quilled bodies. The screaming and the shouting was too much for me, especially as a squadron of Scottish cavalry, maddened to fury, charged our position. I suddenly remembered valour has its own day, dropped my bow and fled. I hid beneath a wagon until the slaughter had finished and came out with the rest of the English Army to claim a great victory.

God, it was a shambles! Scots dead carpeted the entire field. We heard that James IV was killed. Indeed, Catherine of Aragon sent the corpse's bloody surcoat to her husband in France as proof of her great victory. She should never have done that! Bluff King Hal saw himself as a new Agamemnon and did not relish his wife reaping victories whilst he charged like an ass around Tournai. Men say Catherine of Aragon lost her husband because of the dark eyes and sweet duckies of Anne Boleyn. I know different. Catherine lost Henry when she won the victory at Flodden Field – but that was in the future, mine as well as hers. Little did I know, as we marched back to London, how the ghosts of Flodden Field would follow me south.

The army was disbanded and, after tasting the delights of London, I decided to return to Ipswich. I came home, a Hector from the wars. I even nicked my face with a knife to give myself a martial air. This brought me many a meal and rich frothing tankards of ale but they all tasted sour for my mother was dead. She had gone the previous summer − silently, as in life, without much fuss. I went to the cemetery, through the old wicket gate, down to where she would sleep for all eternity beneath the overhanging sombre yew trees. I knelt by her grave and, on one of those rare occasions in my life, let the hot tears run scalding down my cheeks as I begged for her forgiveness and cursed my own villainy.

My step-father was a mere wisp of what he had been, broken in spirit, shuffling and stumbling round his house like a ghost. He told me the truth: how mother had been ill of some abscess in her stomach which had bled, turning malignant, but there had been hope. Hope, he sighed, his eyes pink-rimmed, the tears pouring down his sagging cheeks; hope which died when the physician, John Scawsby, arrived on the scene. Now Scawsby was a well-known doctor and a man of repute. In fact, he was a charlatan, responsible for more deaths than the town's headsman. He had concocted some rare potions and strange elixirs for my mother but the situation had worsened and within weeks she was dead. A wise woman, a herbalist who dressed her corpse, said the malignancy had not killed her but Scawsby's elixirs had. My step-father could do nothing but I lurked in the taprooms of Ipswich, plotting my revenge.

I studied Scawsby most closely: his great black-and-white-timbered mansion which stood on the edge of town; his stables full of plump-haunched horses; his silken sarcenet robes; his ostentatious wealth and sloe-eyed, honey-mouthed, tight-waisted young wife. One day I struck, plunging for Scawsby as sure and as certain as a hawk on its prey. Scawsby used to like to dine at the Golden Turk, a great tavern which fronts the cobbled market square in Ipswich. He was a lean, sour-faced, avaricious man who liked to gobble his food and slurp his wines. He had not read his Chaucer or remembered the Pardoner's words, 'Avarice is the root of all evil', and I played on this. I dressed in my finest: a shirt of sheer lawn with embroidered bands at neck and cuffs, a doublet of rich red samite, dark velvet hose and a cloak of pure red wool. I also borrowed from my step-father a costly bracelet encrusted with precious stones very similar to one Scawsby wore.

At noon on the appointed day, I entered the Golden Turk, and espied Scawsby and a friend sitting beneath the open window conversing deeply, as men full of their own self-importance are wont to do. I went over, my clean-shaven face wreathed in a smile of flattery, and with kind words and honeyed phrases gazed round-eyed at the great physician Scawsby. My flattery soon won a place in his heart and at his table and, raising my hand, I ordered the taverner to bring his best, the costliest wine and the most succulent meat of roasted capon. I played Scawsby like a trout, sitting open-mouthed before stories of his great medical triumphs. At last, when our cups were empty and our bellies full, I admired the bracelet on his wrist. I compared it to the one I wore, cursing how the clasp had broken and saying I wished a goldsmith would fit mine with a similar lock to his. Of course, Scawsby seized the bait. I placed ten pounds of silver on the table as guarantee while I borrowed his bracelet to take to a nearby goldsmith so he could copy from it when he mended mine. I also gave a ring as surety and, pleading I had no horse, asked if I could borrow his from the stable. The old fool promptly agreed and off I went, begging him to stay until I returned.

I mounted his horse and rode like the devil to Scawsby's great mansion on the road out of town. His hot-lipped, full-bosomed wife was at home and I explained my errand: her husband wished for three hundred pounds in silver to be given to me so I could take it back to him in town. Of course, the saucy wench demurred so I plucked out her husband's bracelet which I said was his guarantee of my good faith, as well as pointing out the horse which a groom was now taking round to the stable. After that it was as easy as kicking a pig's bladder. I was taken up to her privy chamber, and given the money in clinking sacks whilst all the time I flattered and teased her. To cut a long but merry story short, I soon had her in her shift and we indulged in the most riotous romp on the great four-poster bed. After that, a cup of claret and back to the Golden Turk where Doctor Scawsby was even deeper in his cups. I returned his bracelet, took back my pledge and walked out of the tavern a much richer and more contented man.

I had extracted my revenge and what could the old fool say? If he issued a bill of indictment against me he would become a laughing stock – which, of course, he did when I passed the story round the taverns and ale houses of Ipswich. I didn't give a damn. I still grieved for my mother and felt the anger boiling in my heart at Scawsby's ineptitude and my own neglect of her. I thought of my mother more often then; her brown, friendly face, her eyes soft as the breeze on the most beautiful summer day. Why is it, I wonder, that the women I have loved I always lose?

Naturally, I went back to my evil ways. I spent my ill-gotten gains and turned to poaching. I had forgotten Scawsby and I made the mistake of thinking he had forgotten me. In March 1515 I was out on one of my nocturnal excursions, helping myself to good fresh meat during the lambing season. I was stopped just after midnight by the bailiff of the local squire who asked to see what I was carrying under my cloak. In spite of my indignant reply he found a young lamb. He accused me of stealing and ignored my explanation that I had found it wandering by itself and was now looking for its mother. I was thrown in gaol and appeared before the local magistrates. I thought I would just be fined but in the gallery I saw Sir John Scawsby's evil mug and a similar face sitting behind the great bench in the Sessions House. Oh, God, I prayed and whimpered.

Scawsby's brother was the principal justice and the full force of the law came to bear on me. I was declared guilty and almost fainted when he placed the black cap on his head and ordered me to be hanged. Lord, I screamed, but Justice Scawsby just glared back, his skull-like face an impassive mask of hatred.

'You are to be hanged!' he roared. He grinned evilly and looked round the court. 'Unless someone here can stand maintenance for you?'

Of course, his words were greeted with a deadly hush. My step-father was now sickly, doddering and senile; and who would bail old Shallot and risk the massed fury of the Scawsbys? I gulped and gagged as if the rough hempen necktie was already round my throat. Suddenly the Clerk to the Justices, a tall stooped figure dressed in a dark russet gown, rose and addressed the bench.

'I will, My Lord!' he announced. 'I will place my bond as surety for Shallot!'

Old Scawsby nearly exploded with apoplexy, so surprised he fixed the bond much lower than his own malice should have allowed: a hundred pounds, to be redeemed by the following Martinmas. I gripped the iron rail and stared in utter disbelief at my saviour: his long solemn face, hooked nose and calm grey eyes. Benjamin Daunbey had saved me from a hanging.

It's hard to define our relationship. Master and servant, close bosom friends, rivals and allies . . . do you know, after seventy years I still can't describe it. All I remember was that I was saved and walked free from the Sessions House. Other felons, not so lucky as I, were put in the stocks, tied to the triangle for a whipping or placed in the pillory, their ears nailed to the block until they either tore themself free or plucked up enough courage to cut them off.

In time I moved house, joining Benjamin in his narrow, dark tenement in Pig Pen Alley behind the butchers' shambles near Ipswich Market − a pleasant enough place inside with its low-ceilinged rooms, buttery, kitchen, small hall and white-washed chambers above. Behind it, however, Benjamin cultivated a paradise of a garden, laid

19

out in rectangular plots, each protected by a low hedge of lavender. Some contained herbs – balm and basil, hyssop, calamine and wormwood – others flowers: marigolds, violets, lilies of the valley. There were stunted apple and pear trees as well as pot herbs growing along the wall to season the meat in winter. Benjamin, taciturn at the best of times, always used this garden as the setting in which to share his deepest thoughts. My master never explained why he intervened to save my life so I never asked him. One day he just sat in the garden and declared: 'Roger, you can be my servant, my apprentice. You have broken so many laws, you are probably more of an expert on justice than I am. However,' he wagged one bony finger at me, 'if you appear before Scawsby again, you will undoubtedly hang!'

I never did but Scawsby had not seen the last of me. Benjamin intrigued me, though he never discussed his early life.

'A closed book, Roger.' He smiled.

'Why haven't you married?' I asked. 'Don't you like women?'

'Passing fancies, my dear Roger,' he replied, and remained assiduous in his pursuit of his duties, even persuading me to join the choir at the local church, my bass an excellent foil to his tenor. I lustily bawled out the hymns whilst watching the heaving breasts of our female companions. Since then I've always had a soft spot for choirs.

At first, life was plain sailing. I kept my head down, doing the occasional errand, staying away from those areas where the powerful Scawsby family had a measure of influence. I feared for my master but one thing I had forgotten though Scawsby knew it well: Benjamin was a nephew of the great Lord Cardinal Thomas Wolsey, Bluff Hal's principal minister. Now the Lord Cardinal was a hard man, not known for his generosity. A butcher's son from Ipswich, he had not forgotten his obscure beginnings but was equally determined that none of his relatives should remind him of them. When the rest of his large family came begging for favours, they were whipped off like a pack of hounds but Benjamin, the son of his favourite aunt, was cossetted and protected. My Lord Cardinal was determined that if he could be saved from the shambles of Ipswich and rise to be a royal favourite, Archbishop of York, Lord Chancellor and a Cardinal of the Roman Church, so could Benjamin.

Well, we all know about Wolsey. I was there when he died, in the Cathedral House at Lincoln, his great, fat fingers scrabbling at the bed clothes as he whispered, 'Roger, Roger, if I had served my God as well as I have served my King, he would not leave me to die like this!'

Now, old Wolsey fell when he failed to secure Bluff Hal's divorce from Catherine of Aragon and place him between the sheets with the hot-limbed, long-legged Anne Boleyn. I never told Benjamin this (indeed very few people knew it) but the Lord Cardinal did not die by natural causes — he was murdered by a subtle, deadly poison. However, that's another story for the future. In 1516, by subtle fetches, Wolsey had crept into the ear of the King. A brilliant scholar, Wolsey had gone to Magdalen College, Oxford, where he became fellow and bursar until his hand was found dipping in the money bags. Anyway, with his crafty mind he soon became chaplain to long-faced Henry VII, buying a house in St Bride's parish in Fleet Street. When Henry VII went mad and died, our new young King, the golden boy, Bluff Hal, saw the craftiness in Wolsey and raised him high. He bought a house near London Stone in the Walbrook, becoming Almoner, Chancellor and Archbishop until all power rested in his great fat hands. Some people said Wolsey was the King's bawd, others his pimp, alleging he kept young ladies in a tower built in a pleasaunce near Sheen for the King's entertainment. Others claimed Wolsey practised the Black Arts and communed with Satan who appeared to him in the form of a monstrous cat. A great man, Wolsey! He built Hampton Court, his servants went round in liveries of scarlet and gold with the escutcheon 'T.C.' on their back and front – 'Thomas Cardinalis'. And, all the time, the Lord Cardinal never forgot his favourite kinsman, young Benjamin.

My Lord Cardinal did not give Benjamin actual honours but rather money, as well as opening the occasional door to preferment and advancement. At least that was the Cardinal's plan though it came to involve treason, conspiracy, murder and executions . . . but that was for the future. If I had known the end of the business at the beginning, I would have run like the fleetest hare. There, I speak as lucidly and clearly as any honest man!

Benjamin was twenty when I met him again as Clerk to the Justices. I was two years younger and quickly learnt to play the role of the clever, astute servant, ever ready to help his guileless master. Well, at least I thought him guileless but there was a deeper, darker side to Benjamin. I did hear a few rumours about his past but dismissed them as scurrilous (I never really did decide whether he was an innocent, or subtle and wise). Do you know, I once met him in a tavern where he sat clutching a small wooden horse to his chest, gazing at it raptly, his eyes full of religious fervour. Now the toy was nothing much, any child would play with it. This particular one looked rather old and battered.

'Master, what is it?' I asked.

Benjamin smiled like the silly saint he was.

'It's a relic, Roger,' he whispered.

Oh, God, I thought, and could have hit him over the head with a tankard.

'A relic of what, Master?'

Benjamin swallowed, trying hard to hide his pleasure.

'I had it from a man from Outremer, a holy pilgrim who has visited Palestine and the house Mary kept in Nazareth. This,' he lifted it up, eyes glowing as if he was Arthur holding the Holy Grail, 'was once touched and played with by the infant Christ and his cousin, John the Baptist.'

Well, what can you say to that? If I'd had my way,
I'd have smashed the toy over the silly pedlar's head but
my master was one of those childlike men: he always
spoke the truth and so he believed that everyone else did.
After that I decided to take him in hand and help him
make full use of the Lord Cardinal's favours. In the spring
of 1517, Wolsey granted Benjamin a farm, a smallholding
in Norfolk on which to raise sheep, and my master gave
me gold to buy the stock. In an attempt to save money
I bought the sheep from a worried-looking farmer who
pocketed my silver at Smithfield, handed over the entire
flock and ran like the wind. No sooner had I returned
these animals to my master's holding than they all died
of murrain which explained the farmer's sudden
departure. Of course, I did not tell my master about their
former owner or how I had kept the difference between
what he gave me and what I had spent. I am not a thief,
I simply salted the money away with a goldsmith in
Holborn in case Benjamin made further mistakes.

Cardinal Wolsey's rage can be better imagined than
described. He angrily despatched his nephew to serve Sir
Thomas Boleyn, a great landowner in Kent. You have
heard of the Boleyns? Yes, the same family which
produced the dark-eyed enchantress, Anne. Now she may
have been a bitch, but once you met her father, you knew
the reason why! Lord Thomas was a really wicked man
who would do anything to advance his own favour with
the King – and I mean anything. Of course, like all the
arrogant lords of the soil, he hated Cardinal Wolsey and
plotted with the other great ones to bring the proud prelate
low. Although a powerful landowner, Lord Thomas had
still married above himself, one of the Howards, the kin
of my old general the Earl of Surrey who slaughtered the
Scots at Flodden Field. Now Boleyn's wife, Lady Frances
Howard, was the proverbial drawbridge, going down for
anyone who asked her. Bluff King Hal's hands had been
under her skirts and well above her garter many a time.
The same is true of her eldest daughter, Mary, who had

the morals of an alley cat. She bore Bluff Hal an illegitimate child but even he had grave doubts about its parentage and locked it away in the convent at Sheen. Mary and her sister Anne were sent as maids of honour to the French court. That's a gauge of Lord Thomas Boleyn's stupidity − it was like putting two plump capons down a fox hole.

King Henry may have been lecherous but King Francis I of France was the devil incarnate when it came to lewdery. Well, he was in his younger days. I met him later on when he had lost all his teeth and suffered from great abscesses in his groin as his whole body rotted away with syphilis. In his youth, Francis brought the best and the worst of Italy to Paris: Italian painters, Italian tapestries and Italian morals.

In his heyday he was tall, sardonic in looks and temperament, high-spirited, a virile devil with a grand air, smiling, insouciant, glittering in his gem-encrusted doublets and shirts dripping with lace. He was surrounded by women, in particular three voluptuous brunettes who formed his little band of favourite bedfellows. He was always most anxious to know about the love affairs of his ladies, being especially intrigued to hear of their actual joustings or any fine airs the ladies might assume when at those frolics, the positions they adopted, the expressions on their faces, the words they used. Frances even had a favourite goblet, the inside of which was engraved with copulating animals but, as the drinker drained it, he or she saw in its depths a man and woman making love. Francis used to give this cup to his female guests and watch them blush.

Now Anne Boleyn kept to herself but Mary took to this lechery like a duck to water, even acquiring the nickname of the English Mare, so many men had ridden her! Nothing abashed her, not even when Francis's fiery young courtiers played evil jokes by placing the corpses of hanged men in her bed.

Now, I told all this to my master, giving him a detailed

description of the morals and habits of the Boleyn women, and what does he do? One night at supper he innocently turns and asks Lord Thomas if my tales had any truth in them? An hour later we left Hever Castle, and the world-weary Lord Cardinal, hearing of the incident, decided his nephew needed further education. We were despatched to the halls of Cambridge. However, a year later, when my master came to give his dissertation in the Schools, a parchment was found in his wallet containing quotations from the Scriptures, St Cyprian as well as the other fathers of the Eastern church. Benjamin was accused of cheating and promptly sent down. I never confessed that I put it there in an attempt to help him. The Lord Cardinal, so Benjamin reported later, informed him, in language more suitable to a butcher in a shambles than to a man of God, exactly what he thought of him, and we were dismissed to our own devices at Ipswich. Suffice to relate, many was the occasion when my master would grasp me by the hand.

'Roger,' he would declare proudly, 'God is my witness. I don't know what I would do without you!'

In a way I am sure he was right and I constantly prayed for an upturn in our fortunes. My step-father died but his house and possessions went to others and I became rather worried because Benjamin had given up his place as Clerk to the Justices and Scawsby would scarcely hand it back. Moreover, he must have listened to the tittle-tattle of the court and realised Uncle Wolsey was now not so sweet on his blessed nephew. Nevertheless, in the late summer of 1517 my prayers in the Chantry chapel of St Mary the Elms were answered. The great Cardinal, in one of his many pilgrimages to Our Lady's shrine at Walsingham, decided to stop at the Guildhall in Ipswich on his way home. He arrived in the town in an aura of splendid pomp, flaunting his purple cardinal's robes, his tall, silver crosses and heavy gold pillars carried aloft before him. A vast army of gentlemen and yeoman tenants arrayed themselves on either side of him. His arrival was heralded by criers wearing splendid livery who parted the crowds in the streets shouting, 'Make way! Make way for Thomas – Cardinal, Archbishop of York and Chancellor of England!'

After these came heavy carts and carriages, loaded high with his baggage. Young boys scattered rose water to lay the dust, then came the Cardinal himself, tall and massive, mounted on a mule. By tradition this is a humble beast but My Lord Cardinal's was carefully groomed, caparisoned in crimson and velvet and carried stirrups of gilded copper. His attendants took over the main chambers of the Guildhall. Benjamin and I watched them arrive but my master did not expect the personal summons he received from the Cardinal later in the day.

We changed into our best doublets, slops and hose and hurried to the Guildhall where yeomen wearing the Lord Cardinal's livery took us along to the audience chamber. I tell you now, it was like entering Paradise. The floors were strewn with carpets, the most modest being of pure lambswool, the richest of silk imported by Venetian merchants from Damascus. Rich jewels and ornaments, images of saints, fine cloth of gold, damask copes and other vestments lay scattered round the chamber. There were chairs upholstered in crimson velvet, others in black silk, all embroidered with the Wolsey coat of arms. Tables of cypress and chairs of pine were covered with a great number of cushions, appropriately decorated with cardinals' hats, dragons, lions, roses and gold balls. Oh, how my fingers itched to filch something!

The prelate himself sat in robes of state on a high episcopal chair stolen from the nearby cathedral. He was dressed from head to toe in pure purple silk, a small skull cap of the same colour on his head, and even his cushioned slippers bore a coat of arms. He was as proud as he looked with his square-jawed, heavy face, skin white as snow, lips full and sensuous but eyes half-closed black pools of arrogance.

On the Cardinal's right, like a spider, sat a black-garbed

figure, cowl thrust back to reveal a cherubic face and shining bald pate. This was Doctor Agrippa, envoy and spy for the greatest in the land. I studied him curiously.

'A strange man, Doctor Agrippa,' Benjamin had once remarked. 'He has personal acquaintance with the Lord of the Cemeteries, a man steeped in magic who dabbles in the Black Arts.'

On closer inspection, I could hardly believe that: Agrippa's face was smooth and kindly, the eyes steadfast and sure in their gaze, though I did glimpse the silver pentangle hanging round his neck. People said he was Wolsey's familiar, his link with the demons of the underworld. On the other side of the Lord Cardinal was a bland young man with sandy hair, sea green eyes and a boyish, freckled face. He smiled at us in a gap-toothed way. I asked Benjamin who he was but my master hoarsely told me to keep quiet. Wolsey waved one purple-gloved hand and Benjamin hurried forward, kneeling at the footstool to kiss the heavy gold ring slipped over the Cardinal's silken glove. Wolsey ignored me, flicking his fingers at us to sit down on two quilted stools. I kept bobbing my head vigorously to placate the Lord Cardinal who sat studying us pensively.

'Benjamin, Benjamin, my dearest nephew.'

My master squirmed uneasily.

'My favourite nephew Benjamin,' Wolsey continued in a silky voice, 'and, of course, Shallot, his faithful amanuensis.'

(To those who don't know Greek, that means secretary.)

Wolsey abruptly leaned forward in his chair. Oh, Lord, I was so frightened, my heart as well as my bowels seemed to turn to liquid. Had the Lord Cardinal found out about the sheep? I wondered.

'What am I going to do with you?' the Cardinal snapped. 'Failed farmer! Failed merchant!' (That was another undertaking which went wrong.) 'Failed scholar! Failed spy!' (I'll tell you about that presently.) Wolsey

27

brought his hand crashing down on the arm of his chair. I glanced sideways at Benjamin. His face was pale but he was not frightened; those curiously innocent eyes gazed steadily back at his uncle. I detected no smell of fear. (Believe me, I know that perfume well!) No, my master was serene, undoubtedly drawing strength from my presence. I quietly preened myself.

'When,' the Lord Cardinal barked, 'are you going to rid yourself of that?'

I heard Agrippa giggle. I thought Wolsey was pointing at my master's cloak for, as I've remarked, I have a slight cast in one eye, then I realised the Cardinal meant me. Doctor Agrippa giggled again whilst the young man on Wolsey's left looked embarrassed.

'Dearest Uncle,' my master replied, 'Roger is both my secretary and my friend. He is shrewd, learned in the arts, of prodigious character and a strong protector. I will always value his companionship.'

'Master Shallot,' Doctor Agrippa intervened smoothly, 'is a lying, base-born rogue who disgraced himself at Flodden and, by all rights, should be drying out in the sun on the town's scaffold!'

I was hurt by Agrippa's words. The Cardinal smiled and stared at his nephew. God be my judge, I saw a look of rare tenderness and gentle irony in the Cardinal's eyes.

'You wrong Shallot,' Benjamin spoke up. 'He has his vices but also has his virtues.'

(A rare perceptive man, my master.)

Wolsey made a rude sound with his tongue and flicked his hand at Agrippa. The magician rose and took three chessmen from a lacquered board on the table beside him.

'You may still redeem yourself,' Wolsey began. 'Explain, Doctor Agrippa.'

The fellow crouched in front of us, his black cloak billowing like a dark cloud around him.

'There are three strands to this tapestry I paint,' he began.

I stared, fascinated by Agrippa's eyes which seemed to change colour from a light blue to a liquid black whilst his voice grew deeper and more soporific.

'This,' Doctor Agrippa remarked, holding up a small white pawn, 'represents the Yorkists driven from power in 1485 when their leader, the Usurper Richard, was killed at Bosworth by the present King's father. This,' the doctor now held up the white king, 'is our noble lord, Henry VIII, by the grace of God our King. And this,' he held up the white queen, 'is our beloved King's sister, Queen Margaret, widow of James IV, who was killed at Flodden, now unjustly driven from her kingdom of Scotland.'

I stared, half listening to Doctor Agrippa, now convinced I was in the presence of a powerful magician. As he spoke Agrippa's voice changed timbre and his eyes constantly shifted in colour, whilst sometimes as he moved I sniffed the rottenness of the kennel, and then at others the most fragrant of perfumes. The magician turned and grinned at Wolsey.

'Shall I continue, My Lord?'

The Cardinal nodded. Agrippa cleared his throat.

'The Yorkists are traitors but they survive in secret covens and conspiracies, calling themselves *Les Blancs Sangliers* after the White Boar, the personal insignia of Richard III. They were once shown favour by James IV of Scotland, and now they plot and threaten England's security.'

'Tell them about the White Queen,' Wolsey interrupted testily.

Doctor Agrippa licked his lips and smirked. 'Queen Margaret always objected to her late husband's involvement with *Les Blancs Sangliers* and eventually persuaded him to withdraw his support for them but not his enmity against England. Then came Flodden.' Doctor Agrippa shrugged. 'James was killed. Queen Margaret, desolate, was left alone with her baby son and pregnant with another. She was distressed and vulnerable. She looked for friends and found one in Gavin Douglas, Earl

29

of Angus. The Scottish Council was furious and, led by the Duke of Albany, attacked Margaret who fled into England.'

[God's teeth, looking back it's a wonder the fellow didn't choke on his words! Never have I heard such a farrago of lies!]

'Naturally,' Wolsey intervened, 'King Henry protected his beloved sister, who now repents of her hasty marriage and wishes to be restored to Scotland.' He paused and stared at his nephew.

'Dearest Uncle,' Benjamin began, 'what has that to do with me? How can I help Her Grace the Queen of Scotland?'

Wolsey turned to the young man who had been sitting silently beside him.

'May I introduce Sir Robert Catesby, clerk to Queen Margaret's privy chamber? He, together with the Queen's personal retinue, now resides in the royal apartments in the Tower.' Wolsey stopped and sipped from a goblet.

(Here it comes, I thought.)

'In a different part of the Tower,' Wolsey continued slowly, 'held fast in a prison cell, is Alexander Selkirk, formerly physician to the late King James. The fellow was brought there by my agents in Paris.' Wolsey smiled sourly. 'Yes, dear nephew, the same man I sent you across to find and whom you let slip so easily between your fingers. Anyway, Selkirk is captured. He holds information which could assist Queen Margaret's return to Scotland. We also think he is a member of *Les Blancs Sangliers* and could give us information about other members of that secret coven.'

[My chaplain mutters, 'What was Benjamin doing in Dieppe?' I rap him across the knuckles, I'll come to that!]

'Selkirk is not a well man,' Sir Robert continued. His voice was cultured but tinged with a slight accent. 'He is weak in both mind and body. We make no sense of him. He writes doggerel poetry and stares blankly at the walls of his cell, demanding cups of claret and alternating between fits of drunkenness and bouts of weeping.'

'How can I help?' Benjamin replied. 'I am no physician.'

'You are, Benjamin,' Wolsey answered, his voice warm with genuine kindness, 'a singular young man. You have a natural charm, a skill in unlocking the hearts of others.' The cardinal suddenly grinned. 'Moreover, Selkirk has fond memories of you, even though his wits do wander. He said you treated him most courteously in Dieppe and regrets any inconvenience he may have caused.'

Oh, I thought, that was rich, but I let it pass. The hairs pricking on the nape of my neck were alerting me to danger. There was something else, a subtle, cloying menace beneath the Cardinal's banal remarks. Why was Selkirk so important? He apparently knew something which the Cardinal and his bluff royal master wanted to share. Benjamin and I were on the edge of a calm, clear pool but, no doubt, its depths were deep, murky and tangled with dangerous weeds. I would have run like a hare from that chamber but, of course, dear Benjamin, as was his wont, took his uncle at face value.

'I will do all I can to assist,' he answered.

The Cardinal smiled whilst his two companions visibly relaxed. Oh, yes, I thought, here we go again, head first into the mire. Wolsey waved a hand.

'Sir Robert, inform my nephew.'

'Queen Margaret and her retinue, as the Lord Cardinal has already stated, are now in residence in the Tower. Queen Margaret wishes to be close to Selkirk, who holds information valuable to her. Her household is as follows: I am her secretary and chamberlain; Sir William Carey is her treasurer; Simon Moodie is her almoner and chaplain; John Ruthven is her steward; Matthew Melford is sergeant-at-arms and her personal bodyguard, whilst Lady Eleanor Carey is her lady-in-waiting. The rest are servitors.'

'All of these,' Doctor Agrippa interrupted, 'including

Sir Robert, served Queen Margaret when she was in Scotland. I will also join her household. Now, Sir Robert's loyalty can be guaranteed though it is possible – and Sir Robert must take no offence at this – that any of the exiled Queen's household could be allies to her opponents in Scotland and any one of them could be a member of *Les Blancs Sangliers*.' Agrippa frowned and looked at me. 'There is one further person whom I believe, Master Shallot, you know well. His Majesty has been pleased to appoint a new physician to his sister's retinue – a Hugh Scawsby, burgess of this good town.'

Wolsey smirked, Catesby looked puzzled, whilst my master rubbed his jaw.

'I am sure,' Doctor Agrippa continued, 'Master Scawsby will be delighted to renew his acquaintance with you.'

I looked away. I don't like sarcastic bastards and I didn't relish the prospect of having old Scawsby peering over my shoulder. None the less, I nodded wisely like the merry fellow I pretended to be.

'Nephew,' Wolsey extended his hand as a sign that the meeting was over, 'prepare yourself – and you too, Master Shallot. On the day after Michaelmas, Sir Robert and Doctor Agrippa will meet you here at noon and escort you to the Tower.'

Wolsey straightened up, a silver bell tinkled and behind us the door was flung open. Both Benjamin and I backed out, heads bobbing, although Wolsey had already forgotten us and was now talking to Catesby in deep hushed tones. Outside the chamber, I noticed Benjamin's face was flushed, his eyes glittering. He spoke never a word until we cleared the Guildhall and entered the musty darkness of a nearby tavern.

'So, Roger, we are to be gone from here in two days.' He looked anxiously at me. 'I know there's more to my uncle's business than meets the eye.'

He sighed. 'Yet it's the best I can do. We are finished here, there's nothing for us in Ipswich.'

'What was this business about Dieppe?' I asked.

Benjamin drained his cup. 'Before your appearance at the Sessions House, Uncle sent me on a mission to arrest Selkirk. I captured him just outside Paris and took him to Dieppe. The seas were rough so we sheltered in a tavern.' He sighed. 'To cut a long story short, the fellow's a half-wit. I became sorry for him and released him from his chains. One morning I rose late, Selkirk was gone, and all I had to show were a set of rusty manacles.' He smiled at me. 'Now Uncle wishes me to finish the task. We have no choice, Roger, we have to go.'

I stared around the tavern, now full of farmers and stall holders making merry and drinking the profits of their day. Yes, we were finished here. Still, I shivered as if some invisible terror, a cold hand from the grave, had rubbed its clawlike fingers down my back. The real terrors were about to begin. The ghosts of Flodden had finally caught up with me.

Chapter 2

Two days later we packed and, as arranged, found Sir Robert and Doctor Agrippa waiting for us outside the Ipswich Guildhall. They greeted us merrily enough, insisting that, before we leave, we should dine at the Golden Lion, the costliest eating house in Ipswich. I am proud to say I made a complete pig of myself on succulent capon, gold-encrusted pastries, roast plover garnished in a rich egg sauce, crackling pork and cheese tarts covered in cream. I drank generously from deep-bowled cups full of wine from the black grapes of Auvergne. After that Doctor Agrippa did not seem so menacing although I kept an eye on him: sometimes I caught him making strange signs and gestures in the air as if he was speaking to someone we could not see. Young Catesby, however, proved to be the most amiable of companions. He diverted us with the gossip of the court about the masques and mummers' plays, the dancing and the revelry, as well as the new wench in the King's bed, Bessie Blount, with her corn-coloured hair, saucy eyes and luscious body.

I suppose you take things as they appear. Catesby seemed a good man, albeit a dark pool with shadowy currents. A good fighting man who showed himself adept with sword and dirk when some mountebanks attacked us on the London Road, Catesby was left-handed, a subtle device, for what the fools thought was his blind side proved to be the place they died, choking on their blood as his sword rose and fell in a hissing arc of silver steel. For the rest, our journey was uneventful and on the morning of 2 October, the Feast of Christ's Holy Angels, we passed St Mary of Bethlehem Church and entered London along Bishopsgate Street.

We found the city in the final, lingering embrace of a terrible plague which caused a great sweating and stinking, redness of the face, a continual thirst and a crushing headache. At the last, pimply rashes would appear on the skin, small pricks of blood. After this the only consolation was that death followed swiftly. People fell ill on the streets, at work, during Mass, and went home to collapse and die. Some perished opening their windows, some playing with their children; men who were merry at dinner were dead by supper time. I saw people massed as thick as flies rushing through the streets away from the presence of an infected person. Fortunately, I remained in good health but Catesby, whilst at our inn, the Red Tongue on Gracechurch Street, fell ill. Doctor Agrippa bought mercury and nightshade mixed with swine's blood, infusing in it a concoction of dragon water with half a nutshell of crushed unicorn horn. He forced Catesby to drink this as he made strange signs in the air. Despite all this mummery, Catesby recovered and Doctor Agrippa announced it was now safe to proceed towards the Tower.

We travelled down through Eastcheap and into Petty Wales, the area around the Tower. God save us, London is a dirty place, but after that infection it was reeking filthy: fleas and lice swarmed everywhere, and the unpaved streets were coated with leavings of every kind. Mounds of refuse were piled high, full of the rushes thrown out of houses and taverns, thick with dirt and stinking of spit, vomit and dog turds. The Tower had been effectively sealed off against this miasma of filth and we were only allowed through its great darkened archways after Doctor Agrippa gave Wolsey's name and showed the necessary letters and warrants.

It was the first time I entered that bloody fortress with its soaring curtain walls, huge towers, drawbridges and moats, embrasures, sally ports and fortified gateways.

Once you were through these concentric rings of defences, the broad expanse of Tower Green, the half-timbered royal apartments and the sheer beauty of the great White Tower, caught the eye and pleased the mind with the cunning of their architecture. You see, in my youth the Tower was still a palace, old Bluff King Hal had not yet turned it into his own private killing ground where all his opponents would meet a grisly death: Sir Thomas More, joking with the executioner; John Fisher, too old to climb the gallows steps; Anne Boleyn, who died at the hands of a special executioner hired from Calais after she spent the evening before her death talking to me and practising how to lay her head on the block; Catherine Howard, a little figure in black who tripped through Traitor's Gate and bravely met her end on the scaffold in the half-light of a winter's morning. Yet, even then, I suppose the Tower had its secrets: deep, dark dungeons, ill-lit passageways and torture chambers full of grisly mechanisms such as the rack, the strappado and the thumbscrew, all of which would break a man's body and shatter his soul. A narrow, evil place, I did not relish staying in it for long.

Benjamin and I were given a small, musty chamber high in Bayward Tower which overlooked the north bastion and the deep, green-slimed moat. The narrow arrow-slit window was boarded up, with peep-holes pushed through to give some view out as well as to let the air circulate. We each had a pallet bed, a chest with its locks broken, bowls of water and a peg driven into the wall on which to hang our clothes. I felt as if we were prisoners and constantly checked the door to ensure it had not been bolted and locked.

We arrived late in the afternoon as the sun set and a damp mist swirled in from the river, so Benjamin insisted on a heated brazier and logs for the fire. The burly, thick-set Constable, John Farringdon, surlily agreed and stamped off, muttering that he was not a taverner and had too many guests in the Tower. That same evening

37

we met these, the retainers of Queen Margaret's household, as they gathered in the huge hall for supper. A cold, benighted place with bare walls and dirty rushes on the floor, its only consolations were a roaring fire in the great hearth and the food which, though simple, was plentiful and hot.

Doctor Agrippa introduced us to Queen Margaret and I groaned inwardly when I met her. She looked what she was: trouble to any man who came within a mile of her. She sat behind her separate table staring at us as she sipped a little too quickly from a huge goblet of wine. Her blonde hair was covered by a fine veil of white gossamer, and she had a strong Tudor likeness with her fleshy nose and gimlet eyes. Her face was broad and fleshy, the lips full and sensual, and despite the heavy jewel-encrusted dress, her podgy body exuded a hungry sexuality. Oh, a lewd one, Margaret. She gave many a man a good time but they always paid for it. She was hot as a poker and liked the pleasures of the boudoir beyond all others. Her husband had scarcely been killed at Flodden and she *enceinte* with his child, when she raised her skirts to please the Earl of Angus. The Queen frightened me by the way she was studying Benjamin, her mouth half-open, the tip of her tongue slightly moistening her lips as if she was looking at some Twelfth Night gift and was eager to shed the wrapping.

'Master Benjamin,' she said softly, her voice sweet and cultured.

'Your Grace.'

Queen Margaret extended a podgy hand for him to kiss. Benjamin approached, leaned over the table and raised her jewelled fingers to his lips. Of course, she ignored me.

'Master Benjamin,' she murmured, 'I am a queen driven from my country, exiled from my child, cut off from my people. I beg you to use all your skill and wit in this matter. If you do, you shall have my heart as well as my gold.'

Of course, the fat royal bitch didn't utter one word

about murder, assassination or ambush! Oh, no, the bloody liar! My master, like the chivalrous fool he was, mumbled a solemn promise. I dismissed her as a hypocrite and I wasn't too keen either on her maid-in-waiting, Lady Carey, who sat nearby, her greying hair stuffed under a ridiculous-looking bonnet, her beanpole figure encased in dark heavy velvet. She had the sanctimonious, bitter face of a kill-joy. Oh, a precious pair, Queen Margaret and Lady Carey, believe me, Gog and Magog in petticoats! Anyway, after the introductions, the Queen simpered at Benjamin and snapped her thick white fingers for us to withdraw. Lady Carey bestowed one last sour smile and we walked down the hall to meet the rest of the company.

This merry gang of exiles sat round the wooden table and barely spared a glance for us until Doctor Agrippa, sitting at the head, rose and rapped on the bare boards with his knuckles. The introductions were made: Sir William Carey, the Queen's treasurer, was a tall, sinister-looking man with close-cropped hair and a beetling brow. With one eye covered by a patch, the other glared furiously around as if he was constantly expecting attack. A redoubtable soldier now past his fiftieth summer, Carey had been a friend of the dead King James, one of the few who had managed to survive Flodden and fight his way out of the bloody mess. Mind you, having seen his wife, if I'd been in his shoes, I would either have stayed there or taken ship for foreign parts.

Simon Moodie was next, chaplain and almoner to the Queen. He was small and nervous with mousey hair, a thin pallid face, and the scrawniest beard and moustache I've ever clapped eyes on.

John Ruthven, the steward, was red-haired with a bloated drinker's face. He had ice-blue, goggling eyes and a nose which beaked like a hook over thick, red lips. A man who would know every penny he had and could tell you at a minute's notice what he and everyone else around him was worth. He constantly stroked a black and white cat, feeding it tidbits from the table, even talking to the bloody thing. Where Ruthven went, so did his cat and I privately wondered if he was a secret warlock and his pet a demoniac familiar.

Then there was Captain Melford, a burly individual with hair cropped close to his head, which seemed as round as a cannon ball. Melford's pale blue eyes were milky like those of Ruthven's cat and his tawny-skinned face was made all the more fearsome by a small pointed beard and a scar which ran across one cheek. A man of indeterminate age and questionable morals, Melford wore the royal tabard of Scotland over his shirt; unlike the rest of us he did not wear hose but black, woollen leggings pushed into high-heeled leather riding boots. What caught my attention was his codpiece which jutted out as monstrous as a stallion's.

Melford was lean, sallow, and undoubtedly vicious. He sat at the table with an arrogant slouch. The naked dagger pushed through an iron ring on his belt proclaimed him a mercenary, one of those professional killers who see murder as an everyday occurrence and the anguish it causes as merely an occupational hazard. Like the rest, his reception of Benjamin and myself was cool and distant, hardly looking up when Doctor Agrippa spoke.

Finally, there was Scawsby. At first he didn't recognise me but, when he did, he threw me such a look of loathing. Lord save us, I thought, if I fall ill, I'll call up Satan himself to tend me rather than allow Scawsby near my sick bed. Of course, the doctor greeted Benjamin fondly.

'Benjamin! Benjamin!' he called out once we had taken our seats. 'You were sorely missed at Ipswich.' The smile on the old bastard's face broadened. He rose, pushed back his taffeta cloak and extended his hand. 'It is good to see you returned to your uncle's favour.'

Benjamin clasped the old quack's hand. 'Good Master Scawsby, thank God you are with us! We Ipswich men . . .' Benjamin let the sentence hang in the air.

Scawsby threw another look of contempt at me and turned away.

The rest of the household turned back to their dishes of meat and vegetables.

'In God's name, Master,' I muttered, 'why did the Lord Cardinal appoint Scawsby to be Queen Margaret's physician? His answer to everything is leeches, and more leeches!'

'Master Scawsby has his good points,' Benjamin replied. 'Some people just misunderstand him.'

'Aye,' I whispered, 'including his patients. They can do very little about it because most of them are dead!'

My master smiled faintly, shook his head and began to eat. I looked around our motley crew: a harsh, unwelcoming collection of rogues with their dark, faded doublets and sour faces. They were a small, hostile group bound tightly together by their hankering after former glories. They were all English-born and had travelled to Scotland with Margaret when she had married King James. They spoke of their dead king with respect, even awe. At first I couldn't determine the true nature of their relationship with their exiled Scottish Queen. I thought it was fear tinged with respect, for Margaret kept her distance, but within days I had changed my mind: they were terrified of her, yet still bound to her as their only path to wealth and comfort. Of course, there were exceptions. Melford seemed impassive rather than afraid; he also took his duties seriously. Where the Queen went so did he, and I idly wondered whether he gave her more than just protection. Just after our arrival at the Tower, I confided this thought to Benjamin and he looked surprised. He sat on the edge of his bed in our musty chamber and shook his head.

'Queen Margaret is not sexually satisfied,' he announced to my stupefaction.

'How do you know that, Master?'

'Oh,' he replied airily, 'her face betrays her. Melford may sleep with her but he gives her no satisfaction.'

41

I gazed back in mock wonderment. I knew Benjamin had his secrets but I did not regard him as an expert on the female kind.

'You see, Roger, men regard women as an instrument of great pleasure.' He cleared his throat. 'Or, at least, some do. Few men see it as part of their *devoir* to give women pleasure and fully satisfy them.' He wagged a finger at me. 'You remember that, Roger.'

I nodded solemnly, lay down on the bed and, turning my face to the wall, wondered where in the world Benjamin drew his theories from. Of course, I was arrogant. My master proved the old adage: 'Still waters run deep'.

Now, I did say the Queen's household in general was terrified of her, but there were two other exceptions. Doctor Agrippa treated Queen Margaret almost with disdain, capping her remarks, quipping with her, and not showing the least trace of fear, never mind respect. The other person not to show fear was Catesby and I soon discovered he was a deep fellow. His relationship with the Queen was rather mysterious. Sometimes at table he would go up and sit beside her. Lady Carey and Melford would withdraw and the Queen and Catesby would sit, heads together, locked in deep discussion as if they were man and wife or brother and sister, bound by deep bonds of affection. Catesby had already proved himself to be an expert swordsman on our journey from Ipswich, now he demonstrated his skill as a politician. On our first night in the Tower, I asked him why the Queen had chosen the fortress when there were more comfortable places on both sides of the Thames. He smiled.

'The Queen didn't choose it — I did. First, we are near Selkirk. Secondly, we are free from infection. And finally,' he looked slyly at me, 'it's easy to keep an eye on everyone when we are all together in one place!'

A clever, subtle fellow, Catesby!

On our third day in the Tower we were shown up into Selkirk's prison cell, high in Broad Arrow Tower. The

room was more comfortable than ours; it boasted two
braziers, a faded tapestry on the wall, a desk, chairs, and
a comfortable four-poster bed. Nevertheless, it smelt fetid
and rank. I noticed with distaste how the chamber pot
full of turds was sitting in the centre of the room where
everyone could see and smell it. Selkirk himself was not
an attractive man: white-faced and skeletal with tawny,
grey-streaked hair which fell in a tangled mess to his
shoulders. His eyes were light blue and full of madness.
Benjamin hardly recognised him as the fellow he had
seized in Dieppe but, strangely enough, he remembered
Benjamin and greeted him like a long-lost brother.
Catesby, Farringdon the Constable, and Doctor Agrippa
showed us up. They treated Selkirk with mock deference
and then, once the introductions were completed and
Benjamin and I seated, withdrew, the door being locked
firmly behind them.

I studied that poor madman and wondered why he was
so important. Ruthven, the only member of the Queen's
household who treated us with any friendliness (for the
rest regarded Benjamin as the Cardinal's spy), had told
us a little about Selkirk: how he had been King James's
physician and journeyed with him to Flodden. After the
King's death there, Selkirk had fled abroad, first to the
Low Countries and then into France.

'God knows what turned the poor fellow's mind,'
Ruthven had murmured.

Now I, too, wondered that as Selkirk sat at his desk,
his long, bony fingers moving pieces of parchment about.
Benjamin talked to him, reminiscing about their meeting
in Dieppe. Sometimes the madness would clear and
Selkirk would reply in a sensible, lucid fashion but then
his mind would wander off. He would jabber in Gaelic,
or pick up the scraps of parchment from his desk and
start reading them as if we were no longer there. He
allowed Benjamin to look at these.

'Scraps of poetry,' Benjamin murmured. He looked
up at Selkirk. 'Who wrote these?'

43

'The King was a bonny poet,' the fellow replied. 'He and Willie Dunbar.' Selkirk smiled slyly. 'Some are composed by me.'

He handed over a few more scraps of paper and I studied them. God forgive me, they were as meaningless as some forgotten language; mere phrases and sentences, some in English, others in Scots, none made any sense. Nevertheless, Benjamin treated the prisoner gently, like a child, talking softly, asking questions, creating a bond of friendship. Every day we returned. Benjamin always brought a huge flagon of wine and a tray of cups. Each time the guards posted on the chamber door inspected the cups and tasted the wine, whilst Farringdon the Constable always escorted us in. Eventually I grew tired of this.

'The poor fellow's mad!' I exclaimed. 'Who would want to hurt him?'

Farringdon frowned, bringing his thick, black brows together. 'God knows.' He scowled. 'But orders are orders, and they come from the highest in the land.'

I also asked Catesby this but he just shrugged and murmured, 'Selkirk is more important than you think.'

So I let the matter rest. I confess I admired Benjamin's skill and wit. Usually he would let Selkirk ramble on but when the man became lucid, Benjamin would quickly pose his questions.

'What do you know that is so important? Who are *Les Blancs Sangliers*? Why are you in the Tower?'

Selkirk would straighten in his chair and shake his head.

'I have secrets,' he would whisper. 'I can count the days. The walls have eyes and ears.' He would stare around apprehensively, then giggle. 'The walls also have secrets.'

'What do you mean?' Benjamin asked.

And so the questioning would continue. I watched Benjamin and began to understand why his uncle had chosen him for this task. One night as we walked arm in arm around the great White Tower, I put this to him.

'Master Benjamin, you seem most gifted in dealing with that poor madman.'

44

Benjamin stopped, his body tensed and he looked away into the darkness.

'Yes, yes,' he murmured. 'I have had some experience. Uncle knows that.'

He stared at me and his eyes were full of tears. I let the matter rest.

At length I grew tired of visiting Selkirk so excused myself and spent days wandering the Tower. The royal apartments were eerie and sinister; galleries which ended abruptly at blocked passageways, spiral staircases which led nowhere. I asked one of the guards about this.

'Some people come here,' he muttered, shaking his head, 'and die in their cells, or on the block or at the gibbet. Some arrive and just disappear, not only them but their cells too. The doors are removed, the openings bricked up, and they are immured until death.'

Oh, yes, a dark satanic place the Tower. Sometimes at night I heard strange screams which plagued my dreams and caused nightmares. I wondered if they were the unfortunates in the torture room or the spirits of those bricked up in the walls of that great fortress.

Yet if the buildings were frightening, so were the people who lived there. The shadowy Doctor Agrippa flitted in and out of the Tower like a bat as he scurried around the city on the Lord Cardinal's business. On one occasion Benjamin sent me to see Agrippa in his lodgings which overlooked the chapel of St Peter Ad Vincula. The afternoon if I remember correctly was quite warm, the pale sun breaking through a cloying river mist which seeped over the walls and gateways of the Tower. I tapped on the doctor's door. There was no answer so I opened it. Agrippa was sitting on the floor. He turned to me quickly, his face a mask of rage.

'Get out!' he roared. 'I thought the door was locked!'

I hastily retreated but not before I had caught the whiff of burning as if an empty pan had been left over a roaring fire. And yet the room was cold, as freezing as a wasteland on an icy winter's day. I waited outside the door. After a few minutes Doctor Agrippa opened it, his face wreathed in angelic smiles.

'My dear Shallot,' he beamed, 'I am so sorry. Do come in.'

When I entered, the chamber was warm and filled with a cloying sweet perfume. I gave him my master's message and left as quickly as I could, now convinced that the good doctor was a perfect practitioner of the Black Arts.

I also decided it was safer to stay in our own chamber. As the days passed, Benjamin began to win Selkirk's confidence.

'He's not as mad as he seems,' my master remarked, his long, dark face lined with tiredness, the deep-set eyes screwed up in concentration.

'Has he told you anything?'

'Yes, he babbles about Paris and a tavern called Le Coq d'Or.'

'And his secrets?'

Benjamin shook his head. 'He said they are contained in a poem but he has only told me the first two lines.' Benjamin closed his eyes. 'How does it go? "Three less than twelve should it be, Or the king no prince engendered he." ' He opened his eyes and looked at me.

'Anything else?'

Benjamin shook his head. 'In time, perhaps.'

Time, however, had run out for Selkirk. About ten days after we had arrived at the Tower, Benjamin came back late in the evening. He described his latest meeting with the prisoner, claimed that the Scotsman was as fond of claret as I and, rolling himself in his blankets, promptly fell asleep. The next morning we were roughly awoken by one of the guards hammering on the door.

'You must come now!' he bawled. 'To Broad Arrow Tower. Selkirk is dead!'

We hastily pulled on our clothes and, wrapping cloaks around us against the early morning mist, hurried across the green, forcing our way through the press of servants, scullions and guardsmen who stood around the doorway of the Tower. We hastened up the stone spiral staircase and into Selkirk's chamber. Most of the Queen's household was there, grouped around the huge four-poster bed where Selkirk's corpse lay shrouded by its sheet.

'What happened?' shouted Benjamin.

Catesby shook his head and looked away. Doctor Agrippa was sitting on a stool, a strange smile on his round, fat face; Carey, Moodie and Ruthven huddled together whilst Farringdon was interrogating the four guards. Benjamin's question created a momentary silence.

'Selkirk's dead!' Agrippa quietly announced. 'Scawsby thinks it's poison.'

Benjamin immediately went across to the tray of goblets and jug of wine he had brought up the previous evening.

'Don't touch that!' barked Scawsby.

The old quack had re-entered the room behind us, a bag in his hand full, I suppose, of the usual rubbish — knives, charts and a cup for blooding.

'What makes you think it's poison?' Benjamin asked.

Scawsby smirked. Going over to the bed, he pulled back the stained sheet. One look was enough. Selkirk had been no beauty in life; now, brutally murdered by poison, he looked ghastly. His hair straggled out across the grimy bolster, his thin white face had turned a strange bluish colour, the mouth sagged, the eyes stared sightlessly up.

'Good God!' my master muttered. 'A terrible death after a terrible life.' He bent down and sniffed the dead man's mouth. 'Have you determined what poison it is?'

Scawsby shrugged. 'Belladonna, digitalis, nightshade or arsenic. The only consolation is that death must have been quick.'

'And you suspect the wine?' I retorted.

Scawsby went over and sniffed both the flagon and cup. The bastard took his time. He knew who had brought them up. So I filled a cup and downed it in one gulp.

'My master is not responsible for the poison!' I shouted.

[Do you know, that's the bravest thing I have ever done in my life.]

'I hope not,' Scawsby sardonically replied, 'otherwise you will be dead within the hour.'

'I look well, Master Scawsby,' I replied, 'and feel well — which is more than can be said for you!'

'No quarrels,' Doctor Agrippa interrupted. 'And no one leaves this room. There is more, is there not?'

Farringdon went to the table, removed a piece of parchment and tossed a faded white rose on to the floor.

'Selkirk was discovered half-lying on the bed. On the desk we found this white rose.'

'The White Rose of York and the mark of *Les Blancs Sangliers*,' Catesby muttered.

His words stilled the room but Benjamin, a determined look on his face, refused to be overawed.

'We have a problem here,' he announced. 'Selkirk had his evening meal before I joined him last night — yes?'

Farringdon nodded.

'I came up with a flagon of wine. Now, both Selkirk's food and wine were tasted by me and the guards?'

'Yes, that's so,' Farringdon replied.

'After I left, did anyone visit Selkirk?'

'No!' the guards chorused.

Benjamin shook his head. 'Impossible. Surely someone visited him?'

'There were two guards at the foot of the steps,' Farringdon replied. 'And two guards outside the prisoner's chamber. The door remained bolted and locked.'

'Except for the usual procedure,' one of the soldiers interrupted.

'What's that?' Catesby asked.

'Well, after Master Daunbey left, we always wait a while, then we open the chamber door to ensure all is well.'

'And?' Benjamin asked.

'Nothing. Selkirk was just sitting at the desk humming to himself.'

'Is there a secret passageway to this room?' I queried.

Farringdon snorted with laughter. 'For God's sake, man, this is the Tower of London, not some brothel! See for yourself.' He waved at the grey granite walls. 'And, before you say it, not even a dwarf could climb thirty or forty feet of sheer wall and slip through these arrow-slit windows!'

'Perhaps it's not murder,' Agrippa announced. 'Perhaps it was suicide.'

'Impossible,' Farringdon replied. 'Master Catesby and I have searched the room. There is nothing here.'

Benjamin took me by the sleeve and we went across to Selkirk's desk but there was nothing amiss: shards of parchment, greasy pieces of vellum and two dirty quills, cracked and dried, littered its surface. Benjamin picked these up and sniffed at them, shook his head and threw them back.

'I have already said,' Farringdon shouted, 'I have searched this room – there's nothing amiss!'

Catesby suddenly pushed forward, an anxious look on his face.

'Here's a merry mystery. A man sits in a locked and guarded chamber. He has no poison and no potions are brought in to him, yet in the morning he is found murdered with no trace of the physic which killed him.'

'Or the assassin,' Benjamin added. 'He must have been here to leave that white rose.'

'The only answer,' I interrupted, not giving a damn but staring hard at Agrippa, 'is that Selkirk was killed in a manner which defies any natural law.'

'Selkirk,' Doctor Agrippa replied smoothly, 'was murdered – and I believe his murderer now stands in this chamber.' He raised a hand to still any protest. 'This is not the time or the place to discuss this. The Queen must be informed. We shall meet later in her chambers.'

Catesby ordered Selkirk's corpse to be removed and the contents of the chamber to be placed in a canvas sack.

We all left quietly, each of us knowing that Dr Agrippa spoke the truth. One of us was a murderer.

An hour later we met in Queen Margaret's luxurious, silk-draped private chamber in the royal apartments. I remember it was dark; a thunder storm had swept in over the Thames and fat drops of rain beat against the stained glass windows of the room. Beeswax candles made the silver and gold ornaments shimmer with light as we took our seats around a long, polished table. Queen Margaret sat hunched at its head, Catesby and Agrippa sitting on either side of her, whilst behind them stood the dark sinister figure of Captain Melford. All her household, as well as Constable Farringdon, was in attendance. The Queen looked furious. She drummed the top of the table with her knuckles.

'Selkirk was murdered!' she began. 'The murderer is here in the Tower — perhaps in this chamber. The assassin is also a traitor, being a member of *Les Blancs Sangliers*. The question is, why was Selkirk murdered and, more importantly, how? There is no need,' she continued, throwing a venomous look at me, 'to talk of magic and the Black Arts. Murder is something tangible and Selkirk's killer will feel the hempen cord when it is placed around his neck! But first,' she looked kindly at Benjamin, 'did the prisoner reveal anything?'

Benjamin frowned, half-listening to the rain drops falling outside.

'What he told me I have already reported to Sir Robert Catesby. Selkirk was insane, with brief moments of lucidity. Your Grace, he talked of your late husband, the redoubtable King James, and about his own wanderings in Paris. And he kept chanting:

"Three less than twelve should it be.
Or the King, no prince engendered he." '

'Anything else?'
'I asked him why he was imprisoned and on one

50

occasion he replied it was because "I can count the days".'

'Is that all?' Catesby asked.

'Yes, Sir Robert. Why? Should there be more?'

'Then let us account for our movements,' Queen Margaret quickly interrupted. 'Sir Robert and I were in the city. We left, Master Daunbey, at the same time as you went to Selkirk's chamber. Doctor Agrippa was with His Eminence the Cardinal. Where was everyone else?'

I half-listened to their explanations: everyone, including myself, could give a good account of what they had done the night Selkirk had been murdered. I was more interested in Ruthven's expression. He was staring at Benjamin, his mouth half-open, as if my master had revealed some great secret.

'Master Constable,' Queen Margaret snapped when her household had recounted their movements, 'My retainers can give a good account of themselves.'

'As can mine!' Farringdon snarled back.

Carey spoke up, his voice squeaking in protest: 'But how can a man be murdered while locked and guarded in a cell? The assassin must have got in to administer the poison as well as leave the white rose!'

'And if,' Moodie commented, 'the murderer did get in, why didn't Selkirk object or cry out?'

'Perhaps he knew him,' Agrippa replied in dry, clipped tones.

'Master Constable,' Catesby asked, 'you are sure of the guards?'

'As I am that I am sitting here,' Farringdon replied. 'They are mercenaries, seeing Selkirk as merely another prisoner. One guard could be bought but not all four. They watch each other. Moreover, both I and my lieutenant did our rounds last night and found them all at their posts. If there was anything amiss,' he concluded, 'all four would swing from a gibbet and they know it.'

Queen Margaret nodded and smiled sourly. She stared coolly at Benjamin as did the rest. Oh, I knew what they were thinking! He was the last person to talk to Selkirk and the old principle in law still stands: the man who saw the victim last must, *prima facie*, be chief suspect. But Benjamin also knew the law.

'Who discovered the corpse?' he loudly asked.

Catesby pointed at Farringdon.

'One of the guards opened the door and saw Selkirk lying there. He sent for me, and I sent for Catesby.'

'I and the Queen,' Sir Robert murmured, 'had come back to the Tower in the early hours. I was in my chamber talking to Melford. Both of us went across.' He shrugged. 'You know the rest.'

'My Lord Cardinal must be informed,' Queen Margaret interrupted. 'Melford, take a message now.' She rose. 'The rest of you are dismissed, though none − I repeat, *none* − must leave the Tower!'

Benjamin and I walked back across the eerie, mist-laden Tower Green. My master was white-faced and withdrawn, conscious of the unspoken accusations levelled against him. I must admit, God forgive me, there was a doubt niggling in my own mind.

'What are you thinking, Roger?'

Benjamin had stopped and turned to me, pulling the hood of his cloak closer about him.

'Nothing,' I lied. 'Well . . .'

'Speak!'

'Why was Selkirk murdered now? I mean, he has been in the Tower for weeks. Why did the bearer of the white rose only strike within days of our arrival here?'

'Go on, Roger.'

'Well,' I stammered, 'it makes *you* look like the assassin.'

'You mean, I was brought here for that purpose?'

'Either that,' I replied slowly, 'or else you discovered something from Selkirk which meant he had to be killed.'

'True!' Benjamin peered through the mist around us. We stood and listened to the muffled sounds of sentries on the ramparts above us, the neighing of horses from the stables and the rattling of cart wheels across the cobbles.

'What I know, Queen Margaret and her household know also. Yet what is it except a few mumbled phrases?' He stared at me, his mind elsewhere. 'Selkirk said the walls had ears. He also giggled and claimed they had secrets. They have removed his body. Come, Roger!'

We went back to Selkirk's deserted chamber in Broad Arrow Tower which had now been stripped of everything except for a few sticks of furniture. The corpse had already been sheeted and moved to the death house near the Tower Chapel.

[Looking back, I wonder if Selkirk's ghost now joins those regularly seen making their spectral way round the fortress. My chaplain shakes his head. 'There's no such thing as ghosts,' he murmurs. Now isn't that little know-all going to be in for a shock?]

Anyway, back in Selkirk's chamber, Benjamin began to study the walls carefully. Now and again he would find a place where the mortar had been chipped away. We poked and probed each of the crevices but found nothing except a trickle of sand or a few pebbles. I remembered how tall the dead man had been and, at my insistence, we both climbed on the desk and began to examine the holes and gaps high in the wall. After an hour we were successful. We found a gap between the bricks and Benjamin drew out a small, yellowing, twisted piece of parchment. We jumped down and, like two schoolboys who had found some treasure, hurried back to our own chamber. Decades later I still recall the lines of that doggerel verse which contained so many secrets and was responsible for such bloody murder.

> Three less than twelve should it be,
> Or the King, no prince engendered he.
> The lamb did rest
> In the falcon's nest,
> The Lion cried,
> Even though it died.

The truth Now Stands,
In the Sacred Hands,
Of the place which owns
Dionysius' bones.

'Hell's teeth, Master!' I whispered. 'What does it mean?'

'The first two lines,' Benjamin replied, 'are what Selkirk was always chanting. Perhaps it's a cipher? Each word standing for something else?'

'At least,' I replied bitterly, 'we have something to show the Cardinal when he sends for us!'

Chapter 3

My words were prophetic. The next morning was clear and bright. A strong sun was burning off the river mist as Melford swaggered into our chamber and announced, 'The Lord Cardinal wishes to see you both. He has also ordered that on the way I should show you something.'

Do you know, I sensed what was coming as we grabbed our cloaks and followed Melford out of the Tower. My worst fears were confirmed when, instead of taking a barge, Melford, striding ahead of us, took us up Aldgate and into the stinking city streets. Benjamin sidled closer.

'What do you think is going to happen, Roger? Where is Melford taking us? Is my uncle the Lord Cardinal angry? I am no assassin.'

'Oh, I am sure there is nothing to worry about,' I lied. 'Melford is going to show us the marvels of the city, perhaps buy us a pastry and a pie from the cookshops. Maybe a visit to a bear garden or a drink in some snug tavern.'

My master smiled, the cloud lifting from his open face. I glanced away in desperation. (He was, in some ways, such an innocent!) We walked on past St Mildred's Church, Scalding Alley and the Poultry Compter. I pointed out the mansion near the Walbrook which Sir Thomas More had recently bought, and the houses of other court dignitaries. I had to chatter to still my nerves. We went through Cheapside where the rickety stalls of the poor traders housed loud-mouthed apprentices who offered us garish threads, fustian hats, trinkets, gee-gaws and other baubles.

55

My master, essentially a country boy, stopped at one stall but Melford spun on his heel and came back, his hand on his dagger. Benjamin, recognising the anger in his eyes, hastily dropped the object he was inspecting and followed on.

At last we came to Newgate Prison, the huge, ugly gaol built on the old city wall — a ghastly sight, made no pleasanter by the smells and smoke from the neighbouring butchers' shambles, whilst the gully in the centre of the street was choked with rubbish. The odour was so foul, Melford took a pomander from his wallet and held it to his nose. A great crowd had assembled, all eyes fixed on the ironbound gates of the prison. A trumpet sounded, its shrill blasts quieting the crowd before the gates opened to a great roar from the throng. Even the costermongers, wheeling their carts laden with baskets of bread, cooked meats and fruit, stopped plying their trade and looked up.

I saw a horse, three black plumes dancing between its ears. A tambour sounded, every beat silencing the clamour around us. The crowd shifted as Melford pushed forward. We saw the drummer walking before the horse which pulled a cart surrounded by guards, halberds half-lowered. The driver was clad in black leather from head to foot, his face covered by a lace-trimmed, orange mask with slits for the eyes and mouth. The cart itself was huge and decorated with the symbols of death. In it stood a man, his red hair shimmering in the sun. Beside him a priest muttered the prayers for the dying. Oh, I remembered my trial in Ipswich and knew the terror that was coming.

I peered between the slats of the cart and glimpsed the cheap pine-wood coffin. My master's face grew dullish pale. I thought he was going to faint or even run away but Melford was now standing between us, forcing us to follow the death cart. We did so, like mourners, as the procession slowly snaked down to the Elms at Smithfield, stopping only at the Angel for the usual bowl of ale for the condemned prisoner.

He looked as if he needed it; his face was one purple mask of bruises. He could hardly stand: there were angry welts across his bare shoulder and one arm hung awkwardly in its socket. At last, the cart trundled up to the great three-branched scaffold raised high on a platform next to a butcher's block in which a huge meat cleaver had been embedded. Another executioner, dressed in a dirty apron, hobbled on one lame leg across the platform and placed the noose round the prisoner's neck. The orange-masked driver whipped up the horse and pulled away, leaving the poor man to dance in the air. Suddenly white roses were thrown from the crowd and an urchin sprang on to the traitor's kicking legs. The boy pulled him down so quickly that, even from where I stood, I heard the click of his neck breaking. The urchin jumped down and scampered off.

Benjamin turned away and vomited, raising a catcall of abuse from some old crones who had gathered there to watch the fun: they were disappointed that the additional punishments of decapitation, castration and disembowelling were now no longer necessary. Melford, his own disappointment also apparent, turned and, with a snap of his fingers and a sharp curt order, indicated we should follow on.

'This was a warning, was it not?' Benjamin whispered, wiping his mouth on the back of his hand.

I praised him for his perspicacity. However, let me assure you, my master was no fool, just an innocent in the wicked ways of the world. I freely admit to my own terror. I felt faint with the heat, the crowd and the sight of that ghastly, twitching body.

We arrived at Westminster. Melford kept showing Wolsey's warrant to various officials until a steward, wearing the Cardinal's livery — three tasselled hats against a scarlet background — led us upstairs to the royal apartments. We encountered more guards and more questions until a great iron-studded door was thrown open and we entered an antechamber which reeked of wealth:

great carved chairs and desks, finely wrought tables with spindly legs and tops cleverly covered with silver and topaz. My fingers itched to caress these valuables but Benjamin and I were ushered on into the Cardinal's presence. He was sitting in his throne-like chair, swathed in his scarlet robes. The light danced on the huge pectoral cross hanging from a chain round his neck and shimmered in the sparkling diamonds which covered his fingers.

Clerks scurried to and fro, bearing piles of documents. There was a smell of fresh wax and resin for the Lord Cardinal was sealing warrants which decreed life, wealth, freedom, prison, exile, as well as bloody death at Tower Hill, or Smithfield Common. Wolsey glanced up and stared at us, his small eyes hard as flint, and I knew what the psalmist meant when he described fear turning his bowels to water. On that occasion, mine nearly did and I quietly thanked God I was wearing thick, brown pantaloons for I did not wish to disgrace myself. The Cardinal picked up a silver bell from the desk beside him and rang it gently. A tocsin itself could not have wrought such an effect: all the clerks stopped their business and the room fell silent. Wolsey muttered a few words and his servants vanished as swiftly as peasants before the tax collectors.

After they had gone, the chamber remained silent except for the buzzing of angry flies and my Lord Cardinal's favourite greyhound busy crapping in a corner under a red and gold arras. Benjamin doffed his cap and swept his uncle a most courtly bow. I followed suit. The Cardinal studied us morosely as his greyhound went to gobble the remains of a meal from a silver dish.

'Benjamin, Benjamin, my dear nephew.'

Melford sidled up, whispered in the Cardinal's ear, grinned sourly at us and quietly left. As he did so, Doctor Agrippa and Sir Robert Catesby slipped into the room and sat on either side of the Cardinal. Once again the bell was tinkled: a servant entered bearing a jewel-encrusted tray. It bore five Venetian glasses, tall and thin-stemmed with bands of precious silver round the rims.

He placed these on a table next to Wolsey and left. The Cardinal himself solicitously served us the chilled wine from Alsace, giving us each a tray of sweetmeats. He returned to his chair, his perfumed, scarlet robes billowing around him as he ordered us to eat. I was only too pleased to do so, gulping noisily from the glass and gorging myself on the thin *doucettes*. Once I had finished, not caring whether Wolsey was staring at me, I also ate my master's for Benjamin had lost his appetite. (I might be a little timid but I do not like being threatened and I was determined to hide my terrors from the likes of Wolsey.) The Lord Cardinal sipped from his own glass, quietly humming the tune of some hymn.

'You saw Compton die?' he suddenly asked.

Benjamin nodded. 'It was not necessary, Uncle.'

'I will deem what is necessary and what is not,' the Cardinal snapped. 'Compton was a traitor.' Wolsey leaned back in his chair, wetting his lips. 'There is a link between his death and that of Selkirk.'

'What was his crime?' Benjamin asked.

'Compton, a member of *Les Blancs Sangliers*, bought a poisonous ointment from a sorcerer. He smeared the walls of a royal chamber with it, hoping to kill the King. He was trapped, questioned, but revealed nothing. Very much,' Wolsey angrily concluded, 'like your meetings with Selkirk. You discovered nothing and now we are faced with a conundrum: how can a man locked in a chamber be murdered, and we find not a trace of the potion or how the poisoner entered or left?' The Cardinal twisted in his chair. 'As Doctor Agrippa relates, the poisoner must have been there to leave the white rose. I believe, at Compton's execution, you saw some bastard throw such roses towards the scaffold?'

'Perhaps it was the same person,' I blurted out.

'Shut up, you idiot!' rasped Wolsey.

'Was Compton questioned by the King's torturers?' Benjamin asked.

'Of course.'

59

'And, dear Uncle, did you learn anything?'

'No, we did not.'

'Then, dearest Uncle, I think it is wrong to tax me with my lack of success with Selkirk. After all, I had no more than ten days.' Benjamin let his words sink in.

I stared at Doctor Agrippa, who was smiling to himself whilst Catesby looked moodily away. Benjamin deftly plucked the piece of parchment from beneath his doublet.

'Before you criticise us further, I did find something. Selkirk hid this in the wall of his prison cell.'

Wolsey almost snatched the document from Benjamin's hand. He did not even let Catesby or Agrippa look at it as he murmured the words aloud, and then peered closely at Benjamin.

> Three less than twelve should it be,
> Or the King, no prince engendered he.
> The lamb did rest
> In the falcon's nest,
> The Lion cried,
> Even though it died.
> The truth Now Stands,
> In the Sacred Hands,
> Of the place which owns
> Dionysius' bones.

'What does it mean?' he asked, handing the parchment to Doctor Agrippa, who read it and passed it to Catesby.

'God knows, Uncle,' Benjamin replied. 'But I believe the secrets Selkirk held are hidden in those lines.'

Wolsey picked up the silver bell and tinkled it. His master clerk came scurrying back into the room. The Cardinal took the parchment from Catesby and tossed it to his servant.

'Copy that, four or five times. Make sure there are no mistakes and have a cipher clerk study it carefully to see if it contains a coded message.'

The man bowed and scurried out. Wolsey glanced sideways at Doctor Agrippa and Catesby.

'Gentlemen, do the words mean anything to you?'

Agrippa shook his head, his eyes on Benjamin, and I caught a gleam of appreciation as if the doctor had realised that my master and myself were not the fools he had thought. Catesby seemed dumbstruck and just shook his head. The Cardinal leaned forward, beaming in satisfaction at his beloved nephew.

'Master Benjamin, you have done well — but now there's more.'

Oh, Lord, I thought. I did not like being near the Great Ones of the land. I also wondered what would have happened if Benjamin had *not* discovered Selkirk's secret manuscript. The Cardinal edged forward on the seat of his chair like a conspirator.

'In a few days' time, on the Feast of St Luke, Queen Margaret will leave the Tower and journey north to Royston, a royal manor outside Leicester. She will stay there until she treats with envoys from Scotland who are coming south to discuss her return to Edinburgh. You will meet these emissaries on Queen Margaret's behalf and listen to what they offer.' Wolsey stared at his nephew. 'And there is more. Selkirk was killed by someone in the Tower. One or more of Queen Margaret's household may be members of *Les Blancs Sangliers*. You are to discover who these are. How and why they murdered Selkirk. And, above all, what are the mysteries concealed in Selkirk's doggerel poem?'

'Any member of the Queen's household could be a secret Yorkist,' Doctor Agrippa spoke up. 'Remember, even old Surrey who defeated James at Flodden once fought for Richard III. Indeed, they could have joined the Queen's household and gone to Scotland in order to plot fresh mischief.'

'Then let's entice them out!' Wolsey remarked. 'Announce that you have found Selkirk's poem, seize your opportunity to read it to the whole company, and see what happens.'

I remembered the strange look on Ruthven's face and

agreed with Wolsey's advice, although I was more concerned for my own skin. Old Shallot's motto is, has, and always will be, 'Look after yourself and all will be well.'

'There's more,' Catesby intervened. 'One of the Lord Cardinal's most trusted agents in Scotland, a Master John Irvine, is coming south. He brings important information, so precious he will not even commit it to letter. Now, near Royston Manor is Coldstream Priory. I have instructed Irvine to meet you there on the Monday following the Feast of St Leo the Great. Irvine will reveal his secrets. You will tell no one what he says but report directly to His Eminence the Cardinal.'

Wolsey grasped Catesby by the arm as the door opened and the master clerk crept back into the room.

'Yes, man, what is it?'

The clerk shook his head.

'Your Grace, the poem is copied but the cipher clerks can trace no code. I also have a message: His Majesty the King expects you now.' The fellow glanced at us. 'And, of course, your guests.'

My heart sank. Take this as a rule from old Shallot – keep away from princes. To you they will always insist on being everything, but to them *you* are nothing but a pawn, a mere straw in the wind. To put it bluntly, I did not want to meet the King, his sister was bad enough! However, Wolsey rose, clapped his hands and Melford appeared at the doorway with two halberdiers. The Cardinal whispered instructions to remain to Agrippa and Catesby as the soldiers led my master and I out of the chamber. We went downstairs behind the Cardinal, across a shimmering black-and-white-chequered floor and, opening a door, entered the royal gardens. They were a feast of colour with their herbs, lilies and masses of wild flowers. In the far corner stood a small orchard of pear trees though pride of place was given to huge raised beds covered with red roses, their heads stretching up towards the sun.

At the far end of the garden was a broad, smooth, green lawn where a group of people dressed in gold, red, silver and pink silks put the flowers to shame. Cloths of lawn had been placed on the grass around a pure white marble fountain. On that clear autumn day, the sound of its tinkling water rose above the gentle hum of conversation and laughter. The area had been cordoned off with screens of cloth of gold nine feet high and in this small enclosure sat the King, Bluff Hal, with the gentlemen and ladies of his court.

Henry rose as Wolsey approached. He stood, his red-gold hair swept back, legs apart, hands on hips, a veritable Colossus of muscled flesh beneath his gorgeous robes. I had once seen the King from afar but now, close up, I could see the reason for the universal admiration of him: dressed completely in white, he gleamed in the sunlight. His hair, burnished by the sun, was grown long, falling in thick locks to his shoulders. Smooth-shaven, his face glowed like precious metal. Only the eyes chilled rather than awed me, set high in his face, narrow and slitted against the sunlight, they exuded a power and arrogance I had never seen before or since.

A golden boy was our Bluff Hal, before he went mad and fat as his great legs became ulcerated and the royal arse became sore with the haemorrhoids which were clustered there. In his later years, the great belly hung down like that of a sow. Henry grew so gross they had to build a special moving chair for him, and so irascible that only myself and his jester, Will Somers, would dare approach him. Of course, you know Henry VIII was murdered, don't you? Oh, yes, they killed him just before they put his swollen body in the coffin, pressing the lid down so urgently the corpse swelled and burst and dogs came to lick the rotten juices. But that was in the future. On that first occasion I met him, I just gawped — so much so that one of the ladies behind the King giggled and I realised that the escort, my master, and even the Lord Cardinal had gone down on their knees.

'You have brought us guests, Thomas?' The King's voice was low, tinged with exasperation.

'Yes, Your Majesty,' the Cardinal replied. 'I spoke of them earlier, you may remember?'

The King turned, clapped his hands and shouted something in French to his companions. The men bowed, the ladies curtseyed and swept out of the garden in a rustle of silk and gusts of fragrant perfume. I recognised Henry's Queen, Catherine of Aragon, dumpy and fat, dressed in dark blue with a necklace of gold carved in the form of Spanish pomegranates around her neck. Her face was sallow though the dark eyes were kind and soft. Sir Thomas More was there, whose house I had shown to my master. A learned scholar Thomas, with his sardonic face and clever eyes. He never had any illusions about the King.

'Do you know, Shallot,' he once remarked, 'if my head could win him a town in France, then it would go!'

In a way poor Tom was right; his head went, not because of a castle but a courtesan – Anne Boleyn.

Once they had all gone, Wolsey rose to his feet with the grace of a dancer. I would have followed but my master gripped my arm and shook his head. I looked up. The pleasaunce was now deserted except for one lady dressed in pink, her blonde hair covered against the sun's heat by a fine veil of white lawn. She was sitting on a small stool sipping rather fast from a huge goblet of wine. Queen Margaret had left the Tower.

'Come, Thomas, come!' the King's voice was brisk. 'Tell your guest to approach. We can't spend all day on this matter.'

Wolsey snapped his fingers. Benjamin rose, went to kneel at the King's feet and kissed his hand. The King raised him from his knees, murmuring a few words of greeting. I went forward, eyes on the ground, and extended my hand to take the King's – but there was nothing there. I glanced up. The King, his arm linked through Wolsey's, was returning to the pleasaunce.

Benjamin walked slowly behind, gesturing with his head for me to follow. I did, trotting like a dog, quietly hiding my own mortification. Apparently, I had been good enough to die for the King in one of his wars but not worthy enough to kiss his hand. In the pleasaunce Wolsey heaved himself on to a chair beside the King. I peered sideways at Queen Margaret. The King was terrifying but that woman would frighten a panther. She was made all the more repellent by her sly cast of features and a grimace which she must have thought was a smile.

'My Lord Cardinal has given you his instructions?' barked the King to my master.

Benjamin nodded. 'Yes, Your Majesty.'

'You are going to carry them out?'

'With all my strength.'

Oh, Lord, I could have clapped my hands over my master's mouth. There he was, a lamb amongst the wolves, openly committing himself (and more importantly, me) to a task which might take us along the same path Selkirk and Compton had travelled. The King nodded and stared down at the sparkling rings of his fingers as if bored by the whole proceedings. I peered closer, glancing sharply at the Cardinal: both he and the King looked solemn but it was like some comedy masque in which Benjamin and I were the jesters. They were laughing at us, though I am not sure if Queen Margaret was party to the joke.

At last the King dismissed us and we went back into the palace where Wolsey suddenly pulled us into an alcove, gesturing with his hand for Melford to walk ahead. The Cardinal was so close I could see the beads of sweat on his fat brow as well as smell the cloying perfume from his silken robes.

'Trust no one,' he whispered. 'Not even Doctor Agrippa. You must go north but, mark my words, your mission will be accompanied by intrigue, mystery, and the most brutal murder.'

[Now, resting against my silken bolsters and looking

back down the tunnel of years, I know that old bastard of a Cardinal was right. The devil himself would strike camp and follow us north.]

As soon as we were clear of Westminster Palace, we headed for the Rose tavern like frightened rabbits to the nearest hole. Our meeting with the King, Wolsey's talk of plots, and his final whispered warning had done little for my indigestion and the sight of my master's white, agitated face afforded me little comfort. Once we were hidden in the dark coolness of the tavern, our noses deep in cups of sack, we relaxed and felt better. Master Daunbey probably drew strength from my calm, devil-may-care attitude.

'What does it all mean, Roger? Poison, secret messages, mysterious meetings and journeys to the wild north?' He looked at the piece of parchment Wolsey had given him, containing a copy of Selkirk's doggerel verse.

'What's hidden in this thrice-damned poem?' he asked. 'Dionysius is Greek. And how can a lamb rest in the falcon's nest? Or a dead lion cry? And what's this business about three less than twelve?'

I could give few answers except a noisy belch and a shout for more sack. The drink soothed Benjamin. He became a little maudlin and began mumbling about a woman called Johanna. I asked him who she was but he shook his head and, in a few minutes, fell into an uneasy sleep. I let him rest for I had become more interested in the coy glances of a serving wench. She showed me more than a smile when I slipped her some of Benjamin's coins and we retired into a chamber at the top of the house. I forget her name. She's probably now just dust and a golden memory but she had lovely eyes, long legs and the biggest breasts in London.

[Bigger than Fat Margot's? my chaplain asks. Oh, yes, like ripe melons. I must give the chaplain a rap on the knuckles; he's far too interested in the lusts of the flesh.]

Anyway, this golden girl took my money but I think she liked me and soon it was hot mouth against warm flesh in the riotous tumble of the bed. When I awoke she was gone; so were more of my coins. I dressed and went downstairs. Benjamin was still sleeping in the taproom so I roused him. He woke cool and calm.

'Master,' I said (as if I had been there all afternoon), 'the day draws on, we must go back to the Tower.'

Benjamin rubbed his eyes. 'Soon we will be gone from London. I must see Johanna.'

'Who is she?' I complained. 'For heaven's sake, Master, I have sat here keeping you company, I am tired and I want my bed.'

Benjamin pressed my arm. 'Roger, you must come.'

Well, what could I do? At heart I am a generous soul so I followed him out to King's Steps and we took a barge up the Thames. I couldn't make any sense out of him so I sat back and left Benjamin to his own thoughts whilst studying the fat carracks of Venice, the big-bellied ships of the Hanse and the gorgeously decorated barges of the noblemen as they skimmed like kingfishers across the darkened Thames down to Westminster or the palace at Greenwich. On the far bank, as the sun set, two river pirates had been hanged, their bodies still jerking at the end of the scaffold rope. Later they would be lowered into the Thames and tied to the wharf for three days and three nights as a warning to other predators on the river. We turned a bend and Benjamin leaned forward, whispering instructions to the oarsman. The skiff pulled in and I stared up at the beautiful white brick convent of the Nuns of Syon.

'Johanna's a nun?' I whispered.

Benjamin shook his head. We disembarked and walked up the gravelled path to the iron-studded convent gate. My master pulled the bell and a postern door opened. Again Benjamin whispered, the white-veiled nun smiled and beckoned us forward. We were led round a flower-filled cloister garth, down white-washed passages into a room furnished with nothing except a bench, a few stools and a large black wooden cross. The nun brought us two cups of watered wine and slipped out, closing the door behind her. Naturally, I was full of questions but Benjamin's face had become cold and impassive, drained of both colour and emotion. Ten, fifteen minutes passed before the door opened and an old nun walked in, leading a girl of no more than nineteen or twenty summers. She had fiery red hair under the dark cowl of her cloak and her face was truly beautiful – marble white with rosebud lips – but her eyes, though a sea-washed blue, were empty and vacant. She stumbled as if finding it difficult to walk and, when Benjamin rose to embrace her, just shook her head and gave him a blank smile.

My master led her over to one of the benches where they sat together, Benjamin caressing her, pulling her close to him, crooning like a doting parent would over a favourite child. The old nun just stood and watched whilst I listened to him mutter sweet endearments but the girl hardly moved, allowing herself to be rocked gently backwards and forwards. I stared but looked away when I saw the tears streaming down my master's face and felt the sheer sorrow of his soul. After a while the nun went across and took Johanna gently out of Benjamin's arms. She and my master whispered for a while, the door was opened and Benjamin and I were left alone.

We did not talk until we were through the postern gate of the Tower and alone in our chamber. By then Benjamin had composed himself.

'Who was she, Master?'

'Johanna Beresford,' he murmured.

The name stirred my own memories. 'There were Beresfords in Ipswich,' I replied, 'an alderman by the same name.'

'Yes, that's correct.'

Suddenly I remembered the rumours I had heard about Benjamin: vague gossip about him being enamoured of an alderman's daughter.

'What happened?'

Benjamin rubbed his face in his hands. 'Some years

68

ago,' he began, 'just after I was appointed as Clerk to the Justices in Ipswich, I fell deeply in love with Johanna Beresford.' He smiled wanly. 'She was rather spoilt, being the only daughter of a wealthy, elderly couple. Nevertheless, I made her laugh and I think she had some affection for me.' He licked his lips and looked around. 'All went well, at least at first. I was received into her father's house where I pressed my suit.' He fell silent.

'What happened then?' I prompted.

'The Assizes came to town, the great judges from Westminster doing their circuit of Suffolk. The captain of the guard was a young nobleman, one of the Cavendishes of Devon.' Benjamin bit his lip. 'To cut a dreadful story short, Johanna became besotted with this young nobleman. Of course, I protested but she was infatuated. Now, I might have accepted that: Johanna was of an honourable family and would have made a dutiful wife, but Cavendish just trifled with her, seduced and then abandoned her. Johanna was distraught with grief. She went down to London but he laughed at her, offering to provide her with comfortable lodgings. He treated her no better than a whore.' Benjamin looked at me, no longer the gentle soul I knew. The skin across his pallid face had drawn tight, his eyes seemed larger, wilder. 'Johanna went mad!' he continued. 'Her parents, distraught, tried to remonstrate with Cavendish but the insults they received only hastened their own demise. Before their death they put her in the caring hands of the Nuns of Syon and left their money in trust to the Order. Alderman Beresford also made me swear that for as long as I lived I would take care of Johanna.' He smiled. 'No duty, Roger, but a sacred trust: Johanna is insane, driven mad by love, witless because of desire. So now you understand.'

I did. I now knew why Benjamin would occasionally hasten down to London on some mysterious errand. Why he was so shy in the company of women. Why he always bore that terrible aura of sadness, and why he'd been so skilled in putting Selkirk at his ease.

'What happened?' I asked.

'To whom?'

'To Cavendish?'

Benjamin rubbed his hands together.

'Well,' he coughed, 'I killed him!'

Now, the Lord be my witness, I went cold with fright. Here was my gentle master, who became sad when a dray horse was beaten, calmly announcing he had killed a young nobleman! Benjamin glanced sideways at me.

'No,' he said tartly, 'not what you think, Roger. No poison-laced wine or arrow in the back. I might not carry a sword but I was taught fencing by a Spaniard who had served in Italy, then fled to England when the Inquisition took an interest in him. Anyway, I sought out Cavendish in a London tavern. I bit my thumb at him, slapped him in the face and asked if he was as brave with Ipswich men as he was with Ipswich women. One grey morning, on thirty yards of dew-drenched grass near Lincoln's Inn Fields, we met with sword and dagger. I could say I meant to wound him but that would be a lie.' He shrugged. 'I killed him clean in ten minutes. There's a law against duelling but the Cavendishes saw it as a matter of honour and accepted that as a gentleman I had no choice but to issue the challenge. My uncle the Lord Cardinal obtained a pardon from the King and the matter was hushed up.' He sighed. 'Now, Johanna is mad and hidden away in Syon, Cavendish is dead, my heart is broken and I owe my life to the Lord Cardinal.' He got up and unclasped his cloak. 'Have you ever, Roger,' he said, talking over his shoulder, 'wondered why I saved you from the hangman's noose in Ipswich?'

To be truthful I had not, accepting Benjamin as a simple, honest, kindly fellow. Now, in that dark chamber in the Tower, I realised that old Shallot had been wrong and fought to hide the cold prickling fear in my heart.

Benjamin slung his cloak down on the bed.

'Well, Roger?'

'Yes and no,' I stuttered.

He knelt down beside me. I tensed, seeing the small knife secreted in his hand. His eyes were still wild in his pale, haggard face.

'I saved you, Roger, because I liked you, and because I owe you a debt.' He smiled strangely. 'Remember that Great Beast of a school master? But,' he seized my wrist in a grip like a steel manacle, 'I want you to swear now, before me and before God, that if anything happens to me, you will always take care of Johanna!' He pulled back the sleeve of his jerkin and nicked his wrist with the knife until a thin, rich, red line of blood appeared; then he took my wrist, the edge of the knife skimming it like a razor. I did not look down but kept my eyes fastened on his. One flicker, one change of expression, and I would have drawn my own dagger but Benjamin harmlessly forced his cut on mine so our blood mingled together, trickling down, staining our arms and the starched whiteness of our shirts.

'Swear, Roger!' he exclaimed. 'Swear by God, by your mother's grave, by the blood now mingling, you will always take care of Johanna!'

'I swear!' I whispered.

He nodded, rose, and tossing the knife on the floor, lay down on his bed and rolled himself up in his cloak.

I waited while the blood on my cut wrist dried, staring across at Benjamin.

Now, let old Shallot teach you a lesson — never presume you know anyone! Benjamin was not the man I thought he was. In truth he was many people: the kindly lawyer, the innocent student, the boon companion . . . but there was a deeper, darker, even sinister side. He was a man who strove to conceal extravagant passions behind a childlike exterior. Outside the Tower, a cold wind from the river cried and moaned like a lost soul, seeking Heaven. I shivered and drew my cloak around me. Benjamin had killed a man! Could he kill again? I wondered. Had his questioning of Selkirk reminded him of Johanna and stirred the demon festering in his soul?

71

After all, my master had been the last man to speak to the prisoner. My mind flitted like a bat around the dark reaches of the mystery surrounding us. Why had the Scotsman died? Would Benjamin do anything for his uncle? Did that include murder? Above all, was I safe?

[I am sorry, I must stop dictating my story; my chaplain, the clerk, is jumping around on his little stool.

'Tell us who killed Selkirk!' he exclaims. 'What were the mysteries of his poem? Why don't you just tell the truth and leave it at that?'

I tell the little fart to sit down. I am a teller of tales and will let my story unfold like a piece of tapestry. After all, why not? Every Sunday my chaplain goes into the pulpit and bores me to sleep with a sermon which lasts for hours about lust and lechery. He wouldn't dream of getting up and bawling out, 'Stop fornicating, you bastards!' and then sitting down, oh, no, and my tale is more interesting than any sermon. Moreover, there's more to come: murder on the highway, terror in the streets of Paris, death by stealth, subtle trickery and evil which would make old Herod himself look an innocent.

Do you know, years later I told Master Shakespeare about Johanna. He was much impressed by the story and promised he would include it in one of his plays about a Danish prince who forsakes his love and sends her mad. I thought he would make a passing reference to me, at least out of gratitude! But oh, dear, no. A sign of the times . . . the laxity in morals! The collapse of truth! I drink from my goblet and turn my face to the wall. In truth, you can trust no one.]

Chapter 4

The days following our visit to Johanna were full of frenetic busyness: Benjamin had to pack our belongings, I had to sell a cup (I'd stolen this from Wolsey) and draw what money I had deposited with the goldsmiths. On 18 October, the Feast of St Luke, we assembled under the looming battlements of the Tower. Servants, porters, farriers and fletchers bustled about. Grooms, scullions and carters carried our baggage and loaded it on to the great wagon: hangings, feathered beds, yards of damask and costly cloth, towels and napkins, were piled into chests. The furnishings of Queen Margaret's chapel — candelabra, heavy missal books with their golden covers and carved stands, cushioned prayer stools — not to mention the pots and pitchers from the kitchen, were piled in great heaps on the cobbled yard. Of course, I avoided so much work, going out to the bloody square on Tower Hill to gawk at the gore-drenched platform where the Great Ones of the land had their heads cut off.

At last we were ready. We left the Tower by a postern gate and went along Hog Street, turning right to hear Mass at St Mary Grace's church. The cavalcade stopped and orders were issued for us to rest in the fields around the church whilst Queen Margaret and her principal attendants went inside. I was all agog with curiosity for I had glimpsed a cart, covered by a black damask cloth, arriving outside the main door of the church. It was protected by yeomen of the guard wearing the royal red and gold livery. The cloth was pulled back and a large casket was taken into the church. Catesby ordered us to follow it.

I wondered what it was as we trailed up the dark nave behind Agrippa, Melford, and others of the Queen's party. The casket was placed on trestles before the high altar. Queen Margaret stood at the head, the rest of us on either side. I craned forward. Queen Margaret, white-faced and with dark-ringed eyes, nodded slightly and Catesby prised loose the lid to reveal white, gauze cloths which gave off a sweet fragrant perfume. These were removed and — oh, sweet Lord, I nearly fainted! The corpse of a man lay there: red-haired, red-bearded, face long and marble-white. The body was clothed in a purple gown and a silver pectoral cross winked in the flickering candle light. The man looked to be asleep though his eyelids were only half-closed. I saw small wounds, red gashes, high on the cheek bones. Immediately the group knelt.

'Who is it?' I whispered.

'Her husband,' Benjamin murmured. 'The late James IV of Scotland, killed at Flodden!'

I stared at the skull-like face, the hollowed cheek bones, the red hair now combed smoothly back from the forehead. I later learnt that the corpse had been badly mauled in battle, the face disfigured by a crashing axe blow. The embalmers had used all their skills to repair the body. Queen Margaret muttered something to Catesby.

'Of your mercy,' Sir Robert intoned, 'pray for the soul of our late King James IV and take your leave. Her Grace wishes to be alone.'

We all filed out of the church, leaving Queen Margaret with her shadows whilst we waited in the warm autumn sunshine.

'Master Benjamin,' I muttered, 'the King's corpse has been above ground for four years.'

'The English generals,' he replied, 'had the body dressed and embalmed after Flodden and sent it south for our King to view.' He smiled and looked away. 'You know our good Henry — he fears neither the living nor the dead. He kept the corpse shut away in a special chamber at Sheen Palace.'

'And the Queen will take it back?'

'No, no!' Ruthven interrupted, sidling up behind us. 'King Henry has decreed that it stays here until she is restored to Scotland.'

I turned and looked at the man's tear-stained face. 'You loved King James?'

'He had his failings, but he was a great prince. Noble-hearted and generous to a fault.' Ruthven looked up at the birds wheeling and twisting against the blue sky. 'Such a noble prince,' he whispered, 'deserved a better end than that.'

Queen Margaret came out of the church, a veil covering her grief-stricken face. Benjamin tugged Ruthven by the sleeve, indicating he wished to talk to him. We walked further away from the group.

'What was your master like?' Benjamin indicated with his head towards the eerie church. 'The late James IV? I mean, as a man?'

'A strange person,' Ruthven replied, 'tinged with the new learning from Italy. King James was interested in medicine and was absorbed in all aspects of the study of physic and the human body.' He rubbed his eyes with the back of his hand. 'Do you know, he even founded a chair of medicine at one of the universities?' Ruthven glanced away, now lost in the past. 'The King's curiosity and hunger for knowledge led him down many strange paths. On one occasion he hired a Satanist, a monk who dabbled in the Black Arts.' Ruthven looked at the party clustered round the church door. 'In fact, Doctor Agrippa reminds me of him, but that was years ago.' Ruthven looked at us sharply. 'Do you know,' he whispered, 'Carey believes his grandfather met Doctor Agrippa in Antioch. But surely it's not possible for a man to live so long?' He sighed. 'Anyway, this Satanist promised he could make things fly. Whether he did or not I don't know, but James loved the good as well as the mysterious things of life – fine wine, beautiful women. He had bastards by at least two of his mistresses, Marion Boyd and Margaret Drummond. He would have lived a long and full life had it not been for Flodden.' Ruthven ground his teeth together. 'He should have heeded the warnings.'

'What warnings?'

'A few days before he joined his army, King James was at prayer in the royal chapel at Linlithgow. A ghostly figure appeared, dressed in flowing robes of blue and white. The spectre carried a great staff and, with his high forehead and blond hair, bore an uncanny resemblance to a painting of St John. In loud, sepulchral tones, this vision warned James to give up war and consorting with wanton women. One of the King's companions tried to seize the apparition but it vanished.' Ruthven gnawed at his lip. 'A few days later the army assembled outside Edinburgh and a ghostly voice was heard shouting at midnight. It seemed to come from the Market Cross. This voice called on James and all his commanders to appear before Pluto, God of the Underworld, within thirty days.' Ruthven shrugged. 'The prophecy was fulfilled. Within a month James and most of his commanders were dead, killed at Flodden.' The steward turned and spat on the ground. 'So, Master Daunbey, you know more about my master. Any further questions?'

'Yes,' I interrupted, 'when my master told you about Selkirk's mutterings, you seemed alarmed, even disturbed.'

Ruthven gazed gloomily at me. Do you know, I really thought he was going to tell me something, but his protuberant eyes refused to meet mine.

'I have said enough,' he muttered as he saw Moodie approach.

'The Queen mourns for her husband,' the chaplain squeaked.

'Does she?' Ruthven quipped. 'How can she?'

'What do you mean?' Benjamin turned as quick as a

76

top, his eyes sharp and questioning. 'What do you mean, Ruthven?'

'I have heard stories, Master Daunbey.' Ruthven nodded towards the church. 'They say King James was not killed at Flodden and that corpse belongs to someone who merely looks like him.'

'Is that possible?' I asked.

Ruthven pursed his lips.

'It's possible,' he whispered. 'First, we always see what we expect to see. Secondly, the royal corpse was mangled; it had been in the hands of embalmers and above ground for four years. Thirdly, at Flodden James dressed at least sixteen of his knights in royal armour and coat of arms. God knows for what reason — he didn't lack courage. And, finally, there were several knights of James's court who looked like him.' He glanced up and saw Agrippa approaching. 'That is all,' he concluded.

I watched him walk away. Benjamin, his arms folded, seemed lost in his own thoughts. He waited until the smiling doctor had passed by.

'An interesting story, Roger. Do you believe it?'

'According to Fabyan's *Chronicle*,' I replied, airing my knowledge, 'when Henry IV fought at Shrewsbury against Hotspur, he dressed several of his knights in royal armour.'

[Oh, by the way, I also told William Shakespeare that and other details. You will read them in his play *Henry IV*. Will was so grateful he said he would base one of the characters of that drama on me. I think it is the Prince, though malicious tongues say it is Falstaff. God knows, I have nothing in common with him!]

We could talk no longer. Catesby was rapping out orders for us to mount and within the hour we had left St Mary Grace's, striking east for Canterbury. Queen Margaret and Lady Carey rode in front of the cavalcade, shimmering in their heavy brocade dresses. Alongside them rode Carey, Agrippa and Catesby, then us followed by the creaking carts and household minions. Melford and a group of archers fanned out before the cavalcade; they cleared the way of the usual merchants, traders, pedlars, students and hosts of vagabonds and beggars who cluster on every road like flies round a horse's arse.

At Canterbury Queen Margaret said prayers before the tomb of Thomas à Becket. Lord, such a sight: the casket which held Becket's body was encased in sheets of solid gold and, over the years, devout pilgrims had brought sapphires, diamonds, pearls and small rubies to be fastened into the goldwork as homage to the saint. Some of these gems were as large as goose eggs but the most precious was an exquisite diamond called the Regal of France. It had such fire and brilliance that even when the church was dark this diamond glowed like a flame in the sanctuary.

[Old Henry put an end to all that. The tomb was wrecked, the gold and silver went to his mint, and the Regal of France on to his large fat hand. Why do I tell you this? Well, the Regal of France caused murder, bloody intrigue and violent death. But that was for the future — you can read about it in one of my journals.]

After Canterbury we took the old Roman Road into Hertfordshire, planning to stop at a royal manor, but the weather turned cold; blustery rain clouds sped in from the sea and we were forced to break our journey at one of the great taverns just outside Canterbury. Melford soon cleared the chambers, telling the irate landlord to shut his mouth and present to the Exchequer, before the Feast of St John the Baptist, whatever bills we incurred. I remember that night well as the evil we had to face gathered and drew closer.

We were all sitting in the great taproom. It was dark and blustery outside and the flames of the candles danced, filling the room with moving shadows. The meal was over, Queen Margaret and Lady Carey had withdrawn and we men sat around the large oaken table, drinking deeply from the wine bowl. Ruthven had his cat with him,

stroking it and muttering something — I could not tell
whether he was talking to himself or his pet.

I noticed his comrades distanced themselves from him.
Indeed, rumours about Ruthven were rife — how he was
a warlock because he was left-handed and talked to his
cat. Ruthven just ignored them.

[In those days, if you were a witch you were safe as
long as you kept away from the common people: once
I saw a group of villagers spread-eagle a warlock, drive
a stake through his heart and bury him beneath a
crossroads gibbet.]

Anyway, back to my companions in that darkened
taproom: Catesby looked bright-eyed and flushed.
Moodie, more like a mouse than ever, nibbled at a bit
of cheese. There was ever-smiling Doctor Agrippa, hawk-
visaged Carey, the thick coarsened face of Melford and,
of course, Scawsby, his face sour as ever as if he had just
broken wind and hoped no one would notice. The
conversation swirled, passing from one topic to another.

Now Benjamin and I, recalling the Cardinal's secret
instructions, had decided to reveal Selkirk's verses as soon
as the opportunity presented itself. Benjamin indicated
with meaningful glances at me that this stark, sombre
evening was such an appropriate time. He skilfully guided
the conversation back to the sinister events surrounding
Selkirk's death for the murder had affected everybody.
Oh, there had been speculation that Scawsby was wrong
and the Scotsman had died because of some strange
seizure. Or again, that his death was the result of the Black
Arts, and many sombre looks were directed at Doctor
Agrippa, Ruthven and even Benjamin. My master bore
all this with his usual tolerance and bonhomie. He had
apparently recovered from his visit to Johanna, hiding
his feelings behind the usual veil of secrecy. Indeed, he
had hardly referred to her except once as we passed
through a small hamlet and had seen children baiting a
poor, crazed woman by the crossroads. Benjamin glanced
sideways at me and grimaced despairingly. However, he

had not forgotten Selkirk's death and, when we were alone, constantly speculated on how the Scotsman had been murdered and what his enigmatic rhyme could mean.

In that taproom he decided to push the matter further and Catesby gave him his chance.

'If Selkirk was murdered,' Sir Robert declared, 'what was the reason?'

'Master Daunbey should have found that out,' Scawsby replied spitefully.

'He questioned the wretch long enough,' Carey barked.

Moodie squeaked in support whilst Ruthven just dismissed them all with one scathing look.

'Oh, but I did,' Benjamin announced.

'You did what?' Carey snapped.

'I may not know how Selkirk died but I think I know why.'

'Nonsense!' Carey retorted. 'What do you mean?'

'Selkirk wrote a poem,' Benjamin continued quietly.

'Mere brainless chatter!' Carey answered.

'Oh, no,' Benjamin whispered.

Outside the wind blustered and beat against the wooden shutters and the huge sign, swinging on its iron pole, creaked and groaned as if calling out across the darkened, rain-soaked meadows.

Benjamin closed his eyes and chanted aloud:

'Three less than twelve should it be,
Or the King, no prince engendered he.
The lamb did rest,
In the falcon's nest.
The Lion cried,
Even though it died.
The truth Now Stands,
In the Sacred Hands,
Of the place which owns
Dionysius' bones.'

Now, the Lord be my witness, Benjamin's words created a pool of watchful silence.

Ruthven pushed his hair wildly back from his face. 'Repeat it, man!' he whispered hoarsely.

Benjamin did while I glanced around. Catesby and Agrippa sat impassive. Moodie's face was a white blur in the candlelight. Scawsby looked frightened, his eyes two small piss-holes. Carey looked dumbstruck, Ruthven strangely excited, whilst even Melford leaned forward and watched Benjamin with amber cat-like eyes.

'Do the words mean anything to anyone?' Benjamin asked.

Ruthven cradled his cat and stroked the back of its head, his hand moving faster and faster across the animal's fur until it stirred restlessly and mewed in protest.

'What else?' Catesby asked. 'What else did Selkirk tell you?'

'He did not give me the poem,' Benjamin replied. 'I found it. But once I asked him why he was in prison, and he muttered about his days at Le Coq d'Or tavern in Paris and said he was a prisoner because he could "count the days".'

Ruthven suddenly rose as if to suppress some excitement inside him.

'Oh, no!' he hissed, speaking his secret thoughts aloud. 'Selkirk was not as mad as he appeared. I suspect he was in the Tower not because he could count the days but was privy to secrets which could rock thrones and topple crowns!' He stood staring at us.

'What do you mean?' Melford snarled. Ruthven's face paled. He shook his head and quietly left the room. After his departure, we all sat silent and uneasy about what to do next until Catesby cracked a joke and the conversation turned to other matters.

The next morning we left for Leicester. I wondered once again what was so important about Selkirk. What did his words mean? Why was he killed? Was the assassin now amongst us? Would he strike again? What did Ruthven know? What mysteries surrounded us? A king who may not have died? A royal corpse not buried? A queen who now sought to return from her self-imposed exile? The intrigue around the White Rose and the mysterious *Les Blancs Sangliers*? I asked Benjamin but he just shook his head and pointed across to the dark fringes of the forest.

'In there, Roger, spirits, witches, dwarfs, Robin Goodfellow and the terrifying boneless creatures lurk. Perhaps Satan himself.' Benjamin nodded towards our companions, now silent after a hard night's drinking. 'Such terrors,' he whispered, 'pale compared to the demons which lurk in the mind of man and feed on the human spirit.'

I still remained puzzled as we travelled north. The journey was uneventful enough; nights spent in some local hostelry, priory or convent where Queen Margaret's influence and the Cardinal's letters obtained us free food and clean but hard beds. We crossed the silent wilderness north of London, the grass withering under a warm sun, and passed eventually into Leicestershire. The weather became cooler under the influences of cold breezes from the frozen north, observed my master. I hadn't any idea what he was talking about but I listened attentively to his description of lands I had never imagined, with their dark green forests, snowy slopes and frozen lakes. Sometimes Benjamin would play on the lute he always carried, whilst I accompanied him on the rebec. (Oh, yes, I had learnt to play this whilst spending a few months in a rotting gaol due to one of the many misunderstandings which plagued my life.) The rest of our party were still silent and withdrawn, openly mistrustful of each other. Memories of Selkirk's death might have receded slightly but the mystery still remained.

Sometimes we met other travellers and conversation with them enlivened the boredom: merchants, wandering friars, the occasional hunting party, clerics or landless men looking for labour. They constantly warned us of the danger of the roads, about the thieves and vagabonds who dressed in green or brown buckram and played Robin Hood in the dark forests or wastelands we passed through. At other times my master, tired by the reticence of Agrippa and the others, continued his absorption with alchemy. Both of us did try to draw Ruthven further on his outburst in the taproom but he openly scorned us. He became withdrawn, chatting only to Moodie.

At last we turned off the main high road and approached the city of Leicester. The mayor and civic dignitaries met us in a blaze of colour at Bow Bridge with the usual greetings and pleasantries. My master studied the bridge carefully.

'Roger,' he whispered, 'you know Richard III, the Great Usurper, passed over here on his route to Bosworth? As he passed, his leg struck the side of the bridge and an old witch prophesied that when he returned his head would strike the same spot.' Benjamin leaned closer. 'Richard's naked corpse was brought back slung across a donkey. Tonight we are to lodge at the Blue Boar inn near High Cross, the same tavern the Usurper rested at before Bosworth. Now I suspect some villainy so when we get there, slip away. Go to the Greyfriars Church, conceal yourself somewhere so you can watch a spot, a place in the Lady Chapel on the left side of the sanctuary. Stay there as long as you can. Only when it is dark should you leave – and be careful! Whatever happens, just observe.'

That's what I liked about Benjamin, always kind and considerate, and of course he needn't have advised old Shallot to stay out of danger! We wound our way through the cobbled streets of Leicester past the great, four-storeyed houses of the merchants, jutting out above us, and into the Newarks. The great Blue Boar inn was a half-stone tavern mansion, its glazed horned windows stared out over the market place. My master pulled me back, watching the riders mill around, paying particular

83

attention to the green-slimed horse trough in front of the Blue Boar.

[You know, of course, the Blue Boar was once called the White Boar but after Bosworth, they changed the colour from white to blue. I once talked to an old retainer of the Usurper who claimed Richard hid five hundred pounds in gold in the great bed there. I have been back to the tavern but have never found this treasure.]

Ah, well! I took a wineskin and went through the alleys and byeways of Leicester to Greyfriars Church. Inside it was cool and sombre, the pillars stretching up into the blackness, the nave and aisles silent except for the birds which nested under the eaves outside. I genuflected before the winking sanctuary lamp and concealed myself in one of the side chapels. From there I had a good view of a beautiful statue of the Madonna and Child lit by the flickering flames of candlelight, as well as of a small raised plinth of stone which I supposed marked the tomb of some notable. I sat, dozed, slurped from the wineskin, said a few prayers and kept my eyes fastened on the Lady Chapel. Some of the devout did come in; a mother and child, an old woman, and a dusty cloaked Franciscan. I watched the light fade outside the windows as the church grew cold, sombre and eerie.

'*Hic est terriblis locus* – this is a terrible place.' The words were scrawled on the frontal of the marble high altar. A terrible place indeed! Night fell, the candle flames flickered out and the ghosts of the dead came back to their resting place (or so the old wives say), somewhere sacred, a fitting protection against the assaults of the demons. The church door remained closed. I shivered and cursed my master. A lay brother came by, keys clanking. He wanted to close the church so I made myself known, claiming I was making a pilgrimage in atonement for my sins. He looked strangely at me, muttered something about coming back within the hour, and sauntered off. I went back to my hiding place. At last the door opened. A dark, cowled figure came in and went up to stand in the Lady Chapel. I crouched down to hide behind a pillar, and watched. The mysterious figure stared down at the tomb and then turned.

'Roger Shallot!' The voice was low and hollow. 'Roger Shallot, I know you are there!'

Oh, Lord, my heart beat quicker and a sudden sweat drenched my body.

'Shallot!' the ghostly figure bellowed. 'Come out!' The voice echoed in the high arches of the church.

I came out, shaking with fright, and watched the cowled figure sweep towards me. I saw a white hand draw back the hood and my master's innocent face grinned at me.

'Benjamin Daunbey!' I snarled. 'My arse and thighs are sore from a day's hard riding. I have lurked like some ghost in this cold, dank church, and now you appear, making a merry jest of it all!'

He laughed and clasped my hand. 'Roger,' he quipped, 'you look as frightened as a gargoyle! I'm sorry I scared you.' He beckoned me closer. 'Did you see anyone come in? I mean, go to the tomb over there? Pay their respects or place a white rose?'

I shook my head angrily. 'Nothing, Master. Why should they?'

He linked his arm through mine and we walked over to the tomb. Benjamin tapped it gently with his boot.

'Here, Roger, lie the mortal remains of King Richard III. His body was brought back to Leicester after the battle of Bosworth Field and thrown into the horse trough at the Blue Boar. The present King's father, his conscience pricked, had the corpse buried here and later erected this tomb.'

[Oh, by the way, when Bluff King Hal broke with Rome because he wanted to get amongst Boleyn's petticoats, the tomb was wrecked and Richard's corpse dumped into the River Stour.]

'So, Master,' I blurted out, 'King Richard lies here? What did you expect?'

Benjamin chewed on his lip and stared up into the darkness.

'What did I expect? Well, here we are in Leicester at the final resting place of the White Boar himself. Members of *Les Blancs Sangliers*, the Guardians of the White Rose, are supposed to be amongst our party. Yet no one comes here to pay their respects . . .' He rubbed the side of his face. 'I find that strange.' He put an arm round my shoulder and walked me back towards the church door. 'See, what do we have here, Roger? A Scottish doctor murdered in the Tower. Why? Because he spoke riddles in verse, or because he didn't believe the story of Flodden? What really happened at that battle? Why did Queen Margaret re-marry so quickly? Why does my good uncle send us to plead for her?' He waved his hand. 'There's a mystery here, Roger, something quite terrible. I don't trust my uncle, and I certainly don't trust Queen Margaret!'

'And Doctor Agrippa?' I asked.

Benjamin let his arm fall away. 'I'm not sure,' he murmured. 'Who is spying on whom? Agrippa is reputedly the agent of the Cardinal, as Carey, Moodie and Catesby are of Queen Margaret. But whom do they really work for? Is it in truth the Cardinal, or our gracious sovereign, or the Earl of Angus? Or even some other foreign potentate . . . ? After all, the present Regent of Scotland is by education a Frenchman. He, too, might be involved in this macabre, mysterious dance.'

We left Leicester and reached Royston Manor late the next afternoon. As a weak sun died and the shadows closed in around us, we saw the high pointed gables and turreted walls of the fortified manor house beckoning darkly to us over the treetops. Royston was a cold, sombre place which blighted our spirits as soon as we glimpsed it. Benjamin and I had been entertaining the group with a French madrigal, my deep bass a smooth foil to my master's well-modulated tenor: a stupid little song about a maid who lost her wealth and her virtue in the great city. Queen Margaret declared the sound was sweet and despatched a small purse of silver in token of her thanks.

As we entered the main causeway which snaked through the trees to the manor's main door, the sight of Royston killed the song on our lips and the joy in our hearts.

My master deepened my unease with a story about the stark, square building's previous owners, the Templars; the monks of war who, two centuries previously, had been brutally crushed by the papacy and the French crown because of their alleged involvement in witchcraft, dabbling in the Black Arts as well as such unnatural vices as sodomy and the worship of a huge black cat. As we dismounted and the grooms hurried about gathering the reins of our horses, Benjamin continued his low-voiced description of the fallen order. (Sometimes, I think, my master liked to frighten me.)

'Do you know, Roger, the Templars worshipped a mysterious image, a dreadful face printed on a cloth.'

At the time I smiled wanly and wished Benjamin would leave me alone. [I only mention this because he was in fact wrong. The Templars were crushed but some of them remained as a secret coven and I have crossed swords with them over the years. I have seen their dreadful face and the stories are true − strong men have lost their reason and wits once they have looked upon it. My chaplain begs me to say more but I shan't satisfy him!]

The inside of Royston Manor was equally grim: it usually stood empty, being used by the court as a place to rest during royal progresses and then left in the tender care of an old steward and a bustling, aged retainer. The steward answered Agrippa's insistent knocking and took us into the main hallway. The house was built in a square, with a broad staircase sweeping up into the darkness. At the top were two galleries, one to the left, the other to the right, which turned again to form a perfect square. On each gallery were chambers and our group was directed into these, servants being left to sleep in the hall, buttery or stables behind the manor house. Sconce torches were fixed in the wall but only a few of these were lit. Now and again we came across the signs and secret symbols of the Templar Order: huge black crosses, thinly covered with whitewash, whilst the arms and escutcheons of long dead knights still hung high on the walls.

The chambers themselves were bleak, containing truckle beds, a few pieces of furniture, a table and a bowl and jug for washing. The windows were mere arrow-slits now blocked by wooden shutters; the air was so damp with a pervasive chill that Queen Margaret insisted fires be lit in her rooms before she retired for the night. A cold meal was hastily served, a few words exchanged, and everyone speedily retired as Catesby insisted that on the morrow we would rise early as there was a great deal of business to be done.

Now it is important for me to tell the story correctly. At first there was a period of confusion as porters, cursing and sweating, brought up bags, chests and coffers. Ruthven was placed in the chamber next to ours and came upstairs just after us. I heard him lock the chamber door and, a few minutes later, the mewing of his cat scratching at the wood for admittance. I went out into the gallery, Ruthven's door opened, the Scotsman came out, picked up the cat, smiled at me and went inside. I heard the key turn. I was going to knock for I was still intrigued by him but Benjamin called me so I let the matter rest.

We retired to bed but I couldn't sleep. I felt restless, uneasy in that haunted, creaking manor house. My terrors would have increased if I had known how once again Murder was stalking us, in that Godforsaken place.

Chapter 5

We were up early next morning. A heavy mist had fallen, drowning the countryside in its white vapour and making Royston Manor even more sinister. We breakfasted in the dingy Great Hall. Queen Margaret came in, leaning heavily on Catesby's arm. The desultory conversation faded. Catesby looked around.

'Where's Ruthven? I ordered everyone to rise early.' He glanced across at me. 'Shallot, be so courteous as to tell Master Ruthven we await him here.'

Carey heard this as he marched in, his bad temper apparent.

'Yes, go and tell him. Hurry up!' he snapped.

Now I would have stood my ground, I wasn't a dog to be sent running hither and thither, but Benjamin added his plea with his eyes.

'Melford, go with him,' Catesby added.

We went back up the staircase and I hammered on the door. There was no answer though I heard the faint mewing of the cat. We tried the door but it was locked.

'Is anything wrong?' Carey called from the hall below.

'No answer,' Melford shouted back. 'Was Ruthven seen this morning?'

Carey hurried up, then Catesby, followed by Moodie and a worried servant.

'Try the door again,' Carey ordered.

Benjamin joined us. We knocked, shouted and pushed. Catesby instructed us to take a bench leaning against the far wall and, though the space was narrow, we began to pound at the door like besiegers breaking into a castle. The old steward came hurrying up, huffing and puffing, but Carey snarled at him so he slunk away. One final shove and the buckled door flew back on its leather hinges.

I'll describe things as they were: Ruthven was slumped across the desk, his head on his arm, his face a whitish-blue, mouth open, eyes staring but sightless. In the far corner, the cat cowered as if it knew it was in the presence of death. On the table near Ruthven stood an empty pewter goblet. Carey lifted the body carefully.

'Dead,' he muttered. 'Dead as a stone! Place him on the bed.'

We carried him across, arranging the cold, lifeless form, trying to impose some dignity for already rigor mortis had set in. The look on the dead man's face was ghastly, as if some phantom of the night had stopped his heart. I wondered where the soul had gone. Was it still with us? Do the souls of the dead stand behind some invisible mirror, watching us who cannot see them?

'Look!' Moodie suddenly yelled.

He pointed to the bolster at the top of the bed where a small, white rose lay like some gift waiting to be presented. We all stood staring at the flower as if it were responsible for Ruthven's death.

'What's the matter?' Agrippa, accompanied by Scawsby, stood in the doorway. Melford pointed to the corpse on the bed and the flower still lying there. Scawsby hurried over, full of his own importance. The fool failed to realise the significance of the white rose, but instead peered down at Ruthven.

'A seizure!' he announced. 'Quite common in a man of choleric humour.'

Melford snorted, mocking him. Agrippa smiled, going up beside the doctor and picking up the white rose.

'I think not, good physician,' he whispered. 'Master Ruthven was murdered and the assassin left his token.' He twirled the rose between his fingers as he looked around. 'The murderer is here in Royston. The question is, who?'

We just stared back. The last time I had seen a white rose had been in that filthy room in the Tower. My master stared at the flower curiously before bending over Ruthven's corpse. He examined the eyes, tongue and nails of the dead man minutely, taking deep sniffs at the gaping mouth.

'Master Ruthven was poisoned,' he declared. 'But how?' He walked over and picked up the pewter goblet, sniffing at it carefully. 'Nothing,' he murmured, 'but the faint tinge of claret. Who brought this up?'

Agrippa shrugged. 'Ruthven did so himself. I saw him as he left the table last night.'

'I smell no potion,' Benjamin replied. He turned to Scawsby. 'Master Physician,' he asked tactfully, 'you would agree?'

Scawsby took the wine cup and held it under his long, arrogant nose.

'Nothing,' he answered.

Agrippa took the cup from him, rubbed his finger around it to collect the dregs and, despite the gasps of Moodie and Carey, licked it noisily.

'Correct, Master Daunbey, no poison.'

'Are you an authority on poisons, Master Daunbey?' Melford asked sharply.

'No,' Benjamin replied tartly. 'But as Physician Scawsby will testify, as Clerk to the Justices I have viewed enough corpses and have some knowledge of . . .'

His voice trailed away as Doctor Agrippa spread his hands.

'Yet,' Agrippa interrupted briskly, 'Ruthven was poisoned, even though he ate and drank only what we all did yesterday evening. So, did anyone else visit him in his room?'

A chorus of denials greeted his question and, because of my sleepless night, I could confirm these. I had heard no human footfalls in the corridor.

Carey stepped forward. 'So Ruthven locks himself in his chamber, he visits no one and no one visits him, but the next morning he is found poisoned and a white rose discovered lying on the bed.'

'Just like Selkirk,' Agrippa added flatly.

'Are there any secret passages?' Moodie squeaked.

Catesby glanced despairingly at the ceiling; still, the old steward was summoned and questioned. The man was frightened, unable to tear his eyes away from Ruthven's corpse, but he shook his head.

'No tunnels,' he declared roundly. 'No passageways or trap doors, but there are ghosts,' he said defiantly. 'The monk knights still walk the corridors.'

Melford sneered in derision.

'Did Master Ruthven go down to the kitchen or buttery or ask for any victuals to be sent up?' asked Catesby.

The old man shook his head and was dismissed.

'Is there anything else?' my master asked.

'What do you mean?' snapped Carey.

'Something in the room perhaps?'

A brief search was made but nothing untoward was found. Ruthven's ink-stained quill was lying on the floor. My master picked it up, scrutinised it carefully then threw it on the table.

'A mystery,' Agrippa announced. He glared round at all of us. 'But someone here is a murderer who knows how Ruthven died!' He sighed and looked at Carey. 'Enough of this, Queen Margaret must be informed.'

We all trooped downstairs, my master staying behind to scrutinise the room once more then joining me outside, shaking his head.

'Doctor Agrippa is right,' he whispered. 'A true mystery. How can a man, hale and hearty before he retired, be found poisoned the next morning, when no one visited him and he remained locked in his room?' He looked at me sharply. 'You saw him?'

I nodded. 'You heard me,' I replied. 'He opened his chamber door, smiled at me and picked up his cat.'

'So how was he poisoned?'

The question dominated our discussions as we gathered in what used to be the long Chapter Room of the Knights Templar.

Queen Margaret sat at the head of the cracked, dangerously shaky table whilst Catesby ordered benches to be brought in for the rest. The King's sister was white-faced and tight-lipped, obviously finding it difficult to control her anger.

'Someone here,' she snapped, her eyes darting round us, 'murdered Ruthven! Someone here is also a traitor, guilty of the blackest treason. Why does the House of York plague us with their romantic dreams and stupid ambitions? The assassins, in their temerity, even left a white rose to mock us! Doctor Agrippa . . .' her voice trailed off.

The good doctor beamed around.

'We must account for our movements,' he said. 'Each and every one of us.'

His prompting was summarily answered. No one had approached Ruthven. Both Master Benjamin and myself had heard nothing amiss and Moodie, who had been in the chamber adjoining Ruthven's on the other side, could also confirm this.

'How was Ruthven?' Catesby asked. 'I mean, in the days before his death? Did he say or do anything untoward?' He looked around. 'To whom did he talk?'

'He talked to Moodie,' Melford observed.

'Well?' Agrippa asked.

The mouse-faced chaplain became even more agitated than usual.

'Ruthven kept to himself,' he stammered. 'He was distant, lost in his own thoughts.'

'What did he talk about?'

'About Selkirk's murder. He found the fellow's mutterings strange.'

'Anything else?'

Moodie licked his lips and looked nervously at Queen

Margaret. Then, placing his hands on the table, he looked down, refusing to meet anyone's eyes.

'We also talked about the days before Flodden – the doings of the late King and the gossip of the court.'

'What gossip?' Queen Margaret asked smoothly.

'Nothing, My Lady. Just memories . . . recollections of happier days. I assure you, that was all.'

'The rose?' Benjamin asked abruptly.

'What about it?' Agrippa retorted.

'Well, there are no roses here!'

'There were in Canterbury,' Scawsby pointed out. 'Small, white rosebuds, the type which come late in the year.'

'So,' Benjamin continued, 'the murderer planned Ruthven's death, then . . .' He let his comment hang like a rope in the air.

'There is no doubt,' Agrippa intervened silkily, 'that Ruthven died by the same hand and in the same way as Selkirk in the Tower.' He took us all in with one sombre glance. 'How Ruthven was murdered, and why, is a mystery.' He looked at Scawsby. 'There was no food or wine in the room?'

The old quack shook his head.

'And you, Shallot, were the last person to see him alive?'

'And I heard no one come up!' I snapped.

Agrippa took a deep breath, placing both hands on the table before him.

'Is it possible, Master Physician, for poison to be administered in slow drops?'

Scawsby grimaced. 'I suppose so, but that would be dangerous. The poisoner would have to infuse the potions many times and, if he was caught . . .'

'Is it possible,' Catesby grated, 'for a poison to be slow acting?'

Scawsby smiled peevishly. 'I have never heard of such a potion. And, even if one existed, Ruthven would surely have felt the effects before he retired.'

'Master Scawsby is correct,' Benjamin added. 'Ruthven was meant to die in that room, behind a locked and barred door.' He waved a bony finger in the air. 'Remember, the door was locked and bolted from the inside. The assassin is subtle and clever. No one heard him come up but he must have got in for Ruthven to die and the white rose to be found.'

'And you, Master Daunbey, were in the chamber next to him,' Lady Carey retorted. She glanced balefully at me. 'Your servant was the last man to see him alive. Isn't it strange that you, Benjamin, were the last person to see Selkirk alive!'

'I am sure,' Queen Margaret intervened smoothly, 'no suspicion of foul play can fall on the Cardinal's nephew.' She glanced angrily at Lady Carey, then smiled falsely at us.

But, oh, that was a clever move by Carey! The damage had been done because when you fling dirt, some sticks. The rest of the group stared at us like a hanging jury before sentence is passed. Benjamin smiled as if savouring a secret joke.

'Lady Carey is correct in some of what she says but her logic is faulty,' he commented. 'Ruthven died because he knew something. He was probably the only one, besides the murderer, to understand all or some of Selkirk's verses.' He leaned forward. 'The murderer is definitely here. I wonder which of us has Yorkist sympathies. Melford?'

The mercenary stirred like a cat alerted to danger.

'What is it, Daunbey?'

'Didn't your family fight for the White Rose once?'

The mercenary smirked. 'Yes, but that's true of everyone here. Isn't it, Carey?'

The old soldier fidgeted as memories stirred. Accusations grew heated, voices were raised. The sum total of charge and counter charge was that every person in the room, besides myself and Benjamin, had some affinity or link with the House of York and the cause of the White Rose. Queen Margaret sat back in her chair watching disdainfully. Catesby looked furious whilst Doctor Agrippa, eyes closed, arms folded, sat like some benevolent friar after a hearty meal. At last he stirred. Drawing a long, thin stiletto from his belt, he rapped the top of the table.

'Come, come!' he shouted. 'You are like children playing a game. These angry words prove nothing. Ruthven could have been killed by magic.' He grinned down at me. 'But we are here on other business.'

'Master Daunbey, we have lost enough time over Ruthven's death.' Catesby interrupted. 'Have your bags packed. You are to leave within the hour. The steward will provide you with a local guide.'

Benjamin tugged at my sleeve. We rose, bowed to the head of the table and left our companions to their baleful conjecturing. Benjamin skipped lightly up the stairs but, instead of going to our own chamber, took me into Ruthven's. The corpse still lay sheeted on the bed. Benjamin scrutinised the room, especially the objects on the desk, picking up the quill, the ink and paper. He sniffed at each, shook his head and put them back.

'What are you looking for, Master?'

'I don't really know,' he replied.

He went across to the bed and pulled back the sheet. He scrutinised Ruthven's corpse, paying particular attention to the hands and closely examining the callous on Ruthven's third finger. Again he sniffed carefully.

'No poison there,' he whispered. He prised open Ruthven's mouth. I stood behind him, trying to conceal my fear and distaste. Surely the dead man's ghost would object to this? Was his soul still earthbound? Would it stay here forever or be freed only when his murderer was brought to justice? Benjamin examined the yellowing teeth. He took a small pin from the sleeve of his doublet and began to scrape between the yellow stumps until he extracted small, grey fragments still wet with mucus.

Benjamin held the pin up to the light, staring at these scrapings.

'What is it, master?' I whispered.

Benjamin shook his head. 'I don't know. It could be food, perhaps some bread.'

'What are you doing, Benjamin?'

Both my master and I turned quickly. Doctor Agrippa and Sir Robert Catesby stood in the doorway. Benjamin beamed.

'Nothing, good doctor. Lady Carey insinuated I might be involved in Ruthven's death. I thought I might find something to show I was not.'

'And have you?' Catesby asked.

Unobserved, Benjamin let the pin drop to the floor.

'No, not at all.'

Catesby waved us forward. 'Then come!'

We went into our own chamber. Catesby, closing the door behind him, told us to sit.

'Forget Ruthven's death,' he began. 'The Scottish envoys will soon land at Yarmouth. They have safe conducts and passes to travel to Nottingham where you will meet them. Queen Margaret's second husband, the Earl of Angus, will be present but the delegation is led by Lord d'Aubigny, one of the Regent's lieutenants. You will treat with him about Queen Margaret's return to Scotland. You will offer nothing, but listen most carefully to what is said. We have arranged for you to be there on the Feast of St Cecilia, the twenty-second of November. However, before that, in two days' time, on the Feast of St Leo the Great, you will meet Irvine, My Lord Cardinal's spy, at Coldstream Priory which lies about thirty miles from here. Irvine's information may well be given in cipher. You will memorise the message and bring it back to me and Doctor Agrippa.'

'Why the secrecy?' I asked. 'Why can't Irvine come here? Why are the Scottish envoys coming by sea? And why Nottingham? Moreover,' I glanced sideways at my master, 'surely the Scottish nobles will want to treat with someone more important than the Cardinal's nephew and,' I added bitterly, 'his manservant.'

Agrippa smirked. 'Shallot!' he murmured. 'Use your head. Irvine cannot come here — there is a traitor and a murderer in the Queen's party. Despite Lady Carey's accusations, you and Benjamin,' he glanced slyly at Catesby, 'are the only ones above suspicion. Moreover, if the Lord Cardinal trusts you implicitly, so will Irvine. As for the Scottish envoys . . . first, a journey by land is too dangerous; secondly, our good King Henry believes this is a Scottish matter and does not wish to intervene officially; finally, Queen Margaret and her household, on the other hand, do not wish to be seen to have anything to do with the men who drove her from Scotland.' Agrippa leaned closer and I smelt that strange perfume he always wore. 'So, Shallot, the pieces of the puzzle fall into place. The Scots will talk with Master Benjamin. They know he acts on the personal authority of the Cardinal.'

'And the rest?' Benjamin spoke up. 'You all stay at Royston?'

Catesby grinned sheepishly. 'Unfortunately, yes, though Melford and I will leave for Nottingham within the hour to ensure the castle is ready for the Scottish envoys.' Catesby smiled. 'You have three days to reach Coldstream Priory. As for Ruthven . . . ' he turned and lifted the latch of our chamber door, 'as Scripture says: " . . . Leave the dead to bury the dead . . ." Eh, good doctor?'

And without further ado they slipped out of the chamber.

We took our leave of a sombre-visaged Queen Margaret and within the hour the steward's guide was leading us out of Royston Manor and into the mist-shrouded countryside. Catesby and Melford had already departed, riding hard for Nottingham, leaving Agrippa, the Careys, Moodie and the old quack Scawsby at Royston.

Our guide was a dour-faced, taciturn, little man who had as much chatter and wit as a dumb-struck oaf though he knew the bridle paths and trackways of Leicestershire like the back of his hand. It was a strange journey. The heavy mist rarely lifted but closed in like a cold, clinging cloud around us. We had the eerie impression that we were the only people alive and the clip-clop of our horses' hooves was the last remaining sound under heaven. Naturally, my master and I reflected on what had happened at Royston.

'I'm puzzled, Roger,' Benjamin kept repeating. 'Two most ingenious murders: both Selkirk and Ruthven poisoned in chambers locked from the inside.' He sighed, his breath hanging like a cloud in the icy air. 'Yet no trace of poison, no one enters their chamber . . . most subtle, most subtle!'

I could only agree and wondered if Agrippa's joke about magic might have some truth in it. I also guiltily recollected Lady Carey's insidious remarks: somehow or other Benjamin was always close to the murdered person. Was he the assassin? I wondered. Did Benjamin carry secret orders from his uncle that Selkirk and Ruthven were to die for the common good? If so, who would be next? I dismissed the thoughts as too disturbing and concentrated instead on Selkirk's poem. The first and last lines especially puzzled me. Benjamin could give no enlightenment but speculated on what news Irvine might bring.

'Perhaps he will provide privy information which will explain it all,' he observed.

I shook my head. I had the uneasy feeling it would not be so simple. Moreover, since leaving Royston I was becoming concerned that we were being followed. Oh, I had no real evidence but a certain wariness, a feeling of unease. Perhaps it was only the effect of the cold, clinging mist but now and again I would catch a sound as if another rider were covertly following our route. We stopped and sheltered in a farmer's barn for the night and the following morning, misty as ever, did little to assuage my suspicions.

'What's the matter, Roger?' Benjamin asked, peering closely at me, his head deep in its woollen cowl. In front of us, the guide also stopped. I listened to the echoes of our horses' hoofbeats fade away, my ears straining.

'Master, we are being followed!'

'Are you sure, Roger?'

'As certain as I am that Queen Margaret has two tits!' I observed crossly.

Benjamin grinned wryly and listened with me. I thought I heard something but then the oaf of a guide urged his horse back, shouting out questions which would have roused the dead. Benjamin shook his head.

'Nothing, Roger,' he commented. 'Perhaps the ghosts of Royston?'

We continued on our way and reached Coldstream Priory just after dark, only being admitted within the convent walls after a great deal of shouting and argument. We waited in the yard until the lady prioress herself came out, a strange woman and rather young for such high office. She was not clad in the garb of her order but attired in a pale blue dress trimmed with the copper hue of squirrel fur. Her head-dress was old-fashioned, two veils of pleated lawn falling down either side of her heart-shaped face and fastened under the chin by a bejewelled gorget. Her skin was as white as milk, her eyes were green flecked with amber, and rather slanted. She looked slyly at my master, just like Queen Margaret had, though she greeted us civilly enough, ordering servants to take our guide and the baggage off to the guest house while she entertained us with cups of wine, fresh-baked bread and huge bowls of hot spicy broth. The prioress read the Cardinal's letters of introduction and listened to my master's questions about the arrangements for our meeting with Irvine. She just shook her pretty head and looked coyly at us.

'No such man has come here yet. Nor have we any warning of his arrival.'

'But My Lord Cardinal said the man would be here

today, the Feast of St Leo the Great,' replied Benjamin.

The prioress pursed her lips.

'No other man has approached our convent walls, nor have travellers or pedlars reported anyone on the roads.' She smiled. 'Perhaps he has been delayed. Perhaps he will arrive tomorrow.'

Tomorrow came and went, 'creeping by' as Master Shakespeare would put it, but no Irvine arrived. We whiled away our time in the convent's comfortable guest house. Our clothes were laundered and, morning, noon and eve, we were invited to partake of fresh-cooked meals and wines even a king would have envied. A strange place, Coldstream Priory: no bells for divine office, just a rather hasty Mass said before noon. The nuns themselves gossiped freely in and out of church. Indeed, as my poet friend would put it, any regulations regarding their life seemed to be honoured more in the breach than in the observance. My master said they had a splendid library, as well they might, but the only work I saw the nuns do was clever and intricate embroidery of curtains, cloths and napkins.

The prioress seemed to regard my master as her chief concern. She solicitously asked if all was well, sending constant messages to enquire if there was anything lacking, or inviting him to walk with her in the sweet-smelling orchard outside the convent church.

My master's main concern was Irvine's non-appearance and when darkness fell on our third day at Coldstream, we both walked out on to the convent wall, peering into the darkness as if willing him to appear. The lady prioress joined us. She pressed close to my master, stroking his hand gently with one of her fingers.

'Master Benjamin,' she said, 'Irvine will arrive tomorrow perhaps. Come – a glass of wine laced with nutmeg?'

My master refused but I cheerfully accepted. The lady prioress glowered at me, shrugged, and with ill grace took me back to her own chamber across the cloister garden where she poured me the smallest goblet of wine I had ever seen. She then busied herself around the room, the implication quite clear: I was to drink up and get out as quickly as I could. I enjoyed making her wait but, just before I left, she called over to me, a false smile on her pretty, hypocritical face.

'Roger, your master − he is a true man?'

'Yes, My Lady,' I replied.

The prioress caught the tip of her tongue between her sharp, white teeth, her eyes sparkling with anticipation.

'A true stallion,' I continued. 'A great romancer where the damsels are concerned but . . .'

'But what?' she asked sharply.

'At times he can be shy and perhaps . . .'

'Perhaps what?' she snapped impatiently.

I nodded towards the bedchamber which I could glimpse through a half open door. 'My Lady, I think he is as taken with you as you are with him. Perhaps if My Lady were to wait for him tonight, there in the dark, he might recite some love poetry . . . a sonnet he has composed?'

The prioress smiled, turned away and opened a small coffer. She threw a clinking bag at me.

'If you can arrange this, Shallot, there will be another purse in the morning.'

'Oh, all My Lady has to do,' I replied with a bow, 'is leave a candle here burning in the window.' I pointed to the high sill which ran just beneath the horn-glazed covering. 'My master will take it as a sign, a beacon to lead him the way you wish.'

I scampered out of the door. Master Benjamin was still on the convent wall, peering into the darkness. I ran up to the guest room, stripped naked and washed myself with a wet rag. I rubbed some of the fragrant perfume my master used into my neck and cheeks, borrowed his best cambric shirt, cloak and hood, and slunk back to the courtyard. I waited a while, hidden in the shadows, watching the convent settle for the night. Ah, yes, the lady prioress was also preparing herself. A candle appeared at her window, its flickering flame a beacon of welcome.

I slipped quietly across the courtyard, pushed open the door and stepped into the darkness. I quenched the candle flame with my fingers and slid into the bed chamber. Praise be, the lady prioress had no light or candle there. My eyes grew accustomed to the darkness and I glimpsed her dark shape on the bed, her long hair falling down to her shoulders. I slipped into the great four-poster bed, whispered a few French endearments I had learnt from a wench and set to with a will. The prioress may have been a lady but she welcomed my rough embraces with groans and shrieks of pleasure. Her body was succulent, slender and smooth. I confess she was one of the merriest tumbles I have ever had.

[Oh, dear, there goes my chaplain again, tut-tutting and shaking his noddle! The little hypocrite! Does he have to be reminded about his long meetings with apple-cheeked Maude the milkmaid at the back of my stables? She certainly came out more red-faced than she went in! He says I lie; the prioress would know the difference between me and Benjamin. He's wrong. Lust, like love, blinds the eyes, otherwise red-cheeked Maude would never let him within a mile of her! Ah, good, he has stopped shaking his head. So, back to the prioress . . .]

'Oh, sweet heaven! Oh, sweet heaven!' she cried as I entered her, my weapon as hard as any spear. Oh, what a night! Two, three times, I had my pleasure of her before kissing her roundly on the cheeks, slapping her on the bottom and whispering a fond adieu.

Next morning a heavy mist had blown in, covering the land with a blanket of gloomy silence. It swirled amongst the convent buildings, dulling the spirit — even mine after such a riotous night. I rose early, pleasantly tired. My master was still asleep, as he had been the previous evening when I returned from my love tryst. I dressed quickly and hurried across the courtyard to the refectory. This was

reached by outside stairs and some of the nuns, ever
hungry, were already filing in. I heard one comment
tossed back.

'Such a gargoyle! A veritable troll of a man!'

I wondered who this unbecoming fellow was and hung
my head in embarrassment when another replied.

'Yes, his name is Roger. Isn't it strange such a
handsome master employs such an ugly servant!'

Of course, nuns have no finesse, no real appreciation
of the true beauty which can lie beneath the surface. I
took my place in the refectory at a separate table near
the dais and watched the lady prioress sweep in. Her face
was pale, her eyes dark-rimmed, and this assuaged some
of my pain at the nun's silly chatter. Master Benjamin
joined me, gaily prophesying that the mist would soon
lift and it would be another splendid day. Out of the
corner of my eye I noticed how the prioress kept sending
him frowning glances at being ignored, interspersed with
coy smiles in an attempt to provoke him into some loving
conspiracy about the events of the previous night.

Her love sighs were suddenly interrupted by a
commotion outside, the screams of women mingling with
the deep gruff shouts of some of the convent's labourers
and porters. The prioress, lips pursed tight, hurried out
and we followed. In the courtyard below, surrounded by
nuns and other members of the convent, sat a strange-
looking man on horseback. His hair was dyed orange and
his white face made ghostly by his dyed russet beard. He
wore a cap of rabbit skin and a dirty moleskin jerkin to
which small bells had been sewn. The prioress muttered
he was a pedlar, but the real source of the commotion
was the corpse slumped across the fellow's sumpter pony.
As Benjamin and I followed the prioress down, the pedlar
shouted in a tongue I could not understand.

'What's he saying?' Benjamin asked.

'He found the corpse,' she replied archly over her
shoulder, 'a few hours' journey from the convent.'

Benjamin went across and pulled back the dead man's

head. I glimpsed sandy hair, a white-grey face, glazed open eyes and slack jaw. What really drew my attention, however, was the ugly, purple-red gash which ran from ear to ear. The prioress chatted to the pedlar in a strange tongue.

'It may be the man you've been waiting for, Master Benjamin,' she called across. 'John Irvine.'

The prioress instructed the porter to take the body into the nearby infirmary, ordered the crowd to disperse and asked one of the sisters to extend hospitality to the pedlar. Inside the low ceilinged, lime-washed sick room the corpse was laid on a straw-covered bed. He had been a young man, quite personable until someone slashed his throat. Benjamin stared as if the victim had been well known to him. We noticed the man's wallet had been cut away from the belt round his waist.

'Robbers!' the lady prioress murmured. 'The roads are plagued with them. The pedlar found the corpse hidden under some bushes.'

I knelt down and went through the dead man's clothing. Sure enough I found what I was looking for: a concealed pocket inside the quilted jerkin. This contained cunningly inlaid pouches holding a little gold and some silver (which I pocketed to have Masses said for the poor man's soul), and a small roll of parchment. On top of this was scrawled the man's name 'John Irvine' and a list of victuals and wine bought from his own pocket at a tavern called the Sea Barque near the Town Wall in Leicester. I walked back to Master Benjamin.

'It is Irvine,' I said.

'Then God rest his soul!' he answered. 'Roger, we have no need to delay here further. We must hasten back to Royston.'

Behind us, the lady prioress gasped.

'Don't you wish to stay, Master Benjamin?' She came closer, her skirts swaying and rustling. 'You are not happy with our hospitality?' she asked archly.

'My Lady,' he replied, 'the food and wine were

excellent.' And, spinning on his heel, he left the woman standing open-mouthed behind him. We summoned our guide, packed our saddle bags and, within the hour, had our horses saddled and ready to leave. The lady prioress, a pure wool cloak wrapped around her, came down to bid us adieu. Benjamin just smiled, raised her white fingers to his lips, kissed them daintily and, like some chivalrous knight, kicked his horse into a canter, almost knocking his would-be-love to the ground. I was less gallant. Ignoring the expression of shock on the woman's face, I stretched out my hand.

'My Lady,' I said, 'you promised me another purse!'

She glared at me, dug beneath her cloak and pushed a purse (much leaner than the one she had given me the night before) into my hand.

'Pimp!' she hissed.

'Oh, sweet heaven! Oh, sweet heaven!' I mimicked in a falsetto voice. The woman's face became pale, her eyes ever widening pools of anger. I laughed and set spurs to my horse and thundered through the convent gates as fast as a deer. I was surprised to see Benjamin keep to a swift gallop, not reining in until a good mile separated us from the convent. Eventually we stopped to walk the horses, the guide going ahead.

'Why the haste, Master?' I asked.

He shook his head and stared up at the sun now breaking through the blanket of mist.

'An evil place, that convent,' he murmured.

My stomach lurched. Did my master know?

'An evil place,' he repeated. He stared at me. 'Irvine was probably murdered there. The lady prioress had a hand in it!'

I gazed back at him, dumbfounded.

'First,' Benjamin continued, 'When we arrived at Coldstream, the prioress said she had not seen Irvine.'

'But the pedlar could have told her.'

'How would he know? His wallet had been taken and it was you who found his concealed pocket. Before you did, the prioress called him: 'John Irvine'. So she seemed to have recognised the corpse and knew his christian name. I didn't tell her that, did you?'

I shook my head. 'But what makes you think he was murdered in the convent?' I asked.

'Ah, that's my second point. When I was on the parapet of the convent wall I saw fresh horse dung lying near the main gate; it was not from our mounts, but the lady prioress said no one had approached the convent.' Benjamin brought his hand up to emphasise his point. 'Did you notice the cloister garden?' he continued. 'The ground was covered with a fine white sand. There were traces of that on Irvine's boots. Finally, the points on his leggings had been tied up wrongly as if done by someone else in a hurry.' Benjamin squinted at me. 'I suspect poor Irvine was murdered in that convent when he loosed his trews, either to relieve himself or . . .' His voice faded away.

I felt a spasm of fear and rubbed my own throat, plucking greedily at the skin. Benjamin was probably right. Irvine had been killed, not preparing for a piss but to carry out the same amorous duties I had. I silently vowed I would not be returning to Coldstream.

'We could go back,' Benjamin muttered, as if he read my thoughts. 'But, of course,' he continued, 'that would prove nothing. The lady prioress would deny the charge, and call in the sheriff or some local justice she has in her power. Anyway,' he sighed, peering away into the mist, 'we have very little evidence.'

'And now, Master,' I answered, 'once again we go back with our tails between our legs! Selkirk was killed before he could reveal anything. Ruthven's dead, and now Irvine.' I had a wild thought but dismissed it: Had Benjamin killed Irvine? Had he gone out one dark night and ambushed the fellow?

'What are you thinking, Roger?'

'I am thinking,' I lied, 'about Irvine staying at the Sea Barque in Leicester.' I took out the piece of parchment I had found on the corpse.

'Strange,' Benjamin commented, watching me closely, 'the murderers did not find that.'

I shrugged. 'The poor fellow had to die quickly. They took his wallet and, after that, he was crows' meat. You do realise,' I added, 'that the lady prioress may have connived at Irvine's death but the murderer must be one of our party from Royston? Only they, as well as the Lord Cardinal, knew Irvine was coming here.'

'But who could it be? Catesby and Melford have gone to Nottingham and we can always establish what day they arrived there. I suppose someone could have come from Royston, perhaps leaving after us but passing us in the mist to plan their ambush . . .'

The guide came over, shouting at us in his strange dialect. Benjamin politely asked him to wait.

'So, Roger, you think we should go to the Sea Barque at Leicester?'

'Yes, Master. We may find something there which could explain Irvine's death and Selkirk's death-bearing verses.'

Chapter 6

We bribed the guide with silver and a promise of more to take us to Leicester. A day later, we were struggling through the runnels and alleyways of that city. The good Lord knows what a dirty, loathsome task it was: the crowded houses, and the stinking sewers which smelt like a boiling cauldron in the heat of the city. At last we discovered the Sea Barque in a rundown market square just under the city walls. The houses on each side of this gloomy square were dirty and ramshackle; an old dog lay panting under the small market cross. Now and again it would rise and lick the feet of a sore-infested beggar fastened tight in the stocks. It was eventide, the market was finished and both the hucksters and their customers were sheltering under the striped canvas awnings of the small ale booths. Benjamin pointed to the Sea Barque, a narrow tenement three storeys high with a great ale stake tucked under its eaves and a gaudily painted sign hanging tipsily over the battered door. Around this entrance were a small group of tinkers and pedlars selling brightly coloured ribbons, gloves, plums and green apples. We pushed through these into the tavern whilst our guide stayed outside to hold the horses.

The taproom of the Sea Barque was cool although musty, its tables nothing but barrels, with a few rickety stools and benches round the walls. We had been warned by a merchant on the road not to drink either the water or the muddy-coloured ales because the plague had recently been raging in the city and the streams might still be infected. My master ordered a jug of wine and questioned the slattern, a pretty, fresh-cheeked wench, who would have been quite comely if she had kept her teeth. Benjamin, courteous as ever, let her sip from his cup and thrust a penny into her small but calloused hand.

'Child,' he remarked, 'do you remember a man called Irvine – fresh-faced, sandy-haired, perhaps secretive and sly? He talked like a Scotsman?'

The girl looked puzzled so I repeated the description and recognition dawned in her bright blue eyes. She nodded her head vigorously and chattered gaily though I could only understand half of what she said. Apparently Irvine had been a constant patron of the place.

'At first he came alone,' the slattern announced. 'He ate and drank generously and was well liked by the other customers, even though he was a Scotsman.' She stopped speaking and winked at my master, taking another sip from his goblet and grabbing the second penny he offered. 'But then,' she continued like a child reciting a story, 'he became secretive and withdrawn and took to meeting in a corner with a sinister-looking fellow.' She screwed up her eyes to remember. 'This stranger had dark brown hair, a patch over one eye and a large purple birth mark which stretched across his cheek.'

'Was he English?' I asked.

She laughed and shook her head. 'A true Scotsman. He could drink like a fish and I couldn't understand his coarse speech.'

'And did Irvine leave anything?' my master asked.

'Oh, no. I cleaned his room.' She looked slyly at me. 'Or, at least, I tried to.'

'Why do you say that?' Benjamin snapped.

'Because he left a drawing on the wall. The landlord was furious and told me to wash it off.'

'What was it?' I asked.

'A large bird,' she answered. 'He drew it with a piece of charcoal. A large bird with a cruel beak and a crown on its head.'

'Like an eagle?' I queried.

110

'Yes, yes,' the girl replied.

'And Irvine's strange companion?' Benjamin asked. 'What did he do?'

'Nothing but chatter to Irvine, then he left, and Irvine shortly afterwards.'

We thanked the wench who could tell us nothing else. We spent some more time moving around Leicester, going from tavern to tavern trying to discover if anyone else had seen Irvine's strange companion. We met with nothing but failure. The end of the second day in the city found us faded, dirty and eager to leave.

We spent two days travelling back to Royston with a guide who was as tired of us as we were sick of him. The manor house, despite a change in the weather, still looked grim: a gloomy, squat huddle of buildings hiding behind a cracked, moss-covered curtain wall. Melford and a group of bowmen greeted us at the gate. Above them, his feet kicking, his hose stained, face black and tongue protruding, danced one of the kitchen minions.

'Hanged!' Melford cheerily announced. 'For stealing household goods and trying to sell them in the surrounding villages.'

The bastard smiled evilly at me as if he would have loved to have put a noose round *my* neck and had me swinging on a branch of the overhanging elm tree. We hid our disgust and made our way up to the main door where the ever-benevolent Doctor Agrippa was waiting for us. Whilst grooms took our horses away, we were led into the dreary Chapter House, now made a little more comfortable with hangings and arras, cushions and chairs, from Queen Margaret's stores.

'Irvine's news?' Agrippa demanded at once as Catesby bolted the door behind us and scrutinised the long, low-ceilinged chamber as if eavesdroppers lurked in its very shadows. He came and stood over us.

'Irvine?' he repeated hoarsely. 'What news do you bring?'

My master flicked the dust from his cloak. 'Sir Robert,

111

I am dirty, tired, saddle-sore and thirsty. I would like some wine.'

Two goblets slopping with wine were hastily served. My master drank deeply while I studied Agrippa's cherubic face and the anxious, worried frown on Catesby's.

'Irvine is dead,' Benjamin announced flatly.

Catesby moaned and turned away. Agrippa fidgeted excitedly in his chair.

'How?' he asked softly. 'How was Irvine killed?'

'He never reached the convent,' my master lied. 'Oh, we waited for him but then a pedlar brought in his corpse. His throat had been cut from ear to ear and his wallet had been filched.' Benjamin shrugged. 'We failed.'

'We were meant to fail!' I interrupted hoarsely. 'Irvine was ambushed. Somebody knew he was coming, and the only people who did are here in Royston Manor!'

'What are you saying?' Catesby demanded.

'That someone from Royston ambushed Irvine and murdered him,' I replied coolly, ignoring the rage which changed Catesby's open-faced, ploughboy looks into a mask of fury.

'How do we know you two did not kill him?'

'Ask our guide,' Benjamin answered. 'Ask the ladies of the convent — we were never out of their sight.'

I remembered the long, graceful legs of the prioress wrapped firmly around me and hid my smile.

'So,' Benjamin continued, 'where was everybody when we were visiting Coldstream?'

'I was at Nottingham!' Catesby snapped. 'We left here the same day you did, November the eighth. Melford and I were in Nottingham on the morning of the ninth. The Constable there will vouch for our movements.'

'And here at Royston?'

Agrippa never took his eyes off mine.

'A good point, Master Shallot.' He spread his hands. 'None of us can account for our movements precisely. Carey was scouring the countryside for provisions.

Indeed, he was away three days. Moodie was sent to Yarmouth by Her Grace the Queen.'

'And you yourself?'

Agrippa grinned. 'Like the good doctor Scawsby, I was completing certain errands – Scawsby was buying medicines for the Queen,' he yawned, 'I, of course, for the Lord Cardinal.'

I stared into those dark, enigmatic eyes. Was he mocking me? Had he been on the Cardinal's business or lying in ambush for Irvine? I remembered the mist-shrouded countryside and shivered. Or had he been immersed in his Black Arts, calling up a demon from hell in some lonely wood or deserted copse? But why should I suspect him? His answer was very clever: no one could really account for their movements but once again Benjamin and I had drunk deeply from the cup of failure. Catesby pulled a stool across and slumped down, burying his face in his hands.

'Selkirk's dead!' he intoned, like a priest beginning the prayers for the dying. 'Ruthven's murdered and now Irvine!' He glanced sideways at Agrippa. 'In time, perhaps, these deaths will be avenged, but the Queen is insistent that we should meet the Scottish envoys.' He glanced at the hour candle burning on the table. 'The situation is this: the Queen fled from Scotland leaving her infant sons, James and Alexander.' He paused. 'Alexander sickened and died. The Queen has no great love for her second husband but she does for Scotland. The Scottish envoys will be led by Lord d'Aubigny, the Regent's right-hand man. The Queen's husband, Douglas, Earl of Angus, has also insisted on coming. You are to demand of them Queen Margaret's return. They should arrive at Nottingham this evening. Tomorrow you must travel there, Master Benjamin and Shallot, and this time the good doctor Agrippa will accompany you.' Catesby stared at us from red-rimmed eyes. 'This time do not fail!' he snapped. 'Now I must tell the Queen.' He rose and left, slamming the door behind him.

'Did you murder Irvine?' I flung the accusation at the smiling Agrippa.

The good doctor threw back his head and laughed merrily, the sound echoing strangely in that dark, forbidding hall. He got up, wiping the tears from his eyes with the back of his hand, and came to stand over me. He cupped my face in small, soft hands.

'One day, Roger,' he whispered, 'you will detect the solution to great mysteries. I have looked into the shadows which are not yet realities. But, oh dear, you still have so much to learn.' He withdrew his hands, smiled at Benjamin and slipped quietly out of the room.

We spent the rest of the day recovering from our journey and doing our best to avoid the other members of the household, who soon learnt of our failure and hid their satisfaction behind smug looks or sour smiles. Dinner that evening was not a happy affair. Queen Margaret and Catesby glowered at us from the head of the table. Melford, now he had tasted blood, seemed to be revelling in some private joke. Moodie looked sanctimonious whilst Scawsby could hardly hide his crows of triumph. Carey looked worried and Doctor Agrippa sat as if a spectator at some masque or mummer's play.

We sat there toying with our food. Perhaps I drank too deeply because one of old Shallot's mottos is, and always has been: 'When you are frightened and there's wine about, drink as much as you can.' At last my master, tired of the ominous silence, tugged at my sleeve. We rose, bowed to Queen Margaret, mumbled our apologies and crept out of the hall.

'Master Daunbey!' Doctor Agrippa's voice called us back. 'We are to leave for Nottingham at first light.'

Benjamin pursed his lips and shook his head. 'No need to summon us, good doctor. You will find us waiting for you outside Royston. The sooner we leave here the better!'

When we returned to our own chamber, I turned drunkenly on Benjamin. 'What did you mean?'

'About what?'

'When Agrippa summoned us back?'

Benjamin chewed on his lip and shook his head. 'You are tired and half drunk, Roger. Go to bed.'

And, without a word more, Benjamin turned his back on me. I staggered off to sleep and was awakened by my master, his face bathed in a pool of candle light.

'Roger!' he whispered. 'Get up – now!'

'What's the matter?' I replied crossly.

Benjamin kept shaking me and half-dragged me out of bed. He pointed to a tray bearing some loaves and watered wine.

'Break your fast!' he hissed. 'The food is not tainted. We may be in danger here!'

I cursed but did as he requested and afterwards we slipped down the darkened stairway out of the main door where Benjamin had ordered a sleepy-eyed groom to bring round the horses. We mounted and rode across the darkened causeway, past the sentry, half-sleeping at the open gates and on to the trackway. The corpse of the household servant still swung from the branch of an elm tree. Good Lord, I remember the scene well to this day. Terror seemed to permeate the very air. It was bitterly cold, at that moment just before dawn when the demons and evil sprites which live under heaven make their final assault against the human soul. I looked round to glimpse the dark mass of Royston Manor and the swaying corpse of the hanged man caught my glance. Panic throbbed through my body and, if I hadn't been made of sterner stuff, I would have dug spurs into my horse and galloped as fast as I could back to Ipswich. The guard did not challenge us and we followed the faint trackway till Benjamin reined in and offered me a bulging wineskin.

'Drink as much as you want, Roger,' he whispered. 'I understand. I found this on our table when I woke.'

He stretched out his hand and I saw the small, faded, white rose lying there. I shivered at the warning. Benjamin threw the rose down.

'Now, Roger,' he continued briskly, 'I apologise for

my rudeness yesterday evening but you do realise we are in great danger? There's something about this matter which could lead us to the gallows or on to the knife of some hired assassin. A dark, sinister masque is being played out and we do not know whom to trust. My uncle? The King? Queen Margaret? Doctor Agrippa? Something does not ring true . . . but what can we do? If we return to London empty-handed, we are finished. If we pursue this, we could very well be placing our heads in a noose. We do not know who are our friends and who our enemies. Two things may protect us: first, the Lord Cardinal treats me as his favourite nephew and that will afford us some protection; secondly, our investigations safeguard us. There are those who skulk behind and let us run hither and thither while they watch what we find out.'

His cool eyes holding mine, he leaned closer. 'We are in a dance of death. As long as the dance continues we are safe, but if we try to step out we will either be pushed back or killed. By whom I do not know but I intend to find out. For what else is there, Roger? Who is waiting for you or me?' He blinked and looked away. 'Who would miss us?' he added softly. 'Who loves you, Roger? Who loves me? Where is our home, where our loved ones? Look at us now, on this wild heathland with only the grass and the sky to keep us company. And our defence? Our health, the weapons we carry and the money we share. That's all there is, Roger.'

For once in my life I admit my master truly terrified me because he was right. My belly rolled in terror. I could have vomited with fear and had difficulty controlling my breathing at the silent horrors my master described. Benjamin took me firmly by the wrist and my horse whickered softly.

'Yet I have you, Roger, your friendship, and you have mine.' He threw back his head and laughed at the grey, lonely skies. 'What more could a man want?' He laughed till the tears ran down his cheeks. 'I mean, Roger, how

many friends does the Lord Cardinal have? Not the King!'
He suddenly sobered. 'Sometimes,' he whispered, as if
the very bushes concealed royal agents or spies, 'I fear
for my uncle.'

'What do you mean, Master?'

'Although he has the King's friendship . . .' Benjamin
was on the point of replying when we heard the clip-clop
of horses' hooves and saw Doctor Agrippa making his
way slowly towards us; his mount, a gentle cob, ambling
along as if it was a balmy summer's day.

'Good morning, Benjamin, Roger.' The doctor drew
back his dark cowl. 'You were in a hurry to leave
Royston.'

Benjamin grunted.

'Why?' Agrippa continues. 'What dangers threaten
you?'

'You know very well,' Benjamin snapped back.
'Murder lurks there. Selkirk, Ruthven, Irvine . . . sooner
or later it will be our turn. I am right, am I not?'

Agrippa's candid eyes rounded in mock amazement.
'But you are the Cardinal's nephew and Roger is your
good friend. Your deaths,' he emphasised, 'would have
to be explained, if not avenged.'

'Don't play games, Doctor. We all stand on the edge
of a darkened ring. There is a great mystery here.'

Agrippa turned to me. His eyes seemed to glow in the
darkness.

'And you, Roger, if your remarks in the Chapter House
mean anything, believe I am at the centre of this darkened
ring?'

My long-suffering patience broke. 'Who are you?' I
accused. 'What magic arts do you dabble in?'

Agrippa shrugged. 'What is magic, Roger?' He pointed
down to his stirrup. 'Many centuries ago, a Roman Army
was wiped out by the Goths at Adrianopolis. Do you
know why?'

I shook my head.

'The Goths wore stirrups and, because they did, could

fight more efficiently on horseback. To many Romans at the time, the Goths were demons who used magical arts to gain victory.' He shook his head. 'And what was their magic? Something we don't even think about today.'

'You weave spells,' I challenged. 'Carey says his father saw you in Antioch years ago! How can a man live so long?'

Agrippa laughed softly. 'You are right, Shallot. Nothing is what it seems to be.' He leaned forward, his face serious. 'Who I am and what I do does not concern you. I am the Lord Cardinal's man!'

'Does the Cardinal need such protection?' Benjamin queried.

Agrippa chewed his lip. 'Your uncle is hated. He needs to protect himself: men say he has a magic ring which he uses to raise demons to control the King. They also claim that the Lord Cardinal has hired a famous witch, a murderess named Mabel Brigge, who has King Henry in thrall through the St Trinian's fast, a three-day period of abstinence from food and drink which leaves the strongest subjects under her control.' Agrippa stopped and looked at a lonely bird shrieking above us as if it was a devil let loose to wander this lonely wilderness.

I shivered as more silent terrors gripped my soul.

'I don't believe that,' my master replied.

'Oh, yes, you do,' Agrippa murmured. 'The only man your uncle should fear is the King himself. You have heard the prophecies?'

Now fascinated by Agrippa's sepulchral tones, I shook my head and wondered what powers he really had. The good doctor looked at us sharply.

'I trust both of you, so I shall tell you. They say King Henry is the Dark One, he is the Mouldwarp, the Prince of Darkness foretold by Merlin, the great wizard of King Arthur's court. According to his prophecies, the king of the twelfth generation after John will be the Mouldwarp, a hairy man whose skin will be as thick as a goat's. At first he will be greatly praised by his people, before sinking down into the dark pit of sin and pride. He is condemned by God to end his reign in gore and destruction. We are the twelfth generation after John and Henry is our King. We see him now as a golden sun but what will happen to him as the day dies and the sun begins to set? Then how long will he tolerate your uncle? And if the Lord Cardinal goes, falling from the heavens like Lucifer, you, the little ones, will be dragged down in his wake!' He spurred his horse. 'That is why we must succeed, not just for ourselves but for the Lord Cardinal. Who knows whether our success or failure might bring the prophecies about?' He glanced over his shoulder. 'We must go on, lest the shadows catch up with us.'

We urged our horses forward. I forget the details of the journey. Both Benjamin and I were lost in our own thoughts and I was mystified by Agrippa's revelations. A strange man whose like you will not meet again in my memoirs.

[Do you know, I lately financed a trip under one of Raleigh's captains to the Americas. When the fellow returned I entertained him here in the manor house. He told me strange stories of red-skinned men who wore eagle feathers, and their wise man fitted Doctor Agrippa's description. A strange world isn't it? My chaplain snorts in derision but what does he know? He lusts after Fat Margot's tits and is jealous because tonight I'll cup them in my hands. Oh, yes, the juices still run hot and I, past ninety, can do what many a thirty year old finds impossible! Do you think I am lying? Read my memoirs. When I was locked hidden away in Suleiman the Magnificent's harem, I satisfied every one of his *houris* but, as I keep saying, that's another story.]

Eventually, Agrippa, Benjamin and I entered Nottingham, going through the main archway into a dirty maze of streets. After the fresh airs of the countryside, we gagged at the smell of stale urine, stinking cats and rotting vegetables. The open sewer in the high street looked as if it had never been cleaned and at times we

119

squelched ankle deep in human excrement. Our horses had more sense and refused to go further so we stabled them at a local inn where we satisfied our hunger on a dish of fish cooked over charcoal before making our way up to the castle.

We crossed the huge market square where a great throng had gathered to witness the execution of two brothers found guilty by the Judges of Assizes of plotting against the King. The press was too great and we found ourselves trapped by the crowd just in front a massive, black-timbered scaffold. The headsman was already waiting. He stood before the rusty, blood-stained block, his face covered by a black hood as he leaned on a great two-edged axe. He was two-thirds drunk but, there again, I suppose any man ordered to discharge such a duty would need some wine to gladden the heart and dull the brain.

The two brothers were conducted in a cart to the macabre beat of a single drum. They were dressed simply in hose and open-necked shirts. The captain of the guard led them on to the scaffold, a scrawny-faced clerk gabbled out the sentence of the court. The younger man pressed forward, his hands tied behind his back. He looked grievingly at his elder brother who muttered something. The man became calmer, sank to his knees and allowed the executioner to bend him so his neck fitted over the block. Again the drum beat, the great axe swirling in the sunlight. There was a crunch, the hot spatter of blood and a deep sigh from the crowd. The eldest brother refused to have his hands tied but coolly watched as his brother's carcase was rolled away. He then knelt at the block like a priest before his prie dieu. He positioned his head, made a gesture with his hand, the axe swirled again, his body jerked, the head bounced on to the scaffold in a great spurt of scarlet. A guard kicked away a dog who tried to run under the scaffold to lick the dripping blood.

My master, pale-faced, his forehead covered with a sheen of sweat, groaned and turned away. Agrippa beckoned me to follow. A cook, sitting in the shade of a market stall, cackled with laughter and performed his own minor execution of a hapless chicken, slicing the neck and allowing the headless corpse to totter for a while before it collapsed in a heap of bloody feathers. My master hurried away to vomit in a corner. Agrippa waited for him to regain his composure.

'I told you,' he murmured, 'the blood letting by our King is just beginning. The Kingdom will be covered by dark pools of blood.'

Agrippa urged us on and we climbed the hill towards the main gates of the castle where the Red Lion Rampant banner of Scotland fluttered in the wind. A wild thought occurred to me and, for the first time, one of the threads in the mystery of Selkirk's poem began to unravel.

We crossed the lowered drawbridge and went under an arched entrance depicting the wonderfully carved scene of the Annunciation. A burly captain of the guard arranged for our horses to be stabled and immediately took us upstairs into what Agrippa called the Lion Chamber, a long, wooden-panelled room with black and white floor tiles which shimmered in the torch light. These were lozenge-shaped and I remembered them particularly because they were decorated with golden love knots. At the south end of the hall was a huge canopied fireplace and, above it, a blue and gold tapestry bearing the royal arms of Scotland. Beneath this was a large, oaken table and two high-backed chairs, also of oak, cushioned with cloth of gold and fringed with silver silk.

'The Scottish lords have made themselves at home,' Agrippa muttered.

The captain invited us brusquely to sit on a bench before the table and hurried out of a side door. We must have waited half an hour. A serving wench brought us flagons of watered beer. Both my master and myself took in our surroundings, whilst Agrippa, perched on the edge of the bench, hummed softly to himself, rocking to and fro like some cheerful sparrow.

At last the captain re-entered, accompanied by three

soldiers. Behind them were two men. One was dressed in a dark blue jerkin and hose. He was an elegant fellow with steel-grey hair and bronzed face, his sensuous mouth fringed by a neatly trimmed beard and moustache. His companion, swathed in a dark tawny robe as if he felt the cold, was a different kettle of fish: jet black hair framed a white face. He would have been handsome had it not been for the close-set eyes and the petulant cast to his mouth.

'My Lord d'Aubigny and Gavin Douglas, Earl of Angus!' Agrippa hissed as we rose to greet them.

I must say this openly: d'Aubigny I liked immediately, a gentleman born and bred, a true courtier like myself. All Angus did was pull his robe tighter around him and slump in one of the high-backed chairs to glower at us. D'Aubigny, however, came down from the dais and shook Agrippa's hand vigorously before allowing the doctor to introduce both my master and myself. He talked to us kindly, his grey eyes dancing with amusement as he questioned us about our journey. Had it been safe? What troubles had we encountered? His English was very good, though tinged with a pronounced French accent. I looked at him curiously for Master Benjamin and Doctor Agrippa had told me about him on our journey to the castle. He was a distant cousin to James IV but his father had been exiled to France so he had been reared and educated in the French fashion. D'Aubigny waved aside our letter of introduction and called for more refreshments before joining Angus on the other side of the table.

'Well, Master Daunbey,' d'Aubigny began, 'a representative of the English King is always welcome but doubly so when he is the nephew of the great Lord Cardinal.' He leaned forward with his hands clasped together on the table. 'So, Master Envoy, what messages do you bring?'

My master looked nervously at the Earl of Angus who had hardly moved except to gulp noisily from a goblet of wine. D'Aubigny himself acted as if Angus was scarcely there.

'Queen Margaret,' my master began bluntly, 'wishes to return to Scotland.'

D'Aubigny spread his hands. 'There is no obstacle,' he replied. 'The Queen is always welcome back. I have said this many times, Doctor Agrippa, have I not?'

The good doctor nodded his head vigorously. When I glanced sideways I noticed how his face had changed; the air of bonhomie and lazy good humour had disappeared. His eyes were hard now, glaring at d'Aubigny with the occasional sideways knowing glance at the sulky Angus.

'I repeat,' d'Aubigny continued, 'the Queen is welcome back. I will take an oath over a casket of the most sacred relics on this. I have explained to King Henry many times that his worthy sister left Scotland of her own accord — or, should I say, fled? We did not separate her from her children, but the Council cannot allow our infant King to wander where he will.'

D'Aubigny shifted in his seat. Perhaps he was disturbed by Agrippa's hard glance. He began to emphasise his points with one hand.

'The Lady Margaret was appointed Regent by no less a person than her late husband in his will. However, she infringed that mandate by marrying My Lord of Angus within a year of her husband's death!' D'Aubigny turned to his companion. 'My Lord, you would corroborate that?'

Angus slouched like a spoiled brat, nodded and began to tap noisily on the table top with his fingers. Again d'Aubigny repeated the question, this time a little more harshly.

'My Lord Douglas, you will corroborate that?'

This time d'Aubigny waited and would have done till the Second Coming. Angus stirred.

'Och, aye!' the fellow replied sourly. 'I will confirm that. Perhaps we were too hasty. The marriage brought neither of us happiness, especially when my lady wife insisted on hiding in one castle or the other so I could not follow her.' He smiled sardonically at Agrippa. 'You know the Douglas motto — "Better to hear the lark sing in the woods and fields than the mouse squeak in the corridors and chambers of the castle." '

'What My Lord Douglas is saying,' d'Aubigny said meaningfully, 'is that the Queen hid herself away, first in Stirling, then in other castles. There was an attempt,' he added, 'aided and abetted by other nobles, to rescue the Queen's children from the rightful custody of the Council. But this came to naught and so Queen Margaret slipped over the border into England.'

'Your Grace,' Agrippa interrupted harshly, 'a mother's place is with her children. In your custody her second babe, Alexander, Duke of Ross, died!'

'A Queen's rightful place,' d'Aubigny tartly replied, 'is in her kingdom with her children, one of whom, although still a bairn, is the appointed King.' D'Aubigny's eyes softened. 'C'est vrai, Alexander did die, but he was a sickly boy, born two months early. Anyway, I do not think we should discuss the young Duke of Ross, should we?'

I looked sideways. Do you know, the little bugger Agrippa actually blushed whilst Douglas lost his solemn look. Indeed, the fellow became agitated. I saw my master stiffen, those mild, blinking blue eyes had caught something, though God knows what. D'Aubigny sensed he had triumphed in this repartee and stood up, smiling kindly at us.

'You see, your mission is ended. Master Benjamin, Her Grace is most welcome back. Indeed, I could invite the Archangel Gabriel from Heaven — but it would be up to him whether he came or not!'

My master rose and bowed.

'Your Grace, I thank you for your time.'

'Tush, man,' d'Aubigny replied, 'it was nothing. In the morning we will meet again.' He looked at Angus and his smile faded. 'This time alone.'

I tried to question my master on what he had learnt from d'Aubigny, once we were shown up to our chamber, but Master Benjamin was in one of his more withdrawn moods. He wandered off then came back to lie on his bed, staring up at the ceiling. Now and again he would glance at me.

'There is a mystery here,' is all he would murmur. When I looked again, he had fallen fast asleep. Thankfully, the good Doctor Agrippa did not share our chamber. I padded round the room and quietly filched any precious object there: a small set of silver candlesticks, two finely chased pewter goblets and a cunningly wrought steel crucifix which hung on the wall. Satisfied with the day's proceedings, I went to bed and slept like a child until awoken, long after dawn, by my master. He smilingly proffered me a cup of watered wine in one of the goblets I had hidden away the previous evening. I gazed quickly around the room and sighed bitterly. Benjamin had replaced everything. As usual, he paid no thought to the future and the prospect of where our next mouthful of bread might come from. He went across and began washing himself at the lavarium.

'Come, come, Roger!' he said in reply to my glare. 'We cannot take from our hosts. D'Aubigny is the perfect gentle knight. We have enough silver. Remember the scripture − "Sufficient for the day is the evil thereof." '

I felt tempted to tell him that I had begun to glimpse some of the mystery behind Selkirk's verses but my anger kept me silent.

Benjamin smiled at me. 'I think,' he continued as if he could read my thoughts, 'logic has shown me a way to solve the murders of Selkirk and Ruthven.'

I started up. 'And Irvine?'

Benjamin shook his head. 'No, but Catesby must be innocent of that at least. Last night, I went to see the Constable: Catesby and his manservant arrived here on the morning of October the ninth. In no manner could they have delayed to ambush poor Irvine.'

'And the other deaths?' I asked crossly.

Benjamin put his fingers to his lips. 'Not now,' he replied, 'as yet I detect only faint glimmerings.' He sighed. 'As I said, "sufficient for the day . . .".'

I felt like murmuring the verses about Judas going out and hanging himself, and that he should go and do likewise, but Benjamin looked so quietly pleased with himself that I bit my tongue. I threw some of the water from the bowl over my own face and drank the rest for I was thirsty, then followed him down to the Great Hall. Thankfully, Doctor Agrippa had made himself scarce, realising that d'Aubigny's invitation did not extend to him. He was probably closeted with that sullen turd, Angus. Good riddance, I thought. A steward wearing d'Aubigny's livery, blue with silver fleur de lys, announced His Lordship was waiting for us outside. I thought the fellow meant the bailey but he took us out into a garden which ran down towards a small river. The Scottish envoy was waiting for us, sitting on a fallen tree trunk, talking to one of his clerks who tactfully withdrew as we approached. D'Aubigny was dressed simply in a dark brown tunic like a forester and I gathered he was about to go hunting. He seemed vulnerable but then I heard the chink of armour and, looking carefully through the trees which swept up from the river, caught a glimpse of colour and steel and knew that help, if he needed it, was never far away. Nottingham Castle may have been put at his disposal but d'Aubigny did not trust our Henry. A wise man!

D'Aubigny rose, greeted us civilly and indicated we should sit with him. He looked round, first towards the trees where his bodyguards were grouped and then, tilting his head back, listened carefully. There were no sounds except the soft cooing of wood pigeons, the gurgle of the water and the strident cry of the snow white peacocks rising above the castle walls. He came swiftly to the point. Opening a small casket, he took out copies of letters sent by Queen Margaret in the year following her husband's death. If they had come from any other man or woman in the kingdom of Scotland, they would have been considered treasonable; writing to her brother Henry, Margaret made constant pleas for the English to send troops into Scotland to restore her as Regent and crush any opposition to her and the Earl of Angus. Henry's replies were equally blunt; he offered help but said it would take time and, if matters should prove too difficult, she was to return immediately to England. My master read these through carefully like a clerk marking up a ledger.

'Why are you showing me these documents?' he asked when he had finished reading them and passed them to me.

D'Aubigny shrugged. 'I am tired of Queen Margaret's constant stream of invective. We did not drive her from Scotland, and her infant son died because he was born too early – her eldest boy is hale and hearty. Queen Margaret is most welcome to return but she must not bring an army of twenty thousand English "advisers" with her. Scotland is an independent sovereign nation. Queen Margaret's brother, the great Harry himself, has no authority there.' He bit his lip. 'We begged the Queen to return. Even when she crossed the border and stayed at Hexham, messengers carried importunate pleas to her, all of which were ignored.' He sighed. 'You may wonder why Queen Margaret does not return.' He blew out his cheeks in exasperation. 'The Council and I are continually speculating on that.' He pointed to the letters. 'Perhaps she knew we had proof of her treachery, but there is no need for her to fear our vengeance.' He screwed up his eyes and stared into the middle distance. 'No, there is something else . . .Why will she not return? What is she so frightened of?'

'Who could threaten her?' my master queried innocently.

'The Earl of Angus for one!'

'He seemed most amenable last night.'

127

D'Aubigny grinned. 'His Grace now knows how to behave. He will not try and seize her son again.'

'My Lord,' I blurted out.

D'Aubigny looked at me quizzically. 'What is it, fellow?'

'Last night, when you mentioned the Queen's second son, the child who died, Alexander, Duke of Ross . . .His Grace and Doctor Agrippa appeared . . .'

'Discomfited?' D'Aubigny added.

I nodded. He grinned at Benjamin.

'Your servant is no fool. There is a great deal of mystery about that child.'

'Such as what, Your Grace?'

D'Aubigny just grimaced, rose and dusted the grass from his hose. 'James died at Flodden in September 1513. Alexander, Duke of Ross, was born before his time on the thirtieth April 1514!'

On that abrupt note, d'Aubigny extended his hand for my master to kiss as a sign that the audience was finished. He added that we must be his guests at the great banquet he was holding that night for other Scottish lords who had come south with him. My master watched him go.

'A strange man,' he murmured, and looked at me. 'There is something terrible happening here,' he added. 'Something very dangerous. All is not what it seems to be.'

'Like what, master?' I asked.

Benjamin shook his head. 'I don't know,' he muttered. 'But I think the darkness is about to lift.'

Chapter 7

We returned to our chamber and spent the rest of the day preparing for the banquet or listening to Doctor Agrippa. He joined us full of his customary bonhomie and scurrilous jokes about the French and Scottish courts. My master listened to him half-heartedly, more engrossed in studying a piece of parchment on which he was writing cryptic notes in a cipher even I did not understand.

At last the sun began to set and Agrippa took us down to the courtyard to watch the other great Scottish lords arrive. Each was accompanied by a fearsome retinue of men armed to the teeth with sword, mace, dagger and small shields or targets. Most of the latter were Scottish but a few were mercenaries from Denmark, Ireland, and as far afield even as Genoa. The Great Hall had been specially prepared for the festive occasion. Huge cresset torches were placed high on the walls, the tables had been covered with white linen and the only plate used was of the best thick silver.

D'Aubigny held court from his chair on the great dais. He was dressed in a rich robe of gold, fringed with black velvet, over a doublet of blood-red silk and black and white hose. On his head was a rakishly set bonnet, pinned to his hair by a silver brooch fashioned in a shape of a fleur de lys. When he took his seat, the trumpets blew and the dinner was served by a long line of servants who carried in plates of steaming hot boar's meat, brawn, beef, sturgeon, fish, bowls of cream containing sugared strawberries, and jug after jug of different wines.

We were placed near the dais on d'Aubigny's right; the

conversation, the strange accents and oaths washed around us like water. Agrippa did the talking for us, I ate as if there was no tomorrow whilst Benjamin seemed fascinated by someone further down the hall. After the banquet an Italian performed a subtle and cunning rope trick, then a troupe of girls danced a vigorous whirling jig which left the faces of the spectators, as well as theirs, red with excitement as they kicked their legs high and let their skirts go up, revealing to all and sundry what lay beneath. I noticed there were no other women present and later learnt this was the Scottish custom. Not that they treat their women badly – rather both sexes go their own way, the ladies of the nobility preferring to take their refreshment by themselves in another chamber. Once the festivities were over and d'Aubigny rose to withdraw, so did my master, refusing Agrippa's invitation to stay and talk awhile.

I wanted to tarry. One of the dancing girls with flame-red hair, skin as soft and white as silk and large dark eyes, had caught my fancy. She smiled at me and I wondered if she would be interested in another type of jig! Benjamin, however, squeezed me by the wrist and I followed him, taking some consolation in the fact that I had hidden two knives, three spoons and a small silver plate used for sweetmeats inside my jerkin.

We had turned off the main passageway into a narrow corridor leading to the stairs of our room, when our way was suddenly blocked by two savage creatures who seemed to step out of the darkness. Both looked very similar, faces and hair as white as snow whilst their eyes were strangely blue though red-rimmed. They were dressed in leather jerkins and thick, woollen green and black skirts which the Scots call kilts. On their feet were sandals very similar to those worn by a friar, but there was nothing peace-loving about this pair of demons. They were armed to the teeth with dagger, sword, dirk and a small array of throwing knives strapped in broad leather belts across their chests. One of them approached my master and tapped him gently on the chest, speaking in a high sing-song fashion. My master smiled, looked at them and shrugged.

'No thank you,' he said, trying to step aside. 'We have eaten enough and now we wish to retire.'

The man smiled and shook his head. I felt queasy with fright for his teeth had been filed down as sharp as dagger points. He had no need of knives – his teeth alone could have ripped out my throat. Benjamin stepped to one side as if to pass and both men stood back, their hands going to their swords. The second one shook his head and gestured we should follow.

'Agreed,' my master said softly. 'In the circumstances, I think we will follow you, but let me remind you that we are envoys of His Gracious Majesty King Henry VIII of England.'

The second of our unwanted guests must have understood for he turned, raised a leg and farted like a dog. They took us back into the main passageway, past the hall and into a small chamber where Gavin Douglas, Earl of Angus, whom I had glimpsed during the banquet, now lounged in a chair. He had a brimming goblet of wine in one hand, the other up the skirt of the dancing girl who had caught my eye earlier. Angus was stroking her, caressing her thighs and making her squirm and moan with pleasure. Of course, he was as drunk as any sot on May Day, his scarlet damask robe, green jacket and purple hose stained with gross globules of meat and large drops of wine.

'Ah, the envoys of my dear wife,' he announced thickly. Unable to use his hands, he raised a leather-booted foot towards us. I would have fled if the Earl's retainers had not been standing right behind me. I stood still. I did not know where to look; at the girl now moaning with pleasure or Angus's slack-mouthed face. Benjamin, however, smiled coolly at the Earl as if the Scottish bastard was his long-lost brother.

'My Lord, what can we do for you?' he asked.

Angus pursed his lips. 'Oh, what can I do for you?' he mimicked in reply. 'First, if you or your misbegotten entity there,' he gestured towards me, 'plot any design against me, then the two gentlemen standing behind you have orders to slash your throats!' He smiled falsely. 'You have met them? They are Corin and Alleyn, two killers from the clan Chattan: they do not give a donkey's arse whether you have been sent by the Pope himself!' He drank the wine in the goblet in one noisy gulp and threw down the cup.

My master bowed. 'Your Grace,' he said softly, 'I thank you for your courtesy and your . . .'

Angus, his face now red and glistening with sweat, got up and stood before us.

'I have news for you!' he grated. 'Tell my beloved wife I know her secrets!' He clicked his fingers and the two Highlanders stepped forward. 'Whether you like it or not,' Angus rasped, 'I have instructed Doctor Agrippa that Corin and Alleyn will go south with you. They have their orders. I hate my wife but we are bound by a bond which these two will defend.'

He turned to the Highlanders and stretched out a hand. Immediately the two brutes knelt, licking his fingers as if they were pet dogs. Angus talked to them in a strange tongue. The two rogues, their blue eyes gleaming with pleasure, nodded and repeated some secret oath. Benjamin, however, refused to be abashed. When the two Highlanders stood, he sauntered up and touched each gently on the chest.

'You must be Corin and you must be Alleyn?'

The two assassins, a curious look in their eyes, stared back and did not resist even when my master shook them vigorously by the hand.

'Good night, gentlemen!' he called out merrily, and humming a hymn, led me out of the room.

Once the door was closed, I remonstrated angrily but Benjamin just shook his head.

'Forget Angus!' he said. 'Come with me. I saw

something in that hall tonight which I have kept secret. Let us wait in the shadows.'

He refused to answer my persistent questions. We went out and stood in the bailey, taking advantage of the bothies and the huddled tenements built against the castle wall which provided shadows deep enough to hide Satan's Army. We lurked for hours as different revellers left, Benjamin diligently watching each go. At last a lone figure staggered out, singing raucously as he swaggered in a drunken stupor. Benjamin turned and nudged me alert.

'The quarry's in sight, Roger. Now let's follow!'

I didn't know what he was talking about but I dutifully obeyed and we trailed the shambling figure as he made his way drunkenly out through a postern gate and down the steep, narrow alleyways of Nottingham. We crossed the market square, passing the makeshift scaffold where the bloody corpses of the men executed earlier still lay bound in dirty canvas sheets. Our quarry stopped in front of a tavern, light and noise pouring stridently through its open windows. The fellow swayed on his feet and staggered through the doorway. Benjamin and I followed a few minutes later.

Inside the din was terrible. Revellers, their tankards frothing to the brim, shouted and sang. Our quarry secured a table in the far corner and, as soon as I glimpsed him, I could have laughed for sheer joy. He was one-eyed with a great purple birthmark across his face; he must be the same fellow who had been closeted so secretly with Irvine at the Sea Barque in Leicester. Benjamin turned and smiled at me.

'Now you see, Roger. When the Scots came south, this fellow was probably in their retinue and must have searched Irvine out.' He nudged me like an urchin planning a prank. 'Let's see if he can babble to us as much as he did to Irvine.'

We pushed our way through the throng and stood before the fellow as he slouched over the grease-stained table.

'May we join you, sir?'

The man looked up. In the flickering candle light, his twisted face looked as ghastly as a gargoyle's.

'Who are you?' he slurred.

'Benjamin Daunbey and Roger Shallot, two English gentlemen, close friends and acquaintances of the Lord d'Aubigny.'

'And what do you wish with me?'

'A few words and the offer of deep cups of claret.'

The fellow's good eye gleamed. 'And what else?'

'Oh,' Benjamin replied, 'we can commiserate over past glories and dead friends.'

'Such as?'

'The glories of Flodden and the murder of John Irvine.'

The fellow became more watchful.

'What do you mean?' he rasped.

Benjamin leaned over the table. ' "Three less than twelve should it be," ' he chanted, ' "Or the King, no prince engendered he." '

Well, the fellow's face paled!

'Sit down,' he hissed.

'What's your name?' Benjamin asked.

The drunkard grinned, displaying rows of blackened stumps of teeth. 'You can call me Oswald, a mosstrooper now serving the Lord d'Aubigny.'

Benjamin turned and shouted for more wine. Once the slattern had served us, Benjamin toasted our newfound friend.

'Now, Oswald, tell us what you told Irvine.'

'Why should I?'

'If you do,' Benjamin replied quietly, 'you will leave Nottingham a rich man.'

'And if I don't?'

Benjamin's smile widened. 'Then, Oswald, you will leave Nottingham a dead man!' My master leaned across the table. 'For God's sake!' he whispered. 'We are friends. We wish you well but Irvine is dead. What do you know?'

The villain studied Benjamin carefully, his one eye shining gimlet hard. At last he dropped his gaze.

'You look an honest man,' he mumbled blearily. He stared quickly at me. 'Which is more than I can say for your companion. Anyway, you said I would be rich?'

Benjamin drew three gold coins from his purse and placed them in the centre of the table. 'Begin your story, Oswald. You were at Flodden, were you not?'

'Aye, I was,' Oswald replied, a distant look in his eye. 'Somehow or other I had been placed near the King. It was a massacre,' he whispered. 'A bloody massacre! Forget the stories about chivalrous knights and the clash of arms — it was one gory, blood-spattered mess. Men falling everywhere, writhing on the ground, huge gashes in their faces and stomachs.' He drank deeply from his cup. 'I glimpsed the King in his brilliant surcoat standing before the royal banners, the Lion and the Falcon. He fell, and so did they.' Oswald sat up, shaking his head as if freeing himself from a trance. 'I was knocked unconscious. In the morning I awoke, thick-headed and a prisoner. Surrey, the English general, forced me and other Scots to comb the battlefield for King James's body.'

'Did you find it immediately?'

'No, it took some hours before we dragged the body from beneath a mound of soggy corpses. There was an arrow still lodged in the throat. The face and right hand had been badly mauled.'

'What then?' my master asked. 'What happened to the corpse?'

'Surrey had it stripped. The bloody jacket was sent south as a trophy and the mangled remains turned over to the embalmers. The stomach and entrails were removed and the corpse stuffed with herbs and spices.'

'You are sure it was the King's corpse?'

Oswald smiled evilly. 'Ah, that's the mystery. You see, James used to wear a chain round his waist as an act of mortification.'

'And?'

'The corpse bore no chain.'

'Was it the King's body?'

'Well, it could have been . . .'

'But you say it did not have the chain on it?'

'Ah!' Oswald wiped his mouth with the back of his hand. 'Just before the battle, James is supposed to have made love to Lady Heron. During his lovemaking, the damsel complained bitterly about how the chain round the King's waist chafed her skin, so James removed it.' Oswald's hand crept out to seize the gold. Benjamin fended him off.

'Oh, there's more than that, surely? Don't play games! What happened to the corpse?'

'It was sent south.'

'And then what?'

'Then nothing.'

Benjamin scooped the gold back into his hand. 'Well, Master Oswald, nothing comes of nothing.'

[I remembered this phrase and gave it to William Shakespeare. You watch, you'll see it in one of his plays.]

Benjamin made to rise. 'So, Oswald, you are no richer but we are wiser. What profit now?'

The fellow gazed suspiciously round the crowded tavern. 'What do you mean?' he slurred.

' "Three less than twelve should it be," ' I chanted, ' "Or the King, no prince engendered he!" '

'Not here!' the fellow muttered. 'Come!'

He rose and staggered out and we followed him into a stinking alleyway a short distance from the tavern.

'Well, Oswald, what do these verses mean?'

'At Kelso . . .' the fellow slurred, then suddenly he went rigid, chest out, face forward, and I watched fascinated as the blood gurgled out of his mouth like water from an overflowing sewer: his eyes rolled in their sockets, his tongue came out as if he wished to talk, then he collapsed, choking on his own blood, on to the shit-strewn cobbles. Benjamin and I turned, daggers drawn, staring into the shadows, but only silence greeted us as if assassination and murder were common events. Indeed, the dagger could have come from anywhere: a darkened window, a shadowed door or from the top of any of the low squat buildings which stood on either side of the alleyway.

'Do not be frightened, Roger,' Benjamin whispered. 'They have killed their quarry.'

He bent over and prised out the dagger embedded deep between Oswald's shoulder blades. It came out with a sickening plop and a gushing gout of blood. I turned the man over. He was not dead; his lips bubbled with a bloody froth and his eyelids fluttered.

'A priest!' he murmured.

Benjamin leant closer.

'A priest!' Oswald whispered again.

His eyes opened, staring up into the dark night sky.

'Absolution,' Benjamin whispered, 'depends on the truth. Tell us what you know.'

'At Flodden,' the fellow murmured, 'at Kelso . . . Selkirk knew the truth.'

Oswald opened his mouth again as if to continue but he coughed, choking on his own blood and his head fell to one side, his solitary eye fixed in a glassy trance. Benjamin felt his neck for a pulse or any sign of life and shook his head. I crouched down, trying to ease the spasms of fear in my own body.

'Come, Roger,' Benjamin whispered. 'He's dead. Let us walk back to the tavern as if there is nothing wrong.'

Of course, I agreed. There is nothing like the sight of death and blood to make old Shallot want a cup of sack or a goblet of wine! We pushed our way back into the tavern and ordered fresh cups. Benjamin leaned across the table, ticking the points off on his long fingers.

'First, let us forget the murders – Selkirk, Ruthven, Irvine and now Oswald. They are merely bubbles on a dark pool. What else do we know?'

I decided to show my hand.

'Some of the meaning of Selkirk's verses is now apparent,' I replied. 'The first line is still a mystery but the falcon is James. That's why Irvine sketched the rough drawing on the tavern wall — a huge bird, the wench said, with a crown. James IV's personal emblem was a crowned hawk or falcon.'

Benjamin smiled. 'And the lamb?'

'The Earl of Angus,' I replied. 'Play with the letters of his title and Angus becomes Agnus, the Latin for lamb.'

Benjamin nodded. 'Of course,' he whispered. 'That explains the lines, "And the lamb did rest in the falcon's nest".'

'In other words,' I answered, 'the Earl of Angus bedded where once the falcon had, between the sheets with Queen Margaret.'

Benjamin's eyes narrowed as if, for the first time, he was judging me at my real worth.

'Go on, Roger!'

'The Lion,' I whispered, 'is also James. The royal banner of Scotland is the Red Lion Rampant.'

Benjamin pursed his lips. 'Agreed,' he replied, 'but how could this Lion cry even though it died?'

'I think Oswald was about to tell us,' I replied, 'before someone's dagger took him firmly in the back. Who do you think his killers were?'

Benjamin swilled the wine around in his goblet.

'God knows,' he replied. 'It could be anyone. Agrippa, Angus, his hired assassins, or someone under orders from the arch murderer at Royston.' He leaned back against the wall, oblivious to the raucous din around us. 'Recite the verses again,' he said.

I began to chant quietly:

'Three less than twelve should it be,
Or the King, no prince engendered he.
The lamb did rest,
In the falcon's nest.

The Lion cried,
Even though it died.
The truth Now Stands,
In the Sacred Hands,
Of the place which owns
Dionysius' bones.'

Benjamin sat forward. 'We know James is, or was, the
falcon and the Lion; the Earl of Angus is the lamb. But
the rest?' He paused and shook his head. 'I wonder,' he
continued, 'what Selkirk meant by the phrase he could
"count the days"?' He stared round the noisy tavern.
'And why are we envoys?' He looked anxiously at me.
'You heard d'Aubigny – Queen Margaret is welcome
back in Scotland so why this farce of a meeting with the
Scottish envoys? The Queen must be frightened of
something. What secrets does she share with her second
husband, the Earl of Angus?'

'The dead child,' I answered. 'Alexander, Duke of
Ross. There's a mystery there.'

Benjamin tapped the table top with his fingers. 'Aye,'
he said, 'I wonder . . .'

'What, Master?'

'Nothing,' he replied. 'Just a wild thought.' He rested
his head between his hands and stared at me. 'But,' he
continued, 'I think I know how Selkirk and Ruthven died.
Still, I must reflect further, look around, marshal my
facts.' He straightened up. 'One thing is certain – we
cannot stay with Queen Margaret's party. We have
already been warned by the white rose left in our chamber.
It's time we left!'

'We cannot run back to Uncle!' I mocked.

Benjamin grinned. 'Oh, no, not that, Roger! We must
separate. Agrippa has blank warrants and letters from
the Cardinal. We will return to Royston for a while but
then it's Scotland for me and France for you. Paris, in
fact!'

'France! Paris!' I yelled. 'Master, surely not?'

Benjamin grabbed my hand. 'Roger, we are finished here. What more can we discover? So far we have gone where other people have sent us, being told to go here, go there, like children in a maze. It's time to take some control of events and do what is not expected.'

'But why Scotland?' I queried. 'And why me to Paris?'

'Our dead friend Oswald mentioned something about Kelso. Some Scots fled to the abbey there after Flodden.'

'And Paris?'

'Selkirk lived there. Remember, he talked about Le Coq d'Or tavern? You know some French?' he challenged.

'A little,' I replied, 'culled from a horn book. But let's go together.'

Benjamin's face grew serious. 'We cannot waste the time, and you'll be safer in Paris than Scotland. The Earl of Angus would not interfere with the Cardinal's nephew, and the French have no interest in this. So, you will be secure, provided you keep your own counsel and stay well away from any English envoys there.' He smiled. 'Not that any would have anything to do with you! Look,' he said, 'you are to be in France by the beginning of December. I shall join you at Le Coq d'Or by the fourth Sunday in Advent.' His dark eyes beseeched me. 'You will go?'

'Yes,' I replied, 'I will.' And added my own selfish after-thought that the whores in Paris were the most skilled in the world, whilst cups of claret were as cheap as water there!

We returned without incident to the castle and slept safely in our own chamber. The next morning Benjamin rose early and said he wished to watch the clerks at work in the scriptorium. He came back an hour later, looking as smug as a cat who'd stolen the cream. I asked him why but he just smiled, shook his head and said he would tell me in his own good time. The castle was now a hive of activity. The Scots, their mission completed, packed coffers and chests and prepared to leave, intending to go under safe conduct to Yarmouth where their ships would take them back to the Port of Leith in Edinburgh. Doctor

Agrippa, who surprisingly had kept well out of our way, now came to dance attendance on us. We made no mention of Oswald or his murder; he seemed totally oblivious of that, being more concerned to hear about our private conversation with Lord d'Aubigny. The Earl of Angus, too, had not forgotten us. His two silent assassins, Corin and Alleyn, attached themselves to Agrippa like dogs to a new master and where he went, they followed. The magician didn't seem to mind, especially as the two clansmen seemed very much in awe of him although they studied Benjamin and myself like two hawks would chickens, as if savouring the thought of a meal to come.

The following day Agrippa announced we would leave and we slipped quietly out of Nottingham and took the road south. Behind us, loping along like two white wolves, trotted Corin and Alleyn, seemingly oblivious to the miles we covered, padding silently behind our horses without murmur or protest. At night, when we slept in taverns, they stayed in the outhouses, fending for themselves like two animals. If Agrippa gave an order they obeyed with alacrity, but sometimes I caught them watching me and shuddered at the amusement in their icy, pale-blue eyes.

We found Royston much as we had left it. Of course, Queen Margaret and Catesby questioned us, paying particular attention to how d'Aubigny looked, what he said and how he treated us, until my head reeled with their constant petty questions. Strangely, never once did they mention the mysteries of Selkirk's and Ruthven's deaths; I got the distinct impression that both of them were relieved by what they heard. Indeed, Catesby seemed quite excited and both he and his Queen openly announced they would return to Scotland as soon as possible.

'We shall go back to London!' Catesby grandly proclaimed. 'Re-order the household, gather our possessions and, when the Council of Scottish lords sends us safe conduct, travel north to the border.'

Now Agrippa looked withdrawn and quietly anxious.

141

'But *Les Blancs Sangliers*!' he protested. 'The deaths of Selkirk and Ruthven, not to mention Irvine − these must be investigated and avenged!'

'Nonsense!' Catesby replied. He pointed to the two killers the Earl of Angus had sent south. 'We have protection enough. Let the Yorkist traitors plot in their secret covens. Such matters do not concern us now.'

I was as bemused as anyone by the sudden resurgence of optimism in Catesby. I also noticed how Corin and Alleyn, once we had reached Royston, switched their allegiance to him. If they obeyed Agrippa, they openly fawned on Catesby and Queen Margaret, with a subservience which belied their previously threatening attitude and hostile intentions towards myself and Benjamin. Agrippa, of course, protested again.

'There are still matters which need to be resolved,' he stormed angrily.

Catesby ridiculed his suggestion and Queen Margaret jubilantly derided it.

'The Council wish me back!'; she announced pompously. 'My young son the King wants to see his mother. Surely,' she added slyly, 'my good brother would not put obstacles between a queen and her throne or a mother and her son?' She turned to us, her fat bottom moving smoothly over the polished seat of her chair. 'Master Benjamin,' she cried, her voice echoing through the Chapter House, 'your uncle the Lord Cardinal cannot object! After all,' she added slyly, 'I shall report how your mission to Nottingham was a great success.'

'Your Grace,' Benjamin replied coolly, 'I thank you for that but I must agree with Doctor Agrippa − there are matters still unresolved.'

'Such as?'

'Selkirk's verse and his death. Ruthven's murder, and the violent destruction of John Irvine, the Cardinal's special envoy to Scotland.'

'And how,' she asked sweetly, 'can these matters be resolved?'

142

Benjamin's gaze held hers.

'I shall go to Scotland alone,' he quietly announced, 'whilst Shallot will travel to Paris. In Scotland I may find some answers. In France Shallot may find the truth behind Selkirk's obtuse warnings.' He smiled. 'Your Grace cannot object? We may be in your household but we work under the direct orders of the Lord Cardinal.'

Of course, the royal bitch agreed. Catesby just smirked. Agrippa, although he objected at first, reluctantly consented to write out the warrants and disburse the necessary silver for our journeys.

The rest of Queen Margaret's household ignored us, taken up with preparations for their own journey back to London. The Careys glared at me, Scawsby sneered and enquired sarcastically after my health whilst Melford, whenever his gaze caught mine, let his hand fall to the dagger at his belt. Moodie was different. He was withdrawn and seemed rather frightened. Just before Benjamin and I left, he searched me out, a small package in his hand.

'You go to Paris?' he asked.

I nodded.

'To Le Coq d'Or tavern?'

'Yes,' I replied. 'Why?'

Moodie shamefacedly extended the package he held. 'In a street nearby,' he mumbled, 'at the Sign of the Pestle in the Rue des Moines, would you leave this? It's for . . .' He looked away, embarrassed. 'It's for a Madame Eglantine who calls there. I knew her once,' he stuttered, 'it's a gift.'

I looked at the little priest and grinned at Benjamin. 'Of course,' I replied. 'Even priests have friends, be they male or female.'

[Now there goes my clerk again, protesting as if he was as chaste as the driven snow. He squirms his little bum on the stool. 'I suppose Moodie's going to be the murderer!' he yelps: I tell the little bastard to shut up. There are more terrors to come, more mysteries and secrets than he could ever know. Something which, if I lived to be two hundred years old then went and announced it at St Paul's Cross, would rock the very throne of England and scandalise the courts of Europe! Good, that's shut the little bastard up. Now I can get back to my story.]

Benjamin and I left Royston in the last week of November, when the days grew dark early and the sun disappeared a few hours after noon. The mist had lifted from a countryside now hard and black under an iron frost. We reached the crossroads. I looked mournfully at Benjamin.

'We part here, Master?'

He looked around as if to make sure Agrippa or any other spy was not lurking in the hedgerow, and shook his head in contradiction.

My heart quickened. 'So I'm not off to France?'

'In due course, Roger, but surely you realise where we must go first?'

'Master, I am in no mood for riddles. I am cold and getting more frightened by the hour. I wish to God this business was done and we were back in Ipswich!'

Benjamin patted me on the shoulder. 'Listen, Roger,' he explained, 'at Sheen Palace lies the corpse of James IV of Scotland. Now, we saw Queen Margaret mourning her husband; we have Selkirk's riddle about a Lion that cried even though it died; Oswald the moss trooper's tale about more than one royal corpse being discovered at Flodden . . .' Benjamin shook his head. 'I know he didn't actually *say* that but it was implicit in his words. Above all, we have his strange reference to Kelso. Roger, I believe all these mysteries are rooted in King James's death at Flodden. Accordingly, we must examine the corpse at Sheen.'

'Hell's teeth!' I exclaimed. 'We just can't march up to Sheen Palace and demand to see a royal corpse!'

Benjamin pulled Wolsey's warrants out of his wallet. 'Oh, yes, we can, Roger. These warrants allow us to go wherever we wish. They order every servant of the Crown, on their loyalty to the King, to give us aid and assistance.'

'Ah, well, Master,' I smiled, 'if you put it like that, of course, it makes sense!'

[Now there's my little clerk sniggering away just because I was frightened. He forgets I can lean forward in this great chair and give him a good whack across the shoulders. On second thoughts, I won't. He's right. I *was* terrified and my fear was born of shadowy terrors yet to come.]

We struck south-west for the old Roman Road which runs from Newark to London. Benjamin had another reason for our sudden change of plan.

'You see, Roger,' he commented, 'you were expected to take the road to Dover whilst I was bound for Scotland. If anyone is preparing an ambush or some stealthy assassin lies lurking in a tavern, their wait will be both long and fruitless.'

Poor Benjamin, he could be so innocent. He forgot we had to travel back!

Chapter 8

Our journey was rather eerie – I mean, travelling south to meet a dead man – nor was it a comfortable one. The weather was deathly cold, the frost nipping at every part of our exposed flesh. I was soon made to feel even more uncomfortable. We stopped at a tavern and, before we ate our evening meal, Benjamin took me up to our flea-infested chamber.

'Take off your doublet and shirt, Roger.'

I stared aghast.

'Don't worry, Roger, I have no designs on your lithe, young body. I merely want you to perform an experiment. Trust me.' He delved into a saddlebag and drew out a long, black chain. 'Don't ask me where I got this from.' He grinned. 'Actually, I found it at Royston. It's a priest's penitential chain to be worn around the waist against the skin. I would like you to wear it for a while.'

'Why me?' I yelled. '*You* wear the bloody thing!'

Benjamin opened his cloak. 'I'm far too thin and angular. You're the proper build. Wear it as comfortably as possible.'

I put the Godforsaken thing on. Strange, at first I didn't notice any difference but that the chain was cold and slipped against my stomach. I only remembered it when I leaned forward or when I tried to sleep at night. (Do remember, these chains were not really a penance, more a sharp rebuke to the pleasure-loving flesh and a curt reminder of vows taken.)

'You cannot take it off, Roger,' my master ordered.

147

'I insist on that. You must wear it as James IV of Scotland did.'

'Why did he?' I asked.

Benjamin explained: 'The King's father was murdered when James was but a boy. However, the King always believed he was partly responsible for his father's death. The chain was a sharp reminder of his guilt.'

'According to Oswald, the corpse at Flodden had no chain about it. So why this mummery and play-acting?'

'James could have taken it off,' Benjamin answered. 'Either at the request of some lady because it disturbed their bouncing on the royal bed. Or, more probably, because he went into battle in full armour. That would fit snugly round his body and make the chain nigh on impossible to wear. Moreover, if James received any blow, it would drive the chain deep into the flesh and inflict a mortal wound.'

I accepted Benjamin's words but, when I questioned him on why I should wear it, he just smiled, waved a bony hand and told me to be patient. We reached London two days later. I advised my master it would be dangerous to go through the city as the Cardinal's spies were everywhere and they might question our journey to Sheen. Instead, I led him in by secret ways, going round the Hospital of St Katherine, past the Tower, to Custom House on the corner of Thames Street near the Woolquay. Oh, I felt tempted to wander, to spend one day, one night in my old haunts or slip across the river to the stews and brothels of Southwark but Benjamin insisted I follow my own advice. We kept our faces deep in our cowls, gave false names at taverns and refused to talk or discuss any matter while we were within a bow shot of anyone else. We went along the river bank: two smugglers were being hanged near Billingsgate and this had attracted a large crowd to watch their last dance. We slipped by these and hired a wherry from Botolph's Wharf.

Despite the cold, I remember, it was a clear, sunny day. I kept silent, sitting back in the wherry to gaze forlornly across at the spires, towers and turrets of the city. We shot under London Bridge. I glimpsed the spiked heads of decapitated traitors, their shredded necks, gaping mouths and straggly hair. All were eyeless for the crows and ravens pluck the succulent pieces first. Once under the bridge the boatmen pulled out to mid-stream. They paused a while to let a fleet of barges, packed with city dignitaries, sweep by as stately as swans. Oh, the splendour of the rich! Minstrels played; the music wafted sweetly across the water from poops and sterns hidden under a dazzle of bright banners and flags. Silver bells tinkled and gold-embossed oars flashed rhythmically up and down. The splendour and pomp seemed to mock our secretive, eerie journey.

We passed Queenshithe, St Paul's Wharf, White Friars and the Temple. Benjamin nudged me as Westminster Abbey came into view. My master knew about my past: the abbey, you see, before fat Henry intervened, had a sanctuary where fugitives from the law sheltered from bailiffs and sheriffs' men. These outlaws pitched their tents in the abbey precincts, fought over stolen goods and, like Jack Hogg and I, stole out at night to rob and pillage the houses of the rich. The great bells of the abbey were booming and I idly wondered what would have happened to my life if Jack Hogg and I had not been taken. (Now let that be a lesson to you! Never protest at fortune: as one door closes, another opens. All you've got to do is make sure there's no trap beyond it.)

At last we reached the Palace of Sheen. The wherry pulled in and we disembarked at the great garden gate. The palace stands far back from the river, its only access being through fields and orchards which protect it against the vagaries of the Thames. Now Benjamin and I were most subtle. Before our journey we had discussed whether the court and its hangers-on would be there. We decided they would not. In autumn, Bluff Hal preferred Windsor and the hunting lodges in the great forest there. We were pleased to find the palace deserted (or so we thought) except for the usual steward and bailiffs who stayed throughout the year to clean the rooms, wash the hangings and sweep out the dirt once the court moved on. Benjamin acted with all the authority he could muster: displaying Wolsey's warrants and issuing orders in such harsh tones that everyone we met was soon running about as if the great Cardinal himself had arrived. We met the steward in his small chamber off the buttery near the Great Hall, a nervous, beanpole of a man with greasy, grey hair and a hare-lip which fascinated me.

'Master,' he whined, 'how can I help you?'

'You can keep secret counsel?' Benjamin asked sharply.

The fellow nodded, round-eyed. 'Of course, Master. My lips are sealed.' He clenched his mouth shut, making his face even more grotesque.

'You are to tell no one of our arrival here. We wish to see the corpse of the late James IV of Scotland.'

The fellow's mouth opened slackly and fear flared in his eyes. He licked his lips.

'That is forbidden,' he whispered.

'I am here on the Lord Cardinal's express orders,' Benjamin repeated. 'You have seen the warrants. Shall I go and tell my uncle you ignored them?'

The fellow's resistance collapsed like a house of cards; bowing and mumbling apologies, he led us out of the main palace building, across a deserted cobbled yard to a small tower built in the far wall of the palace. Two sentries armed with sword and halberd stood on guard. Once again there was discussion but Benjamin had his way. The door was unlocked, we climbed a flight of cold, damp, mildewed steps, another door opened and we stepped into an oval-shaped chamber. It was stripped of all decoration: no furniture, no rushes, no hangings on the wall. The shutters on the windows were firmly closed and padlocked. A perfect mausoleum for the desolate coffin which lay on trestles in the centre of the room.

'Light the torches,' Benjamin ordered. 'After that, sir, you will withdraw.'

The steward was about to protest but my master's gimlet stare forced him to obey. A tinder was struck and the cressets pushed into niches in the wall flared into life. Now, I openly confess, I was terrified. Oh, I have seen corpses enough. Old Shallot's a brawling man: a born street fighter and a soldier who has seen more battles than many of you have had hot dinners. Yet that chamber chilled me. I felt as if we were in the presence of a ghoul, the living dead. The steward closed the door behind him and our shadows danced against the wall as we stood transfixed looking at the coffin lid, half-expecting it to be pushed aside and the corpse to rise and step out. Benjamin must have caught my mood though of course, as always, he drew strength from my presence.

'Remove the lid, Roger.'

I took a deep breath and ran my dagger under the rim of the casket, freeing the wooden pegs from their sockets around the edge of the coffin. We lifted the lid and placed it gently on the floor. The embalmers' perfume filled the room, tinged with a slight sourness which smelt repellent. We then removed the funeral cloths, lifted the gauze veils and stared down at the royal corpse. The heavy-lidded eyes were still half-open, the lips slightly parted; in the flickering torchlight the figure seemed to be asleep. I half-expected to catch a pulse in the throat, see the chest rise and fall and watch those long, white fingers creep towards me . . .

'Come, Roger,' Benjamin whispered.

'Oh, Lord, Master! What?'

'Lift the body out.'

I closed my eyes and grasped the legs as my master picked up the corpse by the shoulders. We gently lowered it to the floor.

'Now, Roger, let us remove the clothes.'

My stomach lurched and my heart began to pound. Now, when I was a prisoner of the French (and, yes, that's another story) I had to clear corpses from the battle field. I was so bloody delighted to be alive I moved corpses minus their heads, legs and arms, and didn't turn a hair. But when you lift a corpse that looks anything but a corpse, it's terrifying. You never really know what to expect.

[I see my chaplain's face has a greenish tinge around those high cheek bones he's so proud of. Good, perhaps he won't be so quick to stuff his fat, little stomach with delicacies from my kitchen!]

Anyway, in that desolate chamber at Sheen I removed soft buskins from the corpse's feet, carefully pushing back the blue robe and the white cotton shift beneath. Benjamin loosened the loin cloth. I could not bear to touch that part of the body.

Now, the embalmers had carefully replaced the face but the torso of the corpse was a mass of wounds and grossly disfigured by a black line which stretched from the crotch to the neck.

'You see, Roger,' Benjamin explained, 'the embalmers first slit the corpse open and remove the heart, stomach and entrails. They drain off as much blood as possible and wash the body with sour wine. After that, spices are packed in and the skin resewn.'

'Thank you, Master,' I replied courteously, feeling quite faint. I tried desperately to keep my gorge from rising and my stomach from emptying the contents of its last meal.

'Master,' I pleaded, 'what does all this prove?'

'Well, the body was badly mauled in battle.' Benjamin pointed with the tip of his finger at the purple-red crosses on the corpse's chest. 'These are arrow wounds. Here,' he gestured to the side of the chest, 'is a lance wound.' He stretched out his hand and tapped the corpse just above the knees. 'These are sword wounds. I suspect the King was surrounded and was lightly wounded by arrows. A spearman tried to bring him down with a lance thrust under the cuirass whilst another took a swing with a sword at the joints in the greaves on his legs. Not enough to kill.'

'Not enough to kill?' I questioned.

'Oh, no,' Benjamin whispered, 'the death wound is elsewhere.' He turned the corpse over on its stomach and pointed to a great ugly bruise at the base of the spine. 'He was killed from behind. Someone crept up and thrust a sword under the back plate of his armour, slicing his spine.' Benjamin gestured to the back of the corpse's head. 'I suspect these wounds were due to the body being trampled in the fury of battle.'

'But is it the King?' I asked. 'Is it James?'

Benjamin turned the corpse on its back. 'Look at the hip bones, Roger. Can you detect any mark?'

I plucked one of the torches from the wall and crouched down, wrinkling my nose at the mild sour odour. 'No graze,' I muttered. I rose and walked to the other side. 'As white and as whole as the skin of a baby!'

Benjamin smiled and took the torch from me. 'Now, Roger, stand up. Push up your shirt and take off the iron chain.'

I did so, feeling rather strange to stand half-undressed in the presence of a mummified corpse. Benjamin pressed the cold steel of his dagger against my stomach.

'The chain has left slight welt marks, yet these will disappear. But,' he asked, 'where is the soreness?'

I pointed to my hip bones, especially the right which had taken the weight of the chain. Already an ugly welt had appeared. Benjamin re-sheathed his dagger.

'Now, Roger, it's obvious – you have worn that chain for a few days and it has left a mark. King James was supposed to have worn it for at least twenty years. The result of such constant chafing would definitely be left on the skin.'

I jumped as one of the shutters suddenly rattled.

'Come on, Master,' I whispered. 'Let's be gone from here. We have seen enough!'

I tied the points of my hose, pushing down my shirt, glad to protect myself against the unearthly chill in that ghastly chamber. I tapped the corpse gently with my feet.

'No need for further proof, Master. This man may have

fought at Flodden but he is not King James. The corpse does not bear the chafing marks of a chain.'

Benjamin sat down on one of the trestles, his hand over the coffin, and rubbed the heel of his hand against his chin.

'Master,' I insisted, 'we should go.'

We re-arranged the funeral cloths and decently restored the corpse to its coffin, pressing the lid firmly down. Benjamin carefully extinguished the torches and I almost shoved him through the door, glad to escape from the miasma of the unburied dead. The steward was waiting for us at the foot of the steps.

'You have seen all you wanted, Master?'

Benjamin slipped two silver pieces into his hand. 'Yes, and remember, keep quiet about this, though I suppose there's no one here. The court is at Windsor?'

The fellow swallowed nervously. 'Yes and no, Master. The King has gone but . . .'

'Who is here?' Benjamin rasped.

'Her Grace the Queen and her young daughter, the Princess Mary.'

'They must not know!' I whispered. 'Master . . .'

Benjamin understood my warning glance. We pushed past the steward, re-crossed the cobbled yard and entered the main palace building. We were almost past the entrance to the main hall when a woman's voice called out: 'Signor Daunbey! Signor Daunbey!'

Benjamin stopped so suddenly, I almost collided with him. A woman stood just within the hall. She wore a gold-fringed dress of red murrey with a white silk head-veil; around her throat was a golden necklace of bejewelled pomegranates. Beside her stood a small, red-haired girl, white-faced and dark-eyed. The woman lifted her veil and came forward.

'Your Grace!' Benjamin went down on one knee, tugging at my sleeve for me to follow suit. 'Roger,' he whispered, 'it is the Queen!'

The woman approached. I stared up into the kind-eyed,

sallow face of Catherine of Aragon. She looked at me and I caught the amusement in her eyes.

'Signor Daunbey, please stand. And your friend?'

Benjamin stood up, looking a little flustered, peering over his shoulder and hoping the steward would not make an appearance.

'Your Grace,' he stammered, 'you know my name?'

She smiled though her eyes became hard.

'I have a memory for faces and names, Signor Daunbey. You are the Cardinal's nephew. I have seen you at court. I am used to . . .' now she stammered, 'to studying what new faces appear.' She pushed the little girl gently before her. 'Though you have never met my daughter, the Princess Mary.'

We bowed and kissed the small white hand.

'Your Grace, I thought you would be at Windsor?'

Now the Queen looked away.

'I cannot,' she answered, her voice guttural, revealing her Spanish background. 'I cannot share the same rooms.' She licked her lips. 'I am the Infanta of Spain and Queen of England. I cannot share a room never mind my husband, with a whore!'

I looked at her dark face, filled with a mixture of anger and hurt, then at little Mary beside her who, over the years, solemnly drank in the insults offered to her beloved mother.

[Do you know, Henry often did that! Dumped poor Catherine and Mary in some deserted palace whilst he went whoring. When he finally divorced Catherine, he sent her to a damp, draughty cottage in the hope that she would die of pleurisy. Of course she didn't! The fat bastard poisoned her. Very few people knew that yet I was there when they opened poor Catherine's dumpy body and took out her heart. Believe me, it was black and blown up like a rotting pig's bladder. Mary, of course, never forgot! Don't you believe the stories about King Henry being buried at Westminster. I was there the night she exhumed her father's body and had his rotting remains tossed into the Thames. God rest them both, two good women viciously treated by a cruel man! However, that was in the future.]

At Sheen Catherine just seemed pleased to see a friendly face. We chattered a while and Benjamin was on the point of leaving when the Queen stepped forward.

'Signor Daunbey, why are you here? Do you bring messages?'

The Queen looked at me and glimpsed the iron chain in my hand.

'You have been to see the corpse?' she asked.

'Yes, Your Grace, on my uncle's orders.'

Catherine nodded. 'I was Regent, you know,' she half-whispered. 'It was I who sent old Surrey north to crush James at Flodden.'

'Your Grace,' I blurted out, 'we have seen the corpse. Would Your Grace be kind enough to answer certain questions?'

Benjamin looked at me in surprise but, I'll be honest, I was tired of this subterfuge and Catherine seemed the friendliest person we had met since this horrible business had begun. The queen smiled and tweaked me gently by the cheek.

'I have heard of you, Shallot,' she murmured. 'The Lord Cardinal has described your escapades until the tears have soaked his cheeks.'

'I am glad to be of service.' I answered sarcastically.

[Believe me, old Wolsey had occasion to cry about me before he shuffled off his mortal coil.]

Catherine waved us into the hall and we sat in the window seat. Benjamin stammered out an apologetic request – how he would appreciate it if no one else was told about our visit. Catherine smiled warmly. Little Mary sat beside her like a doll, her thumb stuck solemnly in her mouth.

'Your questions, Signor Shallot?'

'Your Grace, how was the corpse when it was brought south?'

156

'A bloody mess,' she replied. 'One side of the face was badly mauled. The embalmers worked skilfully, even as they brought it here. The royal tabard was soaked in blood. I sent it to Hen— the King in France as a token of our great victory.' She peered through the mullioned glass window. 'I should not have done that,' she whispered.

'Your Grace,' I asked, 'are you sure it was the corpse of the King of Scotland?'

Catherine shrugged. 'I had never met James alive, so how could I recognise him in death? He wore a ring on his right hand; the tabard and armour were royal.' She made a face. 'The corpse was shaved but the beard and moustache were red. Surrey said it was James, though I have heard otherwise!'

'But no chain?' I persisted.

'Ah, the chain,' she murmured. 'No, there was no chain. But I tell you this – even if the corpse is not James's, Surrey himself assured me that no royal personage could escape from that battle. However, James might have fought in plain armour. It is a common practice.' She smiled at us. I noticed how her teeth were still white, not rotting black like those of the courtiers who constantly stuffed sweets and comfits into their mouth. 'What is your interest in the corpse?' she asked. 'Though perhaps you would be wise not to answer that!'

Benjamin smiled and we rose. We bowed and were about to leave when the Queen suddenly murmured, 'Signor Daunbey, Signor Shallot.' Now she looked solemn-faced. I caught a glimpse of the dark beauty which had once captivated Henry. 'Be most careful,' she warned. 'And be assured, my husband the King has a close interest in these matters.'

We took Catherine's warnings to heart. I dropped the chain in the moat and we fled like the wind from Sheen. It was late afternoon by the time the wherry brought us back to Botolph's Wharf. Benjamin and I had hardly exchanged a word, even when the boat glided by Syon Convent.

We collected our horses from the tavern and decided to skirt the city. We crossed Holywell Road, Deep Ditch, and travelled as fast as we could around Charterhouse and Clerkenwell, keeping well clear of the city before taking the road south to New Cross. We stayed at a splendid hostel there. Of course, I drank deeply from a mixture of relief at the Queen's open support as well as the need to forget the horrors of that grisly chamber. After the evening meal (sweet salmon cooked in white wine), Benjamin and I stayed up long after the taproom emptied. In the main our conversation was about the Queen, and the King's penchant for ever younger mistresses. At last Benjamin stared round the deserted room.

'What do you think, Roger? Did we see the corpse of James IV of Scotland?'

'I don't know,' I replied.

He leaned across the table, ticking off the points on his long, bony fingers.

'Why did we go to Sheen?' Benjamin didn't wait for my reply. 'We were to view the corpse because we suspected it was the body of an imposter. The only proof of our suspicions is the lack of any chain or evidence of one on the body. We discovered that the man in the coffin at Sheen probably never wore a chain round his waist.' Benjamin paused and pushed his platter away. 'I deduce the corpse we have just seen does not belong to James IV. So what did happen to the King?'

I remember trimming the wax from the fat tallow candle in the centre of the table.

'We are faced with a number of choices, Master,' I replied. 'First, King James may have fought in ordinary armour, been killed, and Surrey chose the wrong body. Secondly, James may have been killed either before the battle or at its beginning. Perhaps by assassins sent by *Les Blancs Sangliers*.' I shrugged. 'That could explain the confusion and the poor leadership of the Scottish Army at Flodden.'

'Or,' Benjamin intervened, 'James could have fled, perhaps to the abbey at Kelso.'

'But,' I replied, 'if any of what we have said is true, why does Queen Margaret grieve over the corpse of an imposter? She, of all people, would know the body of her husband!'

Benjamin just stared down at the table, shaking his head. I laughed sourly.

'Can't you see the weakness of our argument, Master? If the corpse at Sheen is that of an imposter, surely it would be safer for Margaret just to get rid of it?'

'Perhaps she hopes people will see what they want to,' Benjamin replied, 'any change detected being dismissed as fanciful or due to the work of the embalmers.' He leaned back in his chair and breathed heavily. 'Yes, Roger, we must remember that. In my days as a Justice's Clerk I saw enough corpses to know that death can grossly disfigure even the comeliest of faces.' He grimaced. 'Indeed, the Queen might not be guilty of deception. Perhaps Margaret just wants that corpse to be her husband's, to give her something to grieve over. She might prefer to accept that rather than face the horror of the idea of her husband, the King of Scotland, being thrown into a pit among commoners.' He looked up. 'What's the matter, Roger?'

'Well, Master, we are building our arguments on the fact that there were men who looked like King James.'

Benjamin rubbed his face. He suddenly looked tired and drawn. 'We have discussed that, Roger. Remember, James belonged to a Scottish clan. It's more than possible that there were a number of courtiers with the same build and looks as he.' He smiled wanly. 'Never forget, nobles love to ape the fashions and styles of their masters. I can think of at least half a dozen of Henry's courtiers who could be mistaken for the King.' He leaned heavily against the table. 'The possibilities are endless,' he muttered.

'How do we know James wasn't taken prisoner by Surrey and hustled down to some secret prison in England?' He toyed with his goblet, watching the lees of wine dance and jump. 'All I do know, Roger, is that all the deaths we have witnessed, all the mysteries we have faced, have their origin in what happened at Flodden.'

'We know a lot of things,' I retorted, 'but we can't prove anything.'

Benjamin fell silent and we sat watching the guttering flame of the candle.

'Perhaps there are other keys which might fit the lock of this mystery?'

My master stared at me.

'Well,' I stammered, 'if we could resolve the White Rose murders . . . ?'

Benjamin stirred and shouted at the slattern to bring a toothpick. The sleepy-eyed girl brought one across and Benjamin began to clean his teeth. I watched him in disbelief for my master was usually keen to observe the finest etiquette at table. Benjamin, however, cleaned his teeth, cupping his hand occasionally as he studied the end of the toothpick.

'Master, are you well? Do you find that toothpick more enigmatic than the mysteries we face?'

He grinned. 'Aristotle, my dear Roger, always claimed that careful observation, coupled with logic, would solve any problem under the sun. Do you remember Ruthven, and the morsels we found between his teeth?'

I swallowed hard. 'Master, I have just eaten!'

'Yes, Roger, so have I. Indeed, over the last few weeks since Ruthven's death, I have been careful, wherever possible, to eat the same foods he did. Do you know, I have never yet found anything which closely resembled what we discovered in his mouth. An interesting thought, eh, Roger?'

'Do you have any solution?'

'As I said at Nottingham, faint glimmerings – all shadow and no substance. But, come, tomorrow I travel north and you go to Dover. Who knows what truth a tavern in Paris and a monastery in Scotland may hold.'

We rose early the next morning. I carefully packed my saddle bags, making sure I had a copy of Selkirk's verse and Moodie's gift. Benjamin travelled with me through the misty, frost-bitten countryside. We chattered about Ipswich and I found the business of Scawsby's treatment of my mother still rankled in my heart. At the crossroads to the south of Norwood we parted company. Benjamin clasped my hand warmly.

'Enough of Scawsby, Roger. Be of good cheer. We shall meet in Paris and be home by Yuletide.' He grinned and I caught the mockery in his voice. 'Whatever happens, Roger, we have been successful. Queen Margaret herself has congratulated us. Such praise,' he added drily, 'cannot be dismissed lightly.'

I pictured the bitch's fat, doughy face and drew small comfort from the memory.

'Remember, Roger, I will be at Le Coq d'Or before Christmas. Be there!' He clasped me once more by the wrist and, turning his horse, cantered quickly out of sight.

I had no choice but to travel south. I did think of making a call at Ipswich to present my warmest compliments to Mistress Scawsby but that would have been too dangerous. Scawsby had killed my mother, nearly had me hanged, and I thought a more subtle revenge would prove a finer dish to serve. So I continued south, making my way along the great chalk road which snaked across the Downs to Dover. Looking back, I suppose I was contented enough, though sad to be parted from Benjamin. Oh, the follies of youth!

Chapter 9

I entered Dover at nightfall just as the sky darkened and
rain began to beat down on my plumed cap. I stayed in
a flea-ridden inn whilst outside the sea began to seethe
and boil under a sudden black storm. By dawn the
weather had abated though the sea was still angry, its
surface broken into dark ridges and furrows by a
treacherously high wind. A sloop took me out to the ship
which dipped and rose wildly in the harbour. Oh, God,
it looked pitifully small and flimsy! I spent the day riding,
or rather bucking, at anchor, the only time in my life I
really wanted to die.

The next day the idiot of a captain decided to make
a run for the open sea. I gave up. I stayed in the darkness
vomiting as the ship veered wildly through the troughs
of high waves. I prayed to every saint I knew and, when
I reached Harfleur, spent a great deal of my time resting
in a seaside tavern. After a few days my condition
improved, the weather changed dramatically, and I made
my way across the cultivated, fertile fields of Normandy.
A week's journey to the Porte of St Denis and into Paris.
At first the city entranced me: the spacious meadows and
dark green woods near the walls; the windmills, châteaux
and palaces being swiftly built in the new Italianate style
with their façades of grey stone, high arched windows
and elegant columns.

My knowledge of French was rather better than
Benjamin knew. I soon found my way around both the
broad boulevards and reeking, rat-infested alleyways.
Now Paris is a city which seethes like a hissing snake.

It is full of intrigue, subtle plots, and traders who could cheat a beggar out of his skin. My store of money began to dwindle but at last I found Le Coq d'Or, a dingy, two-storey building which stood at the mouth of one of the runnels on the far side of the Grand Pont opposite the elaborately carved Notre Dame Cathedral.

The landlord was a snot-nosed, weak-eyed character with greasy, spiked hair and a face as pitted as the track which ran past his dingy tavern. I took a garret there, posing as an English student from the halls of Cambridge. It was the sort of place where you are accepted for what you claim to be, your worth depending on how much gold or silver you have in your purse. After two or three days I bought the landlord a carafe of his own wine − the mean-mouthed varlet picked a costly, unsealed jar, not the usual watery vinegar he served most of his customers − and asked him about Selkirk. The fellow gave me a world-weary look and shook his head.

'I cannot remember everybody, Monsieur.' A piece of silver jogged his memory. 'Ah, yes,' he answered, breathing wine fumes into my face. 'The Scottish doctor − thin as a beanpole with untidy red hair. He and his stupid verses!' The fellow shrugged. 'He was here for a while. But then other Goddams [This is what the French used to call us English] came and took him away.'

'What did Selkirk do?' I asked. 'I mean, before his arrest.'

The landlord made a face. 'He stayed in his room, he went out . . .'

I fidgeted angrily and the fellow licked his lips.

'I think he went to St Denis,' he continued. 'To the abbey there. Or to Notre Dame.' He brought a dirty finger up to his lips. 'He was always carrying a casket, a battered, tattered thing which he guarded with his life.'

'What was it?'

'I don't know.'

'The English who came for him, did they find the casket?'

164

'No, I don't think so. They ransacked his room and were angry because they couldn't find anything. Selkirk laughed at them, jumping up and down here in the taproom. Some of the things he said made no sense so they gave him a crack across the head and took him away. That was the last I saw of him.'

I could make no further headway with the landlord so I made enquiries amongst the other customers: a beggar who whined for alms inside the doorway and a greasy-haired knave, but they only repeated what the landlord had said. The only clue (and one I ignored at the time), was Selkirk's interest in the Abbey of St Denis to the north of the city. I was planning to go there when my descent into the horrors began.

Now, Moodie had given me a package. Of course, I had opened it and found nothing more than a piece of costly silk, blood-red and fringed at each end. A sort of sash for some lady to wear round her smooth, soft-skinned waist. It gave off a fragrant smell which stirred my memory though I could not place it. Anyway, bored by my stay at Le Coq d'Or I decided to go to the shop under the Sign of the Pestle in the Rue des Moines and leave Moodie's present there.

[Yes, yes, my little chaplain is correct. He has pursed his sour lips and guessed my true intentions: if I had not been so bored, I would have sold it. I wish to God I had!]

I found the Rue des Moines and entered the small apothecary's shop, but I was disappointed. There was no Madame Eglantine, only a garrulous old man who chattered like a magpie, took the package and said he would hand it over to the lady next time she visited the place. I told him who I was and where I was staying and then forgot the whole incident. Two days later I was in the taproom of Le Coq d'Or, the slattern beside me half drunk. She pressed up against me, her fingers tickling my codpiece though I knew she was after my purse. My hand was teasing her juicy shoulders and succulent breasts thrust out from a dirty, though very low-cut bodice. A call of nature interrupted my pleasure and I went out to the necessary house behind the tavern, nothing more than a hole in the ground enclosed by a shabby wooden palisade and a door which bolted from the inside. I was squatting there, contemplating my future, when suddenly the door burst open. Three figures, their faces muffled by cloaks and broad-brimmed hats, seized me and began to beat me as if I was some dog.

Now in life there is nothing more defenceless or ridiculous than a man with his pantaloons about his ankles, his shirt tail raised and his mind on other matters. The three ruffians pummelled me, banging my head against the wooden slats. Of course, I fought back like a veritable lion but my sword and dagger were in the garret and who in the tavern would listen to my screams?

Within a few minutes my body was one mass of bruises from head to toe. Two of the ruffians seized me, pushing me against the fence, and I could only gabble in horror as their leader drew a long, thin stiletto and pulled back my shirt to expose my throat. He said something in French about the shop and the Sign of the Pestle. I saw the evil light in his eyes and knew that so far they had only been playing with me: their real intent was to kill. I gave one more scream, I don't know for whom. Benjamin! My mother! My nurse! Wolsey! Anyone! The dagger moved closer, nicking part of my neck just under my left ear.

'I'm too young to die!' I screamed.

[I can see that little bastard of a chaplain laughing again. Does he think it's funny? Look, I'm no hero and, if you had your pants down and three ruffians bent on killing you, you'd bloody scream!]

I closed my eyes and suddenly the jakes door was thrust back and a veritable mountain of a man stood there. He roared in French at my three assailants, brandishing a huge club. They took one look at him and scampered over the fence as quickly as rats over the timbers of a sinking ship. I just slumped and sat down in the mud and dirt.

The Colossus squatted down next to me. I glimpsed a broad, cheery face, a bristling beard and moustache.

'Who are you?' I whispered.

The fellow stood up and I saw the long, brown gown of a Franciscan monk, the rough cord round his waist and the wooden crucifix slung on a piece of string round his neck.

'I am Brother Joachim,' he announced in a voice like thunder.

'You are a priest?'

'I am a Franciscan and a Maillotin.'

'A Franciscan I know. What's a Maillotin?' I mumbled through bloodied lips.

'Never you mind!'

He scooped me up in his great arms, barking at me to make myself presentable and half-carried me back into the taproom. On his orders the tapster broached a good cask of wine and brought across a bowl of water. Joachim cleaned my face, wiping dirt from the bruises whilst I greedily gulped the thick red claret. Perhaps I should have known there was something wrong; the taproom was strangely quiet, the slattern had disappeared and the landlord seemed too busy to care.

'Do you need any more help?' Joachim asked.

'No,' I muttered.

'Then I'll be off!' the friar boomed. 'I have to visit the shrine of the Blessed Dionysius.'

Despite my injuries, I gaped up at him.

'Dionysius?' I queried. 'Who is he?'

'St Denis, of course!' the friar joked back. 'I use the Latin name. You know the monastery?'

He shook my hand and strode out of the tavern. I never saw him again, the man who saved my life. (Do you know, until fat Henry crushed the monasteries, I always had a soft spot for Franciscans. Not just because of Joachim's kindness but that chance encounter put me on the road to solving Selkirk's riddles and the horrible murders they caused.) Once Joachim had gone, the landlord showed renewed interest in me. He came and stood over me, a mock-tragic expression on his face.

'Monsieur, you were attacked?'

'Oh, no,' I sarcastically retorted, 'just some French bravos welcoming me to this Godforsaken city!' I got up. 'I must go to my chamber.'

'Monsieur!' The villain stepped in front of me, two of the thugs he always kept in the tavern to crack the heads of noisy revellers now standing behind him.

'Monsieur, your room has been ransacked. By whom I do not know. Your baggage and silver, they have gone!'

'Hell's teeth!' I snarled but the landlord, the two thugs close to his shoulder, screamed his innocence. He peered closer at me and asked what an Englishman was doing in Paris.

'This Selkirk,' he jibed, 'were you his bum boy?'

[At the time I didn't know what he was talking about. I always was, and have been ever, a devoted admirer of the fairer sex, but after you have made the acquaintance of men like Christopher Marlowe, you really can't trust anyone. Oh, yes, I knew Marlowe the playwright and helped him stage his play *Edward II*. Poor Kit! A good poet but a bad spy. I was with him, you know, when he died. Stabbed to death in a tavern brawl over a pretty boy.]

Ah, well, I had to leave Le Coq d'Or and found myself penniless, freezing in a Paris alleyway without baggage or silver. I thought of going to St Denis, but to what use? More pressing was the need to find shelter, food and extra clothing. I thought of following Joachim but I felt tired, exhausted after my beating. Somehow, my visit to the Sign of the Pestle had caused the attack on me so I dared not go back there. I crouched in that alleyway and prayed for Benjamin to come.

Poor old Shallot! Alone in Paris, in a foreign city on the brink of winter, penniless, hungry, with not an item I could call my own except the clothes I stood up in. At first, I lived on my wits. I became a story-teller: painting my face, filching a gaudily embroidered robe and, not being versed in the French tongue, pretending I was a traveller lately returned from seeing the fables of India and Persia. I took a position on the edge of one of the bridges across the Seine and told, in halting fashion, stories about forests so high they pierced the clouds.

'These,' I cried, 'are inhabited by horned pygmies who move in herds, and who are old by the time they are seven!'

I earned a few sous so I became more fantastical, maintaining I had met Brahmins who killed themselves on funeral pyres; men with monkeys' heads and leopards' bodies; giants with only one eye and one foot who could run so fast they could only be caught if they fell asleep in the lap of a virgin. As the days passed, my wits sharpened and my command of the tongue improved, as did my stories. I had met Amazons who cried tears of gold, panthers which could fly, trees whose leaves were made of wood, snakes three hundred feet long with eyes of blazing sapphire.

At last both the sous and the stories ran out so I sold the cloak and gathered a few objects: bones, shards of pottery and the occasional rag. I became a professional relic-seller. The proud possessor of a fragment of the Infant Jesus's vest, a toy he had once played with (Benjamin would have been proud of that), and a hair from St Peter's beard which could cure the ague or a sore throat. I had the arm of Aaron and, when someone burnt that as a joke, changed my tale and said the ashes were from a fire over which the martyr of St Lawrence died. I earned a few sous but not enough. Paris was full of rogues, card-sharps, brigands, footpads, dice-coggers, pimps, ponces, horse-stealers, bruisers, coin-clippers — the true children of wing-heeled Mercury, the lying patron of thieves and politicians. In a word, the competition became too intense and, in the reeking runnels and smelly alleyways of Paris, I began to starve.

Now Paris may well be the inspiration of poets and

troubadours but I don't remember it as the fabled Athens of the West. All I recollect is a grey, sombre sky and the dark Seine rushing under the bridges; tall, sharp-gabled houses which sprang up from the cobbles and leaned crazily together, storey thrust out above storey; the narrow, winding streets of the Latin Quarter; the pell-mell of ascending gables and tinted roof tiles, the gables of their lower storeys sculpted into fantastic shapes of warriors or exotic animals. Oh, yes, I got to know these well as I slunk past like a hungry fox in a deserted kitchen yard. Above me, the gaily painted signs of the taverns and food shops creaked in the wind and mocked my hunger. At each crossroads the stone fountains with their precious supply of water were guarded by men-at-arms. On one occasion I stopped to pray before the statue of a saint at a street corner and noticed the lamp burning before it. I stole the candle from its socket and sold it for a crust of bread and a stoup of water from an ale wife.

The fourth Sunday in Advent came and went. Benjamin had told me he would return to Le Coq d'Or; every morning and each evening I went there but no Benjamin. I cursed him for a fool. I tried to speak with the landlord but was driven off for what I seemed − a ragged, evil-smelling beggar. My mind, once sound as a bell, became muddled and confused. I thought I saw Selkirk and his damned doggerel tripped through my brain:

> Three less than twelve should it be,
> Or the King, no prince engendered he!

[The vicar wipes away a tear. The bastard had better not be laughing!]

I slept in graveyards or along the steps of the churches and woke hollow-eyed and sick with hunger to the oaths of the men-at-arms, the mocking jeers of cheapjacks and mountebanks, the clatter of hooves and the crazy jangle and flurry of hundreds of city bells. London reeks but Paris is much worse. The stench there is terrible; the alleys and streets caked with mud and shit, and made more pungent by other offal which smelt as if barrels of sulphur had been spilt along every alleyway.

I lived as a beggar, scrounging what I could, but then winter came, not only early but cruelly, one of the sharpest, coldest winters for decades. The roads became clogged and food in Paris began to run out. Even the fat ones, the lords of the soil, the truculent men-at-arms and the tight-waisted, square-bodied wives of the bourgeois, began to starve. The markets became empty and what food was left in Paris was prized more highly than gold. The old died first, the beggars and the maimed; they just froze as they leaned gasping against urine-stained walls. Then the babies, the young and the weak. Snow fell in constant sharp, white flurries. The Seine froze over and the nearby forests, usually a source of food, now gave birth to a new nightmare. Great, shaggy-haired, grey wolves banded together, left the frozen darkness of the trees and crossed the Seine in packs, to hunt in the suburbs. They attacked dogs and cats and savaged and maimed the crippled beggars. They even dug up graveyards, dragging out the freshly interred bodies. A curfew was imposed, archers armed with loaded arbalests patrolled the streets and thick webs of chains were dragged across the entrances to the main thoroughfares.

I thought I was safe. I was weak with hunger but I had a knife and I could still move round the city. Naturally, I heard the stories and one morning saw a bloody trail of gore where the wolves had attacked and dragged away an old beggar woman who used to squat on the corner of the Rue St Jacques. One night I was in an alleyway, nothing more than a narrow, darkened trackway. The night sky was brilliant and the stars seemed to wink like precious stones against the velvet darkness; the streets, carpeted by ice and hard snow, shimmered and glowed under the pale moonlight. I had fallen asleep, squatting behind a buttress of the church of St Nicholas long after curfew, my lips blue, my teeth chattering with the cold.

171

I cried out with the pain which seemed to turn my body from head to toe into one raw, open wound. For the hundredth time I cursed Benjamin and wondered desperately what had happened to him. I walked in a daze trying to keep warm as strange fantasies plagued my mind: Selkirk chanting in a field of white roses all stained by blood; my mother crouching on a step as she used to when I would play and run to her — but, when I drew closer, she was an old cripple, eyes open, face frozen blue. She just toppled over as I touched her.

I walked on, trying to keep warm. The streets were black, the cobbles rough beneath their carpet of ice and a bitter, cruel wind whipped the snow into sudden flurries. I saw a group walking towards me through the ashen darkness. They were leper women, unfortunates from the hospital of St Lazaire, a dozen withered, hideous creatures, embodying foulness and decay. They gathered their filthy, scant rags about them and screamed at me to go away, their putrid breath freezing on their blue lips. I wandered down the Rue de la Carbière then I heard the first soul-searing howl: the wolves were back in Paris, hunting for whatever they could find.

The hairs on the nape of my neck tingled and my tired heart lurched with fear. I hurried on, slipping on the black ice, cursing and praying, hammering at the doors I passed but I was so cold I could hardly cry out. Again the howl, nearer, more drawn out, chilling the heart as well as the blood. I turned, like you do in a nightmare, and down the years the vision of terror I glimpsed still springs fresh in my mind. The long track wound behind me, past dark, high-gabled houses, the hard-packed snow winking in the ivory moonlight. At the far entrance of the street emerged one huge, horrible shape, dog-like, massive and sinister. It just stood there, then others came, massing in the darkness, ears pointed, high-tailed, the fur on their backs raised in awesome ruffs.

Lord, I screamed and ran, heart thudding, my throat so dry it constricted. I wanted to vomit and would have if my belly had not been so empty. I screamed: *'Aidez-moi! Aidez-moi!'*

I prayed, promising to give up wine, warm tits and marble white buttocks. (You can see how desperate I was!) Behind me the wolves howled as if sure of their prey and calling others to join them for their banquet of good English beef. I flew past barred doors and shuttered windows. Nothing but silence greeted my cries. As I hurried I heard the scrabbling patter of the wolves closing in. Another chilling howl and I could have sworn I smelt their hot, sour breath. [Oh, by the way, I have been chased by wolves on two occasions. A few years later in the ice-packed snow outside Moscovy, but nothing was as chilling as that short, desperate run in Paris.] I glimpsed the creaking sign of a tavern with two red apples. I screamed again.

Suddenly the door beneath the sign opened, a hand stretched out and pulled me in. I heard the crash of a body against the door, and angry snarling. Gasping for breath I looked round, noticing the low black beams, tawdry tables and thick, fat tallow candles, their rancid smell cloying my frozen nose and face. A stocky, red-faced fellow with hairy warts round his mouth grinned a gap-toothed smile, pulled open a shutter and let fly with a huge arbalest. I heard curses, the screaming yelps of the animals, then I fainted.

When I revived, Wart-Face (who introduced himself as Jean Capote) and his companion Claude Broussac, rat-faced with a pointed nose, greasy hair and the cheekiest eyes I have seen this side of Hell, were bending over me, forcing a cup of scalding posset between my lips. They introduced themselves as self-confessed leaders of the Maillotins, the French word for 'clubs', a secret society of the Parisian poor who attacked the rich and earned their name from the huge cudgels they carried. Brother Joachim, like many of the Franciscans, must have been one of these.

'You're not going to die,' Broussac said, his eyes

dancing with mischief. 'We thought we'd denied the wolves a good meal. If we hadn't, we'd have tossed you back and perhaps saved some other unfortunate!'

I struggled up to show I wasn't wolf meat. Capote brought me a deep-bowled cup of heavy claret, heated it with a burning poker, and a dish of scalding meat, heavily spiced. I later learnt it was cat. They asked me a few questions and withdrew to grunt amongst themselves, then came back and welcomed me as one of them. God knows why they saved me. When I asked, they just laughed.

'We don't like wolves,' Broussac sneered, 'whether they be four- or two-legged. You're not French, are you?' he added.

'I'm English,' I replied. 'But I starve like any Frenchman!'

They laughed and clapped me on the shoulder. If I had lied, I'm sure they would have cut my throat. I swear this now [never mind the chaplain who is sitting there sneering at me], I saw more of Christ's love amongst the Maillotins than anywhere else on this earth. Their organisation was loose knit but they accepted anyone who swore the oath of secrecy and agreed to share things in common, which I promptly did. What we owned we stole and filched, not from the poor but the merchants, the lawyers, the fat and the rich. What we didn't eat ourselves, we shared; the most needy receiving the most, then a descending scale for everybody else.

I also began to plot my departure from Paris. Benjamin, I reasoned, must either have died of an illness or been killed. Now I would need silver to reach the coast and get across the Narrow Seas. Broussac once asked what I was doing in Paris, so I told him. He was fascinated by Selkirk's murder.

'There is a secret society,' he murmured, 'Englishmen who fled after your Richard III was killed at Bosworth. They have an emblem.' He screwed up his face so it seemed to hide behind his huge nose. 'Their emblem is an animal, a leopard? No, no, a white boar. *Les Blancs Sangliers*!'

At the time I didn't give a damn. In the winter of 1518 all I cared about was surviving and life was hard in Paris. Yuletide and Twelfth Night passed with only the occasional carols in church, for no one dared to go out at night. Mind you, every cloud had a silver lining. The brothels were free, the ladies of the night well rested and more than prepared to accept sustenance, a loaf or a jug of wine, instead of silver. I suppose I was happy enough. I never planned. (I always follow the Scriptures: 'Sufficient for the day is the evil thereof.') I just wish I had practised what I preached! I was full to the gills of roasted cat, which is one of the reasons I can't stand the animals now. Whenever I see one I remember the rancid smell of Broussac's stew pot and the gall rises in my throat.

[The silly chaplain is shaking his noddle.

'I would not eat cat,' he murmurs.

Yes, the little sod would. Believe me, when you are hungry, really hungry, so that your stomach clings to your backbone, nothing is more tasty than a succulent rat or a well-roasted leg of cat!]

I stayed with the Maillotins until spring came. The river thawed and barges of food began to reach the capital. The city provost and his marshals became more organised, clamping down more ruthlessly on the legion of thieves which flourished in the slums around the Rue Saint Antoine. Broussac and Capote refused to read the signs and so made their most dreadful mistake. One night, early in February 1518, the three of us were in a tavern called the Chariot, a cosy little ale house which stands on the corner of the Rue des Mineurs near the church of Saint Sulpice. We had eaten and drunk well, our gallows faces flushed with wine, our stupid mouths bawling out some raucous song and planning our next escapade.

Now Broussac had an enemy – a Master François Ferrebourg, a priest, bachelor of arts, and pontifical notary. He occupied a house at the Sign of the Keg, a little further down the street opposite the convent church of the Order of Saint Cecily. Broussac, on our way home, stopped to jeer in at the lighted windows of Master Ferrebourg's office. Oh, God, I remember the scene well: the black street with its overhanging eaves and gables, the broad splash of light pouring across the cobbles from Ferrebourg's open window. Inside, his clerks sat toiling into the night over some urgent piece of business and Broussac, half-tipsy, taunted them, making rude gestures and spitting through the window. Now, we should have left it at that, but we were too drunk to run, whilst the clerks were sober and quick-witted. They left their writing desks and poured into the streets, led by Master Ferrebourg himself. The notary gave Broussac a vigorous shove which sent my companion sprawling into the open sewer. He picked himself up, roaring with rage, and, before I could stop him, whipped out his dagger and gave Master Ferrebourg a nasty gash across his chest whilst lifting the purse from his belt.

'Run, Shallot!' he screamed.

I was too drunk and, as Broussac disappeared into the darkness, Capote and myself were seized and held until the night watch arrived. Our thumbs were tied together and, in a clatter of arms and a tramp of archers, we were hustled into the dark archways of the Chatelet prison and thrown into a deep dungeon beneath the tower.

We were tried before the Provost of Paris the next morning. Capote, still drunk, farted and belched when the sentence was read out. I tried to reason with them but, in doing so, confessed I was English. My fate was sealed. We were condemned as two of the most troublesome blackguards within the liberties of Paris; rioters, burglars and assassins, hand in glove with some of the most desperate characters of the underworld. We were sentenced to hang the next morning at the gallows of Montfaucon. I tried to plead and argue but was only beaten for my pains and thrown down the steps back into my cell; the dungeon door, grating shut, was locked securely behind us.

Capote immediately fell asleep on the straw. I just sat staring into the darkness, hugging my knees. All I could see was Death, beckoning and grinning before me. In the thick, musty air of the dungeon I felt a creeping graveyard chill. Who would help me this time? The Parisians would scarcely spare a second thought for an Englishman and be only too pleased to see me twitch and shake at the end of a rope. I thought of Benjamin and Wolsey and cursed them. Couldn't they have done something? Made enquiries? Searched me out?

['Put not your trust in princes, Shallot!' my chaplain often quips. I rap the little hypocrite across the knuckles and tell him to keep writing.]

I spent the night before my intended execution listening to Capote's raucous songs. The fellow said he didn't give a fig about life so why should he fear death? He was still brazening it out the next morning when the Provost and his bodyguard of twelve mounted serjeants and ten archers came to collect us. We were roped, hustled up the steps of the dungeon and into the freezing courtyard. The scarlet execution cart was waiting for us, the skulls of hanged men decorating each side. The Provost barked an order and the red-hooded executioner turned, wished us good morning, flicked his whip and urged the cart through the gates of the prison and on to the winding track down to Montfaucon.

We made a brief stop at the Convent of Les Filles de Dieu near the port of St Severin. Here the good sisters comforted us on our last journey with a manchet of bread and a cup of wine.

I chewed the bread and took the wine in one long gulp to control my trembling for I did not wish to disgrace myself. Capote was as raucous as ever, eyeing the sisters, cracking jokes with the executioner, telling the good prioress to have a second cup ready for the journey back. The provost then ordered us forward, the serjeants going ahead, spurring a lane through the mob gathering to watch us die. I glimpsed Broussac, one hand down the bodice of some whore, the other holding a wine cup. He grinned and toasted me silently. I glared back at the bastard. If he had kept his mouth shut I would still be eating rancid meat and plotting my own way out of Paris.

At last we reached the gibbet and, if you should wish to see a vision of Hell before death, go to Montfaucon. A hideous place! A flat, oblong mound fifteen feet high, about thirty feet wide and forty feet long, it stands like some horrible pimple outside Paris on the road to Saint Denis. On three sides of this mound there is a colonnade on a raised platform comprising sixteen evenly spaced square pillars of unhewn stone, each thirty-two feet high, linked together at the top by heavy beams with ropes and chains hanging from them at short intervals. You could hang a small village there. In the centre of the platform gapes an immense lime pit covered by a grating which is used for the disposal of the hanged after they have been gibbeted. (Did you know in summer the gallants take their doxies out there for a picnic? Imagine, wine and pastries under the swinging corpses of the damned!)

When I arrived, Montfaucon seemed to have been busy. At least fifteen crow-pecked corpses, slimed by their own decay, swung from the end of creaking ropes. By now my courage had failed and I had to be helped up the steep, wooden steps, the executioner's assistants whispering that if I made a good show they would make sure I would choke for no more than ten minutes. Behind me the cart creaked away and the executioners busied themselves with the ropes. I glimpsed Capote beside me, now quiet. The thick hempen cords were slung round our necks; a dusty-robed priest appeared as if from nowhere to recite in a precise voice the last prayer for the dying. The provost came to the edge of the scaffold, unrolled a parchment and read the sentences of death. The noose was tightened and I was pushed up a ladder.

'Don't be nervous,' the executioner grinned. 'At least you don't have to go down it again!'

I gazed out wildly over the crowds.

'Not now,' I whispered. 'Surely, not now!'

The ladder was turned, I heard a voice cry out: 'Not that one!'

But I was already choking as the noose tightened around my throat. I heard a terrible pounding in my ears, my heart thudding like a drum, my stomach lurching as I swung on the end of the rope. I turned and twisted. Capote was also dancing in the air. I couldn't breathe, the pain in the back of my head was so intense, then suddenly blackness.

I revived as I felt myself go hurtling through the air and crashed down on to the wooden planks of the scaffold. The noose round my neck was loosened, I retched and vomited. Beside me crouched the provost, looking concerned.

'You are still with us, Master Shallot?'

I retched again, on to his robe, a suitable thanks to the hard-faced bastard. He squirmed in distaste.

'A pardon, Shallot.' He thrust the small scroll under my nose. 'Someone still loves you!'

The provost made a sign. Two of the archers picked me up under the armpits and hustled me down the steps of the scaffold. I glanced at Capote, still dangling, choking out his life. I saw a sea of faces and heard the boos and catcalls of the crowd, cheated of their sport. A serjeant-at-arms, wearing the royal arms of France on his tabard, gestured to the archers to hoist me into the saddle of a horse whose reins he held.

Hell's teeth, I can hardly remember the rest! A bumpy, shaky ride back across Paris. I thought I was being taken to the prison but instead found myself outside the door of Le Coq d'Or. The serjeant-at-arms, hidden behind the guard of his conical helmet, dragged me down and pushed me into a chamber where a candle glowed in the darkness. I smelt the sour odour of sweaty robes and noticed a brazier of gleaming charcoal had been rolled in. I was shoved down on the bed, the soldier left and the slattern bustled in with a small manchet loaf and a goblet of wine. She watched me eat for a while, mumbled something and left. I nearly choked on the bread; my neck and throat seemed to be ringed by a cruel vice. Stars danced before my eyes and I kept shaking with fear at my latest brush with death. Surely you understand? One minute dangling on the end of a rope; the next a reprieve, a bumpy ride through Paris, followed by the sweetest bread and most fragrant wine I had tasted for months.

[Ever since Montfaucon I have always dreaded executions. I mean, sometimes, as Lord of the Manor, I have to order one but my court is well known for its leniency. Of course, I pay the price. At night my fields are more alive with poachers than rabbits. I will grant the most hardened criminal a reprieve rather than see him hang. The chaplain is nodding his little, bald head. Of course, the idiot now understands the reason for my mercy. He probably thought I had a soft heart. Well, he learns something every day, including why I can never bear anything tight round my throat. Even the touch of smoothest silk reawakens the horrors of my journey to Montfaucon.]

Anyway, back to Le Coq d'Or where I lay on the truckle bed and drifted off to sleep.

When I awoke Benjamin was leaning over me, his eyes bright in a face more pallid than usual.

'Roger, I have returned.'

'Of course, you have, you bloody idiot! Just in time!' I snarled. 'Where in Hell's name have you been?'

Chapter 10

Benjamin sat on the stool next to my bed and wiped the sweat from his face. He looked paler and thinner.

'I'm sorry, Roger,' he mumbled. 'It's a long story. I went to Kelso in Scotland.' He looked away, lost in his memories. 'A lonely monastery surrounded by a sea of dark purple heather and deserted, haunted moors. A grey-slated, dark-stoned building.' He smiled thinly. 'Oh, I was safe enough. Agrippa gave me a safe conduct and the Lord d'Aubigny arranged for moss troopers to guard my every step.'

'What did you find?' I asked crossly.

Benjamin rubbed his eyes on the back of his hand. 'Nothing,' he replied. 'Nothing at all. Many Scots fled to Kelso after Flodden, but you know something, Roger? No one could remember a single event from those stormy days.' He furrowed his brow. 'Even stranger, the prior, the sub-prior, all the officials of that monastery, had been changed. Some had died in rather mysterious circumstances, others been sent abroad on this task or the other. The rest,' he shrugged, 'were as silent as the grave. Only one old lay brother, a hoary old man, mumbled about the abbey being the dark pit for the evil deeds of the Great Ones of the land.'

He sighed. 'Then I came south to Royston but Queen Margaret and her party had already returned to London to collect all their possessions so I followed in hot pursuit. I visited the Lord Cardinal at the Palace of Sheen. He already knew about our mission to Nottingham being successful and welcomed my visit to Kelso and your journey to Paris.' Benjamin took a deep breath. 'Then I fell ill. At first I thought it was some ague but it proved to the Sweating Sickness. Uncle sent me to St Bartholomew's and Agrippa brought an old lady who fed me on a concoction of crushed moss mixed with the leavings of sour milk. The fever broke but I was weak.' He patted me gently on the shoulder. 'The Lord Cardinal sent an envoy but the fellow was ambushed, apparently killed by robbers outside Dover.'

'I don't think so,' I tartly retorted. 'He was killed by assassins just like the bastards nearly murdered me at Le Coq d'Or!'

'What do you mean?' Benjamin asked.

I told him my story in sharp, succinct phrases. Benjamin listened carefully.

'I'm sorry,' he apologised. 'I have been in Paris a week. The landlord here swears he knew nothing of you.'

'He's a liar!' I interrupted.

'He may well be. Anyway, I went to the Provost of Paris. I invoked all the Lord Cardinal's power to organise a search for you. Actually, the pardon was issued last night.' He grimaced. 'But you know officials.'

'Yes, I do!' I snarled. 'Only too well. The bastards had me hanged!'

Benjamin bit his lip. 'I agree with you, Roger, but your troubles began with that piece of red silk. It was the signal for your murder. Undoubtedly the demon who dogs our footsteps has agents in Paris.'

'That may well be so,' I answered, 'but Moodie gave me the cloth, so he must be the assassin.'

[Ah, there goes my chaplain again, jumping up and down on his stool. 'I told you! I told you!' he cries. I just tell him to shut up and give him a sharp rap across the knuckles. The little turd doesn't know what he's talking about.]

'Tell me,' Benjamin continued, 'you say the silk had a fragrance. Did you recognise it? Was it like this?'

He undid the neck of a small pouch and held it under

my nose. I sniffed. It was the same fragrance I had noticed around Madame Eglantine's gift.

'Yes. What is it?'

Benjamin smiled and spilled the faded white rose petals which fell soft as snowflakes to the floor.

'*Les Blancs Sangliers!*' I murmured. 'Moodie must be one of them. He killed Selkirk, Ruthven and Irvine, though God knows why or how.'

Benjamin shook his head. 'No, it's more subtle than that.' He looked at me quizzically. 'What are you smiling at, Roger?' The anxiety drained from his face. 'You know something, don't you?'

I grinned. ' "The truth Now Stands In the Sacred Hands of the place which owns Dionysius' bones!" '

'You know what it means?' Benjamin whispered.

'Oh, yes, and it's not far from where we're sitting. Dionysius is not some Greek god!' I cried, forgetting the bruise which racked my neck and the heavy fatigue which still held my limbs in a vice-like grip. 'He's St Denis, the Roman martyr beheaded on Montmartre Hill, who carried his head, so legend says, to where the Abbey of St Denis now stands.'

Benjamin got up, kicking over the stool behind him in his excitement.

'Of course!' he breathed. 'Dionysius is Latin for Denis. The monks there must have Selkirk's secret!'

I swung my legs off the bed. 'Yes, we'll find it there in a battered casket.'

Benjamin looked at me suspiciously. 'Why didn't you go to St Denis yourself?'

I rubbed the weal where the rope had chafed my neck. 'Oh, yes,' I replied sarcastically. 'An English beggar dressed in tatters swaggers up to the abbey gates, asks for a casket to be handed over, and the monks cheerfully comply.'

Benjamin grinned. 'They will now!' He tossed a bundle of clean clothes at me. 'These will not make you a courtier, Roger, but at least you won't be a beggar!'

'I'm tired,' I moaned. 'My neck still hurts. I want food, wine, proof that I'm still alive.'

Benjamin crouched down beside me, his long, dark face drawn with anxiety. 'Roger,' he insisted, 'we must hurry. Time is important. No doubt the murderer already tracks our footsteps, and we must resolve this mystery before Queen Margaret leaves for Scotland. We have to go to St Denis, find Selkirk's secret and return to England as soon as possible.'

I nodded glumly.

Benjamin brought a fresh cup of wine and a bowl of greasy soup. I ate, gulping like a dog, and then changed my clothes. The evil turd of a landlord, a vacuous smile on his slack face, came up to enquire after my health. I grinned wickedly back and told Benjamin to wait for me in the street outside. I made my preparations and joined him as quickly as I could. We walked up the beaten trackway, slipping and cursing on the icy ground underfoot. Behind me, the candle I had so carefully placed in the dry straw in the garret of Le Coq d'Or kindled into life and the flames turned the evil tavern into a blazing inferno. Oh, yes, revenge is never so sweet as when it's deserved.

Although I had escaped from Montfaucon, the ice cold day soon curbed my elation. The city was still held fast by winter and the journey was cruel and hard. I ached from head to toe and the wound in my throat, inflamed by the cold, created a circle of pain around my neck and shoulders.

We passed the gallows, the corpses of the less fortunate now freezing hard at the end of their ropes, then through the gateway of the city and towards the Abbey of St Denis. God knows, it's an awesome, inspiring place; soaring gables of stone, grinning gargoyles, huge windows full of coloured glass, towers which pierce the sky and fretted stonework with a carving on every cornice, turret and pillar. St Denis is the royal mausoleum of France where the white alabaster tombs of the kings lie in quiet hope of Christ's Second Coming. A strange place, cold and sombre. The abbey is a veritable city in itself; its granges, buildings and outhouses sprawl across the countryside, circled by a huge curtain wall which is guarded by soldiers wearing the livery of the royal household. Of course, alone I would have been turned away. Benjamin, however, with his fluent grasp of French and armed with the personal recommendation of the Lord Cardinal of England, soon gained admittance. An austere prior welcomed us into his chamber and listened carefully to Benjamin's request.

'Many people come here,' he replied quietly in perfect English. 'They bring gifts and treasures which they commit to our care. Some return, some do not.' He spread his hands. 'They place their trust in us.' He looked sharply at Benjamin. 'You swear that Selkirk is dead?'

'I do, Father Prior.'

'And his secret is one which may threaten the English throne?'

'Perhaps,' Benjamin replied. 'But it has been responsible for the deaths of at least three good men and may cause the deaths of others, including our own.'

The prior moved uneasily behind his desk. He pointed to the Bible chained to a great lectern beside him. 'Swear that!' he rasped. 'Swear what you say is true, with your hand on the Gospels!'

Benjamin obeyed. One hand placed on the great, jewel-embossed cover and the other held high, he proclaimed in solemn tones that God be his witness, what he said was the truth. Once he had finished the prior nodded and his granite face broke into a thin smile. He rang a small hand bell. A young monk entered to whom the prior whispered hoarse instructions. I heard the name 'Selkirk' and a possible date. The young monk nodded and padded softly away, returning soon afterwards with a small, battered leather coffer sealed with the waxen crest of the Abbey of St Denis. The prior broke this and lifted the lid. He felt around inside, his long fingers picking up scraps of parchment. He looked despairingly at Benjamin.

'You say Selkirk was mad?'

'Yes, Father Prior.'

'Then this may be his last insane joke. There's nothing here but innumerable scraps of parchment. Now my conscience is settled, you may take it.'

We left St Denis as darkness fell and made our way to a tavern outside one of the gateways of Paris on the main road to Calais, a warm comfortable place which had escaped the ravages of famine which still afflicted the city. Benjamin hired a chamber as well as fresh horses for the morning. He also ordered a meal of succulent roast capon cooked in rich sauces and freshly baked loaves of pure wheat rather than the coarse rye bread I had eaten the previous months. I gorged myself to the gills although Benjamin ordered me to be temperate with the wine. Afterwards, we sat in the ingle-nook of the great fireplace watching the roaring flames turn the pine logs to a white smouldering ash. Benjamin opened Selkirk's casket and for a while sifted amongst the pieces of parchment. One was singular: a dirty yellow piece, jagged at the top and bottom; only the heading was discernible, a quotation in Latin from one of St Paul's epistles. It simply said: 'Through a glass darkly'. The rest were a jumble of hieroglyphics and strange signs. There were some complete manuscripts but these were nothing more than a collection of royal warrants written personally by King James and sealed under his signet ring, granting tasks or favours to his 'beloved physician, Andrew Selkirk'. Benjamin studied some of these and so did I but we could discover nothing amiss. My master placed the documents back in the casket.

'Let us refresh our memories,' he said. 'Selkirk was King James's physician. He went with the King to Flodden where James was defeated and killed. Selkirk fled to Paris, left his so-called secret at St Denis and went to Le Coq d'Or where he was arrested and taken to England.' He stared at me. 'You would agree with that?'

'Yes, Master.'

'Now, in Scotland, James's widow Margaret, the mother of one infant, is pregnant again when she hears the news of her husband's defeat and death. By King James's will, she is made Regent but forfeits that position by marrying the Earl of Angus. She also loses the confidence of her nobles and is forced to flee to England, leaving her two boys behind. The Scottish nobles set up a Regency Council with control of Margaret's baby sons, one of whom, Alexander, Duke of Ross, dies soon after his mother's sudden departure for England. Am I correct Roger?'

'A number of matters,' I replied, 'must also be remembered. First, before James went to Flodden, he had so-called visions which warned him against his loose morals and of the dangers of invading England. Secondly, why should Margaret suddenly marry the Earl of Angus and then, within such a short time, desert him; indeed, even hate him? Thirdly, why did she shelter in England away from her kingdom and her sons? We heard from the Lord d'Aubigny that the Scottish Council is more than prepared to welcome Queen Margaret back with open arms.'

'Which,' Benjamin continued, 'leads us to this sudden change in the Queen's mood. It seems that she cannot return to Scotland fast enough. I'm sorry. Go on, Roger.'

'I wonder what Margaret was so frightened of? And what secrets she and the Earl of Angus share? Don't forget, Master, there are other mysteries which may be contained in the documents in that casket. What did Selkirk mean by the phrase he could "count the days"? And why has King James's body not been returned to Scotland for burial?'

Benjamin nodded and stared at the dying flames of the fire.

'Which brings us to Selkirk's verses,' he said. 'We know the falcon is James, the lamb is Angus, the Lion also is the King of Scotland. Is Selkirk saying that somehow King James survived Flodden? Something we suspected when we viewed the corpse at Sheen.'

'Perhaps,' I interrupted. 'The verses do say the Lion cried even though it died. Finally, we have discovered who Dionysius was but not the real secret left with him.'

Benjamin picked up the casket and carefully examined the lining, searching for any secret compartment or hidden drawer.

'Nothing,' he murmured.

'Which brings us, Master,' I said, 'to the murders once more. Both Selkirk and Ruthven were found poisoned in chambers locked from the inside. No poisoned cup or dish was found there.'

Benjamin agreed.

'Whilst Irvine,' he remarked, 'could have had his throat cut by any member of Queen Margaret's household except for four; you and I who were at the convent, and Catesby and Melford who were in Nottingham. We also know that the Queen herself did not leave the manor house.'

'Which means,' I concluded wearily, 'that we do not know who the murderer really is, although we suspect Moodie. We do not know Selkirk's secret, even though we hold it in our hands. Above all, we do not know the meaning of the first two lines of his damnable poem, "Three less than twelve should it be, Or the King, no prince engendered he!" '

On that merry note we both retired for the night. Benjamin spent most of the time sitting in a chair staring at the guttering candle flame, whilst my sleep was racked by terrible nightmares of my visit to Montfaucon. The next morning Benjamin dressed my wounds and we began our journey back to Calais. The weather improved and, although the roads were clogged with icy mud, we soon reached the Channel port where Benjamin used his warrants and his status to secure our passage home on a man-o'-war.

A terrible journey, believe me! If Hell exists, it must consist of being eternally sick on a ship which crosses the Narrow Seas but never reaches shore. I disembarked at Dover, cursing Benjamin, the King, the Lord Cardinal, and heartily wishing I was back in Ipswich, free from the baleful influence of the Great Ones of the soil. Matters were not helped when we found Doctor Agrippa waiting for us in a seaside tavern, cheerful and full of life as a well-fed sparrow. The fellow never seemed to age, nothing changed him; no lines of worry on his cherubic face, while those hard, glassy eyes shimmered with a quiet amusement.

He greeted us effusively, clasping Benjamin warmly by the hand. He insisted we join him for dinner where he regaled us with tidbits of gossip from the court and city.

'How did you know we were coming?' I asked crossly.

He smiled as if savouring some secret joke. 'I have my sources,' he quipped. 'The Lord Cardinal told me to come here. Your return was only a matter of time.' His face grew hard. 'You have news?'

'Yes and no!' Benjamin joked back. 'However, the game is not yet over and, if you'll accept my apologies, we still cannot discern friend from foe.'

That enigmatic little magician ignored this possible insult and deftly turned the conversation to other matters. We stayed one night in Dover, then travelled across a frost-hardened countryside back to London. Only God knows how he knew but Agrippa insisted we arm ourselves. He also warned us that, once we were back in London, we were to be careful where we went, to whom we talked and what we ate and drank.

His warnings proved prophetic. We were on a lonely stretch of road just outside London: it was late in the afternoon, darkness was about to fall and we were arguing about whether we should hurry on to the city or stay at some roadside tavern for the night. Our assailants, muffled and cloaked, seemed to rise out of the ground, running swiftly towards us, armed with dagger and sword. Now, in the ladies' romances, such encounters are full of brave oaths and heroic stances. However, I consider myself an expert in the art of assassination and murder and, I tell you this, violent death always comes quietly.

One minute we were riding our horses, the next we were surrounded by five villains intent on murder. Benjamin and Agrippa drew their hangers and set to with a will, the eerie silence of that lonely road shattered by grunts, muttered oaths and the scraping clash of steel. I drew my own sword, shouting defiance and encouragement to the rest. But, oh, Lord, I was frightened! These were not your ordinary footpads, they would never attack three well-armed, mounted travellers. Oh, no, these were assassins, despatched by the arch murderer we were hunting.

'Roger!' Benjamin shouted. 'For God's sake, man!'

Now I had been hanging back, attempting to develop some strategy.

[No, that's a lie! My chaplain's right, I was petrified. Now you talk to any coward, a real coward like myself, and he'll tell you there's a point where fear becomes so great it actually turns into courage, not out of anger or fury but that marvellous innate desire to save your own skin. On that London road I reached such a point.]

Two assailants were pressing Agrippa whilst the other three had apparently forgotten me and were intent on bringing my master down. I closed my eyes and spurred my horse forward, my huge sword rising and falling as if I was the Grim Reaper himself. It's a wonder I didn't kill Benjamin but, when I opened my eyes, two of the rogues were dead of huge gashes between shoulder and neck whilst Benjamin was on the point of driving his sword straight through the breast of a third. Agrippa, his fat face covered in sweat, had already despatched one but now had lost his sword and kept turning his horse sharply to counter his final opponent. I waited until the fellow turned his back, charged and felt my sword sink deep into his exposed shoulder. The fellow whirled and, as he did so, Agrippa finished him off, plunging his dagger firmly into the man's back.

Death is so strange: one minute noise, blood, screaming and retching; the next, a terrible silence. You old soldiers who read my memoirs will realise I speak the truth. So it was on that fog-bound, lonely London road. Benjamin and Agrippa, chests heaving, cleaned their weapons. I sat like a Hector until I suddenly remembered my stomach and began noisily to vomit. Nevertheless, both my master and Agrippa were loud in their praise of my martial prowess. Naturally, I can resist anything but flattery and lapped it up like a hungry cat does milk. Of course, I glimpsed the wry amusement in Agrippa's eyes but Benjamin looked at me oddly.

'You're a strange one, Shallot,' he murmured. 'I'll never understand you.'

I dismounted and searched the corpses. I found nothing noteworthy except on one, possibly the leader, who had a considerable amount of silver which I pocketed for distribution to the poor. We then continued our journey, pushing on until we reached the city walls and lodged at one of the fine taverns on the Southwark side of the river. Oh, it was good to be back in London! To see and smell the greasy rags of the poor; the silk-slashed, perfumed doublets, velvet hose and precious buckled shoes of the rich. The pompous little beadles; dark-gowned priests; the lawyers from Westminster Hall with their fur tippets; and, of course, my favourites, the ladies of the night, with their hair piled high, low-cut dresses and heels which clicked along the cobbles. A bear had broken loose amongst the stews; a whore was being whipped outside the gates of St Thomas's Hospital; two butchers who had sold putrid meat were riding back to back on some old nag, their hands tied behind them, the rotten offal they had sold fastened tightly under their noses.

[Ben Jonson is right, London is a wondrous city! Within its walls you can see the whole spectrum of human behaviour: the splendour of the rich moving through the streets on damask-caparisoned palfreys and the bare-arsed poor who would slit your throat for a crust of bread.]

Strangely, Benjamin did not wish to visit his uncle who was wintering at the Bishop of Ely's inn just north of Holborn. He insisted we went direct to the Tower. We took the route through Cheapside because the Thames was frozen from bank to bank, past the mansions of the rich, the stalls full of fripperies, the mouldering Eleanor Cross and the great Conduit which was supposed to bring fresh water into the city. I say 'supposed to' for it had been frozen over and, beneath the ice, I glimpsed the scrawny corpse of a dead dog. The city was just recovering from one of the usual bouts of plague which come in late winter; its citizens, however, sensed the worst was over and the streets buzzed like an overturned hive. We reached the Tower through Poor Jewry, passing the house of the Crutched Friars and then through a postern gate which stands near Hog Street. Benjamin and Agrippa had fallen strangely silent.

Only as we entered the Tower did Benjamin lean over and whisper, 'Roger, pretend we discovered nothing. Keep your thoughts hidden and your counsel concealed until we find the truth about this party of knaves.'

Benjamin's 'party of knaves' had re-established themselves in the Tower waiting for spring to dry out the roads so they could travel north. Sir Robert Catesby greeted Agrippa warmly, taking him aside for secret consultations whilst ignoring Benjamin and me. At last I grew tired of such rudeness. The grooms had taken away our horses and I did not wish to stand like a servant on the freezing forecourt of the tower.

'Doctor Agrippa!' I called out. 'What is the matter?'

He apologised and walked back to us arm-in-arm with Catesby, who now gracefully bowed to both of us.

'Welcome back, Master Benjamin, Shallot. I apologise for any offence given but there has been another death, though one which may resolve the mysteries which have plagued us.'

'Moodie's dead!' Agrippa flatly announced. 'Not murder this time,' he added quickly. 'He died the Roman way.'

Benjamin cocked his head quizzically.

'He killed himself,' Catesby declared. 'Asked for a

bowl of warm water from the kitchen, locked his chamber and slashed his wrist.'

'When was this?' I asked.

'Yester evening. His body was not found until late at night.'

I stared up at the grey sky and the black ravens which circled above the battlements like the souls of men condemned to wander the earth forever.

'You said his death may resolve the mysteries?' Benjamin abruptly asked.

I stamped my feet on the cobbles as a sign that I was freezing. Catesby took my point, smiled, and led us up to his own warm, spacious chamber in the Lion Tower. He served us mulled wine sprinkled with cinnamon and heated with a red hot poker and then emptied the contents of a saddle bag on to the table; it contained a few faded white rose petals and pieces of parchment. The latter were passed around for us to examine. Most were notes, drafts of letters or memoranda concerning secret Yorkist plans as well as proclamations written anonymously to be nailed on the doors of churches up and down the kingdom. They were full of the usual childish nonsense about the Tudors being usurpers and that the crown, by right and divine favour, should go to the House of York – in reality a pathetic bundle of faded dreams and failed aspirations. Agrippa studied them with a smile. Benjamin just dismissed them, tossing the documents back on to the table.

'So Moodie was a supporter of the White Rose,' he said quietly. 'A member of *Les Blancs Sangliers*. But why should he kill Selkirk and Ruthven?'

Catesby shrugged. 'God knows! Perhaps he saw them as a threat. Perhaps Selkirk's verses contained information which he wished destroyed.'

'Do you really believe that?' I asked.

Catesby shook his head. 'No,' he answered slowly. 'No, I don't. Perhaps it was just an act of revenge.' He sighed. 'There's neither rhyme nor reason to Moodie's suicide.'

He sat down heavily. 'I don't know how Selkirk and Ruthven died,' he murmured, and looked up. 'Do you?'

Benjamin shook his head.

'Moodie could have killed Irvine,' Catesby continued. 'He did leave Royston for a while at the same time as you, and a priest would be acceptable within the convent walls at Coldstream.'

'What does Queen Margaret say?' asked Benjamin.

Catesby shrugged. 'She mourns Moodie's death and has her own explanation of it.' He paused to gather his thoughts. 'Her late husband, James IV, at one time supported the cause of the White Rose and then deserted it. She believes James was not killed at Flodden.' He coughed, the sound shattering the eerie silence of the chamber. 'Queen Margaret believes,' he continued, 'that her husband was murdered at Flodden by a member of *Les Blancs Sangliers* who have since waged continuous war against those who advised her late husband, such as Selkirk and Ruthven.'

I sat back, surprised because what Catesby said made sense. Agrippa toyed with the tassels on his robes whilst Benjamin just stared into the middle distance, lost in his own thoughts.

'But why,' he asked eventually, 'would Moodie now kill himself?'

'Because,' Doctor Agrippa intervened, 'he probably thought that you or Shallot would have discovered something during your travels in Scotland and France to trap him.'

Again, Agrippa's conclusions were logical; after all, Moodie had arranged the deadly attack on me in Paris.

'How was your mission?' Catesby queried.

I shrugged. Benjamin just laughed.

'Let me put it this way, Sir Robert, if Moodie dreaded our return then he had very little to fear.'

Agrippa sighed noisily, I don't know whether from relief or disappointment.

'Ah, well!' Catesby rose. 'Soon this matter will be

finished and Her Grace will leave for Scotland. She is very busy.' His boyish face lit with a smile. 'But I know she wishes to see you.'

Agrippa excused himself whilst Catesby took Benjamin and me across to the Queen's spacious chamber on the second floor of the Tower just next to St Stephen's Chapel. [Or was it St John's? I forget now.] Well, the fat bitch had made herself comfortable! She had a beautiful room, painted red and decorated with golden moons and silver stars. Tapestries hung on the walls and Turkey rugs covered the polished floor. Margaret herself was dressed in a tight-fitting, damson-coloured gown which emphasised her full, rounded figure whilst her golden hair was unbraided and hung down to her shoulders. She looked warm and comely but her eyes were still black as night and her face spoilt by that false, simpering smile. The Careys were also in attendance: Lady Carey glowered whilst her husband busied himself at the far end of the room, totally ignoring our existence. Melford the killer was there, lounging like an alley cat on a bench against the wall, whilst the bastard Scawsby was mulling a glass of wine for his mistress. He turned away as we entered, shoulders shaking as if relishing some private joke. Queen Margaret took us both by the hand, welcoming us back and handing Benjamin a small purse of silver coins.

'Your work on my behalf is much appreciated, Master Daunbey,' she simpered. 'I would ask you to stay longer, but His Majesty the King has invited me to a masque at Richmond.' She waved a hand to indicate the dresses scattered around the room; some of taffeta, others of damask or cloth of gold. The false smile spread. 'Time is passing and I must go.'

We bowed and left, Catesby showing us to the door. We wandered back into the freezing bailey. Benjamin leaned against a wall watching a butcher at the far end of the yard hack a haunch of beef into huge, steaming slabs, the blood pouring like red streams over the rough-hewn carving block.

'Roger, Roger,' he murmured, 'what is going on here? One minute we are involved in matters of state, murder, Yorkist conspiracies, and the next we are dismissed because Her Grace wishes to attend a masque!'

Catesby had told us we had our old chamber in one of the towers but Benjamin insisted that, before we retire, we should examine Moodie's corpse which had been placed in the death house, no more than a wooden shed built against the walls of the Tower Church, St Peter ad Vincula.

Well, believe me, I have seen corpses enough, bodies piled six, seven feet high, left to steam and rot on battle fields as far flung as France and North Africa. I have seen heads hacked off and stacked high in baskets, and more bodies hanging from the branches of trees than I have apples in an orchard. Nothing, however, is more pathetic than a solitary corpse lying on a cold slab in a disused shed.

Moodie may have been a priest but in death his body had been laid out like some broken toy to lie on a shelf, the grimacing features half-hidden by a dirty cloth; the eyes still open, sightless and empty. Some attempt had been made to straighten the limbs and that was all. Apparently, he was to be interred in the clothes he died in, wrapped in some canvas sheet and either buried in the cemetery of a nearby church or the small graveyard on the other side of the Tower church. Two days dead, the body was beginning to putrefy and the stench made both Benjamin and myself gag. Benjamin muttered the Requiem, stared at the mottled-hued face and carefully examined the wrists of the dead man. The left was unmarked but the right bore a huge, deep gash which must have drained the blood.

'A painful way to die, Master.'

Benjamin shook his head. 'Not really, Roger,' he said, his voice muffled by the hem of his cloak which he held up to cover his nose. 'The wrist is cut and placed in warm water. They say death comes like sleep, a painless way to oblivion. The senators of ancient Rome often used it.'

I took his word for it and we left, glad to be free of the ghastly place. Outside Benjamin stared up at the darkening sky.

'The game is not over yet, Roger,' he murmured. 'Believe me, Moodie did not die in vain.'

He would say no more. We retired to our chamber, made ourselves as comfortable as our bleak quarters would allow, and later joined the rest of the household when they gathered to dine in the small hall. Queen Margaret had already left in a blaze of colour, escorted by Catesby and Agrippa, riding along Ropery, then Vintry Street into Thames Street, where she would meet a troop of her brother's royal serjeants at Castle Baynard.

Catesby, if he had stayed, might have put a restraining hand upon the petty malice of his comrades. Previously they had ignored us: now they let their malice show. Carey (his wife had gone with Queen Margaret), Melford, Scawsby and the two killers from Clan Chattan, Corin and Alleyn, swaggered into the hall. To be truthful, I had forgotten about Earl Angus's gift to his estranged wife but the two Highlanders still remembered us. They smiled, displaying wicked-edged teeth, and once again I was reminded of hunting dogs studying their intended quarry. Benjamin and I sat at one end of the trestle board, they sat at the other, grouped together like stupid boys immersed in their own private jokes. The garrison had already eaten so we were alone. The servants brought platters of over-cooked, rather rancid meat, garnished with herbs, and once they withdrew and the wine circulated, Melford began talking at the top of his voice about sending boys to do men's work. The two Highlanders grinned as if they understood every word, Carey smirked whilst Scawsby gave that neighing laugh which made the blood beat in my temples. Coward or not, I could have plunged a dagger straight into his black treacherous heart. Benjamin ignored them, lost in his own

thoughts, but at last Scawsby, his sallow face flushed with
wine, rose and came to stand over me.

'So glad to see you, Shallot,' he purred. 'Another
errand, another failure, eh?'

Benjamin nudged me with his knee so I looked away.
Scawsby leaned closer and I wrinkled my nose at his sour
breath.

'You are a base-born rogue, Shallot!' he hissed. 'If I
had my way you would be buried like your mother in a
pauper's grave!'

Benjamin seized my wrist before I could grasp my
knife.

'Come, Roger!' he murmured. 'We have eaten our fill.'

He dragged me away for I could have killed Scawsby
on the spot and anyone else who tried to interfere. Outside
the hall, I turned to Benjamin.

'You should have let me kill him!' I accused.

'No, no, Roger, they are full of wine and their own
importance. They think the game is over and we are to
be whipped off like hounds, back to Uncle.'

'If you could prove Scawsby was the murderer!' I
hissed. 'After all, he knows poisons.'

Benjamin looked away. 'Scawsby,' he murmured, 'is
he the murderer or just a spiteful man who rejoices in
the humiliation of others? But I tell you this, Roger,
Moodie was innocent of any crime. He no more
committed suicide than Selkirk or Ruthven!'

Chapter 11

My master still refused to share his thoughts. He spent
the next day closeted in our chamber studying the
manuscripts we had brought from Paris. I grew restless
and said I would leave, so Benjamin warned me to be
careful and stay well away from Queen Margaret's
household. I left the Tower and went to the area known
as Petty Wales, a maze of alleyways and streets which
stretches down towards the Wool Quay. It was a cold day,
late in February; a troupe of gypsies, Egyptians or 'Moon
People', as the country folk call them, were holding one
of their fairs. Of course, they had attracted every villain
in London, including myself: cut-throats, palliards,
pickpockets or foists, professional beggars, and all the
scum of the underworld. I felt at home and wandered
around the tawdry booths and stalls, seeing if I could
catch the eye of some pretty wench or buy some trinket
for one I had not yet met.

Now, as you know, I am a keen student of history and
believe that chance and luck play a great part in the
tapestry of life. If Harold had not been drunk before the
battle of Hastings perhaps he would have won; or if
Richard III's horse had not become stuck in the mud,
the Yorkist royal line might well have continued. So it
is with our petty lives. A fickle change of fortune can bring
about the most momentous events. There I was wandering
the alleys of Petty Wales whilst the hucksters and pedlars
screamed for trade and the cookshops were busy serving
hot eel pies and jugs of mulled wine. There were
sideshows: the stuffed mummy of a Mameluke fresh from

Egypt; a unicorn's horn; a dog with two heads and a lady with a long, flowing beard. What caught my fancy was a young boy screaming that, behind a tattered cloth, stood a giant from the far north.

'Almost three yards high!' he screamed. 'And a yard across! Tuppence and you can touch!'

Of course, it would be the usual trick, a very tall man standing on small stilts. The urchin plucked my sleeve, his eyes rounded in amazement, skeletal face alive with false excitement.

'Come, Lord,' he said, 'see this Cyclops. A veritable wonder!'

I smiled, tossed the lad a penny and asked: 'How come he's so big?'

The boy's master, sensing money, stepped forward.

'Because,' he lied, 'this giant was not nine months in the womb, as you or I, but eighteen!'

My jaw dropped and I turned away in amazement. Nine! Of course, every man born of woman lies nine months or thirty-eight weeks in his mother's womb. I remembered Selkirk's verse: 'Three less than twelve should it be', and his mutterings about how he could 'count the days'. I spun round and ran like a whippet, sliding, slipping and cursing on the wet cobbles back to the Tower. Benjamin, however, was missing and I suspected he had gone along the river bank to the convent at Syon. I had to curb my excitement and kept to my own chamber. I did not want Margaret or any of her household to sense any change in me. Early in the afternoon Benjamin returned, withdrawn and sombre-faced.

'Johanna?' I asked.

'She is well, Roger, as well as can be expected. Stretched,' he murmured, 'like a cobweb in the sun.' He scrutinised my face. 'But you have something to tell me?'

I told him what I had learnt in the fairground that morning and asked him to recall our conversation with Lord d'Aubigny in Nottingham Castle. Benjamin's gloom immediately lifted.

'And I have something for you, Roger!' he exclaimed and went across to his saddle bag. He pulled out the strange manuscript found in Selkirk's casket and picked up a small piece of polished steel which served as a mirror.

'What do the first words say?'

'We know that, Master Benjamin, a quotation from St Paul: "Through a glass darkly".'

He smiled. 'And you remember your Latin, Roger?' He passed the manuscript over to me. 'Hold this up, facing the mirror.'

I did so.

'Now, read the words in the mirror!'

Oh, Lord, it took a few minutes and I marvelled at Selkirk's ingenuity. He had written his confession in Latin but taken great pains to write each word backwards. I made out the first three words. *'Ego Confiteor Deo'* – 'I confess to God.' The rest was easy. In that cold, dark chamber of the Tower Benjamin and I plumbed the mysteries of Selkirk's poem and the terrible truths it contained.

'You see, Roger!' Benjamin exclaimed. 'In the end all things break down in the face of truth.'

'And the murders?'

Benjamin leaned back. 'Listen to this riddle, Roger!' He closed his eyes and chanted. 'Two legs sat upon three legs with one leg in his lap. In comes four legs, takes away one leg. Up jumps two legs, leaves three legs and chases four legs to get one leg back.' He opened his eyes and grinned. 'Solve the riddle!'

I shook my head angrily.

'Roger, it's a child's game yet only logic can solve it. So it is with these murders. We can resolve them by evidence but that is strangely lacking. We can reveal the truth by close questioning and subtle interrogation but that is impossible. Take Irvine's death: we could spend years asking who was where and what they were doing. Or,' he added, 'we can apply pure logic, meditation, speculation, and finally deduction.'

'Like the riddle you just told me?'

'Yes, Roger. Logically it can only have one meaning. Two legs is a man sitting on a three-legged stool with a leg of pork in his lap.'

'And four legs is a dog?'

'Of course, the only logical deduction. Now,' Benjamin leaned closer, 'let's apply logic to these murders.'

Well, it was dark by the time we finished and when we looked through the shutters, the Tower Bailey below was clouded in a thick, cloying river mist. I felt elated yet exhausted. Benjamin and I had not only demonstrated what Selkirk had hidden in his lines but how that poor Scottish doctor had died, along with Ruthven, Irvine and Moodie.

[There goes my little chaplain again, leaping up and down, shouting like a child, 'Tell me! Tell me!' Why should I? All things in due season. Will he reveal what Mistress Burton said in confession? Or would Master Shakespeare interrupt *Twelfth Night* to tell his audience what's going to happen to Malvolio? Of course not! As I have said, all things in due season.]

Benjamin did all the work, translating Selkirk's secret message. After he had finished I studied the transcript carefully whilst Benjamin watched me. I should have interrogated my master for I noticed that enigmatic look which used to flicker across his face whenever he has told the truth but kept something back for his own purposes. [Oh, don't worry, I'll tell you about that later.] However, in that dark, freezing chamber all that concerned me was that we knew who the murderer may be and the true nature of the dark secrets contained in Selkirk's poem.

I pointed to the manuscript. 'This confession mentions one new name?'

Benjamin nodded. 'Yes, yes, my dear Roger, the knight Harrington but he is not important. Like poor Irvine or Ruthven, Harrington was just another victim of our murderer's great malice.'

I studied Benjamin closely. 'Master, is there anything else?'

Benjamin made a face. 'For the moment, Roger, I have shown you all you need to know.' He rose and stretched. 'We have the evidence, what we need to do now is trap the murderer.'

'How can we do that?'

Benjamin shrugged. 'Reveal a little of what we know and choose a place, lonely and deserted, where the murderer, wanting to silence us, will make his presence felt.' Benjamin walked and leaned against the wall staring out through one of the arrow slits. 'It can't be here,' he murmured. 'Or in London.'

I rose and stood beside him. 'I know a place nearby, Master, where we could set our trap and watch the murderer fall into it.'

Benjamin gazed around as if the very walls had ears. 'It could be dangerous, Roger.'

I shrugged. 'Master, we suspect who the murderer may be. We have proof but we must make him show his hand. [I see the clerk sniggering, he thinks my courage was bravado, perhaps it was.] However, my master took me at my word and gently patted my shoulder.

'Then so be it, Roger.' He murmured. 'So be it.'

We did not go down to the hall for dinner that evening but had a servant bring us cold meats and a jug of watered wine from the garrison kitchen. We spent the night like two artificers planning a subtle masque or Twelfth Night game but at last we were agreed. The next morning we left the Tower and went past St Mary Grace's Church to the fields which stretched north from Hog Street to Aldgate, a deserted barren area like the blasted heath in one of Will Shakespeare's plays. Now, in the middle of these wild moorlands was an old, derelict church, once dedicated to St Theodore of Tarsus.

In more prosperous times there had been a village there but, since the Great Plague, all had decayed. The village had gone and the church was in disrepair. The roof had been stripped, the nave stood open to the elements, the chancel screen was long gone to some builder's yard whilst the sanctuary was only discernible by the steps and stone plinth on which the altar had once rested. To the right of the nave, in one of the aisles, were steps leading down to a darkened crypt. Benjamin and I went down these. Surprisingly, the door was still there. We pushed it open on its creaking, rusty hinges and found the crypt dark and deserted except for the squeaking of mice and the rustling wings of some bird nesting on the sill of the open window high in the wall. A rank, fetid place, sombre and cold, I sensed it was full of ghosts. In the far corner were decaying tombs with effigies on top, knights clasping their swords, now crumbling to a white powdered dust. I looked around and shivered.

'This will do, Master?'

Benjamin smiled thinly. 'Yes, Roger, it will. Not for tonight but certainly tomorrow!'

We stayed away from the Tower for most of the day. Benjamin visited a distant relative in Axe Street near the Priory of St Helen but we made sure we were back in the Tower for the evening meal. Queen Margaret and all her retinue were there: Catesby, full of his own importance, issuing orders, loudly declaring how they would be on the road north before the Feast of the Annunciation. Agrippa looked quiet and withdrawn. Melford and the rest chose to ignore us but Benjamin and I, like good actors, had learnt our lines and so waited. Of course, Scawsby, as expected, rose to the bait.

'Master Benjamin,' he asked gaily, 'when we are gone, what then?'

Benjamin shrugged. 'God knows, Master Scawsby. My uncle the Lord Cardinal may have other tasks for us. Once, of course, we have finished this one.'

Benjamin's quiet words stilled the clamour.

'What do you mean?' Carey barked.

Benjamin smiled and turned back to his food.

'Yes,' Agrippa spoke up, 'what do you mean, Master Daunbey?'

'He means,' I said, standing up, 'that we know the mystery behind Selkirk's poem. We know also how Selkirk, Ruthven, Irvine and Moodie died!'

Well, you could have heard a needle drop. They all sat rigid, like figures in a painting: Queen Margaret, a cup hovering half-way to her lips, Catesby about to speak to her, the Careys with their mouths wide open. Melford, Agrippa and Scawsby just sat pop-eyed. The only exceptions were the two Highlanders but they sensed that what I was saying was important. I have never enjoyed myself so much in my life! Agrippa was the first to stir.

'Do explain, Roger,' he said silkily. 'Pray do.'

'When I was in Paris,' I lied, 'I did not find Selkirk's secret but something more important – a man who fought with the late James IV of Scotland at Flodden.'

Benjamin looked strangely at me as I strayed from the agreed text.

'This man,' I continued meaningfully, 'was with James until he died.'

'Who is he?' Queen Margaret rasped, half-rising out of her chair. 'What are you talking about?'

'Oh, he's here in London, Your Grace. Soon we will meet him. He has enough evidence to prove what he says is the truth.'

Now Benjamin rose and took me by the arm. 'You have said enough, Roger. We must go.'

We both swept out of the hall, trying hard to hide our excitement at the dangerous game we were playing. Benjamin pushed me across the bailey.

'Why did you mention this person?' he demanded crossly. 'We did not agree to that.'

I smiled. 'We now play a dangerous game, Master. Fortune has dealt us each a hand. We discovered the truth by chance, so let chance still have some say in what will happen.'

Benjamin agreed though he was both anxious and

angry. 'We cannot stay in the Tower,' he murmured. 'The murderer may strike now and finish the game.'

So we packed our saddle bags, Benjamin managing to draw from the Tower stores two small crossbows and an arbalest as well as fresh swords and daggers. We left the fortress. Benjamin told me to stay at a small ale-house near the postern gate and slipped away. I whiled away the time eyeing the bright-cheeked young slattern and trying to persuade her oafish swain to hazard a few coins at dice. At last I got bored and sat back, sipping from a black jack of ale and remembering what we had learnt from Selkirk's confession. [Oh, I wish my chaplain would stop interrupting. I'll tell him what it said in due course!] I could scarcely believe it and wondered what had become of the knight Selkirk mentioned, Sir John Harrington. I also relished my own subtle trickery and hoped its victim would fall meekly into the prepared trap. Suddenly I recalled my mother and one of her favourite sayings, a quotation from the Psalms: 'He fell into a snare which he had prepared for others.' I took another gulp from the black jack of ale and hoped this would not happen to me. Once again I scrutinised what I'd planned. No, the plot was primed. All we had to do was keep our nerve.

After a while Benjamin returned. His face looked white and drawn but his eyes were feverish with excitement.

'Where have you been?' I snapped.

He stared innocently back.

'To see the Queen, of course.'

I groaned. 'What for, Master? We agreed to leave that fat bitch well alone.'

Benjamin grimaced. 'I had to, Roger,' he muttered. 'You have been thinking of Selkirk's confession?'

I nodded.

'Well, all I did was ask her about Sir John Harrington, a Scottish knight who fought with her husband.' He grinned. 'Let's be on our way!

'I also told Doctor Agrippa about our meeting place,' he muttered as we slipped down a darkened alleyway.

'Was that wise?' I asked.

'We shall see,' he replied. 'As you said, Roger, Agrippa may be the murderer so he must know where the last act of the play is to take place.'

'And the rest?'

Benjamin stopped. 'They will find out, Roger, so we must make sure we are ready.'

We lodged in a small tavern just off Poor Jewry and slept late the following morning. Benjamin went about his business and I seized the opportunity to go about mine. I went to a scrivener in Mincing Lane off Eastcheap, who, for a price, wrote out my message in a good clerkly hand. I also drew three gold pieces from a merchant in Lombard Street and he agreed to send my small package, sealed in a leather wallet, to the Tower. Next I bought an hour candle, a great thick wax article divided neatly into twelve divisions, and went back to our lodgings to clean the swords and daggers and ensure that the arbalest was in good working order. Just before dusk we slipped out of our chamber, made our way up Aldgate Street, across the stinking City ditch into Portsoken, and then turned south across the wasteland towards the ruins of St Theodore's Church.

In day time this had been sombre; in the cold darkness it was positively eerie. Dark-feathered birds rustled at the top of broken pillars, an owl hooted from the surrounding trees, and the silence was broken now and again by the long mournful howl of a dog from a nearby farm.

[A wise hag once told me to be wary of ruined churches. They draw in those restless spirits who have not yet gone to heaven or hell but spend their time in Purgatory on the wastelands of the earth.

Of course, my little chaplain chuckles and titters. As I have said, he doesn't believe in ghosts. He should go to the ruined priories and monasteries, now shells of their former glory, thanks to Bluff Hal — he'll find ghosts enough there. Or walk along the moon-swept galleries of Hampton Court and hear the ghost of Catherine Howard scream as she did in life when Henry's guards came to arrest her.]

Anyway, in that ruined church, Benjamin and I set the scene for the final act. We crept down to the crypt. I fastened the hour candle on top of one of the tombs, struck a tinder, and the thick, white wick flared into life. Benjamin then emptied charcoal at the foot of a tomb and, taking a flame, blew the coals into life. We looked around, pronounced ourselves satisfied and left the crypt, making sure the door remained ajar. From the top of the steps, we could see the light from the candle and the charcoal glow invitingly through the darkness.

We hid ourselves deep in the shadows, growing accustomed to the eerie, mournful sounds of the night. The clouds broke and a full moon bathed the ruins of the church in a ghostly light. At one time I tensed, whispering that I had heard a noise. I crouched, ears straining, but heard nothing else. More time passed and, just as I was about to fall into a deep warm sleep, I heard a sound under the ruined archway. I nudged Benjamin awake and turned to watch a dark, cowled figure scurry like a spider up the nave and scuffle down the steps. Benjamin made to rise but I held him back.

'What time do you think it is?' I asked.

'About eight or nine o'clock!' he hissed. 'Why, what does it matter? Roger, what have you done?'

'Stay awhile,' I murmured.

We heard a movement from the person in the crypt as if he was about to remount the steps. Another shape, cat-like, crept up the nave. Benjamin craned forward.

'As I thought!' he hissed. 'But who's down there already?'

I just looked away and smiled. The second figure slipped down the stairs. We heard the crypt door open and an angry shout followed by a terrible abrupt scream.

'Come on!' Benjamin ordered and, taking the loaded crossbows, we ran to the stairs.

Inside the crypt lay a figure, tossed like a bundle of

rags in the corner. A pool of blood was forming around the body from the great wound caused by the dagger embedded deep in the chest. The dead face was turned away from us. As we entered the other man whirled round, the hood slipping off his head.

'Melford!' Benjamin exclaimed.

The mercenary's face was alive with excitement, like all killers' just after they have tasted blood.

'Master Benjamin and young Shallot!' he murmured. 'How good of you to come.' His hand crept towards the crossbow on top of the tomb next to the candle. He nodded to the corpse. 'Was he one of you?' he asked.

'Who?'

Melford went over and, grasping the corpse by the hair, half-dragged the body up to reveal the haggard, horror-stricken face of Scawsby.

'Secretly,' Melford said, letting the body fall with a crash, 'he must have been one of you. He came from the same town, didn't he?'

Benjamin glanced sideways at me but I watched Melford as he sauntered back to the tomb, getting as close as possible to the arbalest resting there. He smiled wolfishly.

'Or perhaps he wasn't. Perhaps I came down here and found you red-handed, guilty of his murder. Now, what would the Lord Cardinal say to that?'

'Melford!' I shouted.

The mercenary turned. Even as he grasped the crossbow, I brought up my own, releasing the catch. The bolt took the mercenary full in the chest just under the neck. He tottered towards me, his hands going up as if to beseech some favour.

'Why?' he muttered even as the blood swilled into his mouth and bubbled at his lips.

'You're a killer,' I replied. 'And you talk too much!'

Melford's eyes opened, he coughed and the blood gushed out of both mouth and nose. He pitched forward on to the crypt floor.

Benjamin went across and examined both corpses.

'Dead!' he announced quietly. He looked up. 'And you are responsible, Roger.'

I placed another bolt in the crossbow.

'Melford was an assassin's tool. He was as guilty, perhaps even more so, than any man hanged at Tyburn.'

'Did you want Scawsby's death so badly?'

'Yes,' I answered. 'But not as badly as God did or my mother's ghost. Scawsby was a murderer. He killed my parents and nearly had me hanged. As long as he was alive I would never be safe. Nor,' I added, 'would you or yours.'

'How did you get him here?'

'Scawsby was a greedy miser,' I replied. 'I sent an anonymous letter telling him that if he came here, he would find a great treasure and the means to rid the Queen of me. Three gold coins accompanied the letter as surety of the writer's good faith. I knew Scawsby could not resist such a promise.'

'And if Melford had arrived here first?'

'Scawsby would still have died. I am sure Melford's orders were to kill whoever he found here.'

Benjamin stared at me. 'Perhaps you are right, Roger.' He blew out the candle. 'Leave the corpse alone, this masque is not yet over.'

We walked back up the crypt steps. Even then I knew something was wrong. I sensed the menace in the air, the deep cloud of unease, the watching malevolent shadows. We had only walked a few paces when I heard a tinder strike behind me and a low voice chanted: ' "Three less than twelve should it be, Or the King, no prince engendered he!" '

Benjamin and I turned: in the sanctuary two candles had been lit and we glimpsed shadowy figures.

'Place the crossbows on the ground, Master Daunbey. And you, Shallot, your sword and dirk, then come forward!'

I took a step back and a crossbow bolt skimmed the air between Benjamin's head and mine.

'I shall not ask again!' the voice warned. It sounded hollow and unnatural in the echoing ruins of the church.

'Do as he says, Roger!' Benjamin murmured.

We threw the arbalests down and unbuckled our sword belts.

'Now, come forward,' the voice rasped, 'slowly to the foot of the steps!'

Cresset torches flared into life, shedding a pool of light around the old altar plinth where Catesby sat enthroned. On either side of him stood the two Highlanders; like Catesby they were armed to the teeth with sword, dagger and crossbow.

'Well, well, well!' Catesby smiled. In the flickering torchlight he looked older, more cunning. The boyish face had a twisted, crafty slant. [Have you noticed that? How, when the veil drops, the true character is exposed in the face and eyes? I wonder what my chaplain would really look like then?] Catesby's languid posture betrayed a truly evil man, openly rejoicing in plot and counter-plot.

'Benjamin,' he half-whispered, 'you seem surprised?'

'I thought it would be Agrippa.'

I glanced sideways at Benjamin and wondered how Catesby knew where to come.

'Ah!' Sir Robert smiled again. 'And Captain Melford?'

'He's dead.'

'And whom did he kill?'

'Scawsby.'

'Was he . . .?' Catesby broke off and grinned at me. 'That was clever, Shallot, very clever indeed!' The villain shrugged. 'I did not like him, but he had sworn to kill you.' He sighed. 'Now I'll have to do it for him.'

'The Lord Cardinal will miss us,' Benjamin spoke up.

'Now, now, Master Daunbey, don't tell lies. I had you watched. You've sent no letter to your uncle, nor have you visited him.' Catesby sat up straight. 'If you had, the Lord Cardinal's men would be here. Moreover, what could you tell him? You suspected Agrippa, didn't you?'

Benjamin just stared back.

211

'Anyway,' Catesby continued briskly, 'my friends here will kill you, we'll tell the fat cardinal some lie, and within days I'll be over the Scottish border.' He pointed to the ground before him. 'Sit down, Benjamin. Roger, join him!'

Once we did so, Catesby leaned forward like some malevolent school master relishing the prospect of a beating he'd planned for two hateful pupils.

'Let's see how much you know,' he began. 'You claimed Moodie was murdered?'

Benjamin smiled back. 'Yes. You told Moodie, an innocent pawn, to give Roger that red silk sash, a sign to your agents in Paris that he was to die there. When we returned to England you organised the attack outside London and, when that failed, Moodie had to die. Of course, you were in a hurry. I suspect poor Moodie was drugged. You took his wrist, you and your hired killer Melford, and slashed the veins. You would enjoy that, wouldn't you, Catesby? You love the stink of death! But, as I have said, you were in a hurry. You are left-handed; Moodie was right-handed. If he had slashed his wrist he would have held the razor or knife in the right and slashed the left. But you, being left-handed, slashed his right wrist.'

Catesby sat back. 'But his chamber was locked from the inside!'

Benjamin laughed. 'Sir Robert, you are an evil but intelligent man. Do not dismiss me as a complete fool. The only proof we have that the chamber was locked is that you told us so.'

Catesby flicked his hand like a gambler dismissing a bad throw of the dice. 'And Selkirk and Ruthven?'

'Ah!'

Beside me Benjamin pulled his cloak close about him as if he was really enjoying the story he was about to tell. 'Now, their deaths were very cunning. Both were poisoned but no trace of any potion was found in any cup or food. Nor was any poison discovered in Selkirk's cell or

Ruthven's chamber at Royston. Now I thought about that and, when I was in Nottingham Castle, I went down to the scriptorium. I watched the clerks as they used their quills over their accounts and memoranda. Do you know, there must have been a dozen clerks in that hall and each of them, at some time or other, put the end of their quill in their mouth?'

Benjamin paused and I saw Catesby's face harden like some evil boy who senses his terrible prank had gone awry.

'After I had seen Selkirk that evening,' Benjamin continued, 'the poor madman picked up a quill to continue his insane scribblings. The quill was new and coated with a deadly poison. What was it? Belladonna, the juice of nightshade or red arsenic? A few licks of any of these would stop a man's heart; Selkirk would drop the quill, perhaps rise and stagger to his bed before collapsing and dying. The next morning a distressed Constable took you to the chamber. In the confusion you picked up the deadly quill and replaced it with another.'

Benjamin paused, breathing deeply. I was watching the two Highlanders who stood there like statues. Only their eyes, which never left us, betrayed their malevolence and lust to kill.

'At Royston you followed the same plan. You were in charge of the Queen's household, you allocated the chambers, and whilst pieces of baggage were being brought upstairs, it would be so easy to slip into Ruthven's chamber and leave a poisoned quill. Now, that's where you made a mistake. You see, Ruthven always had his cat with him. Whatever he ate or drank he always shared with his pet. Yet the animal escaped unscathed. I reached the logical conclusion that the cause of Ruthven's death was something he put into his mouth which the animal would never share, and that must have been the quill.' He paused but Catesby stared coolly back. 'The chamber door was forced, people rushed in, and of course everyone gathered round the corpse. Once again you, or your creature Melford, must have changed the quill. In that crowded, untidy chamber, even if you had the keen eyesight of a hawk, the swift exchange of something so small would be very difficult to detect.' Benjamin stopped speaking.

'Very good,' Catesby muttered. 'And you, Shallot, you verminous little cretin, you were party to this?'

'I helped my master in his observations,' I replied. 'We examined Master Ruthven's corpse and found a substance caught between his teeth. A morsel of goose-quill. Benjamin experimented by chewing a piece himself, and found it was similar to the substance from Ruthven's mouth. This confirmed our hypothesis that Ruthven's quill had been poisoned.'

Catesby clapped his hands in mocking applause.

'Finally, there's Master Irvine,' I continued. 'Once again, Sir Robert, you were very clever. You ensured that you were at Nottingham though you left orders at Royston which sent the other members of the Queen's household hither and thither. Now, when we were in Nottingham, we learnt that you and your manservant had arrived on November the ninth, so it would appear impossible for you to be involved in Irvine's death.'

My master touched me on the arm and took up the story.

'However, Sir Robert, on my return from Kelso I came back along the Great North Road and revisited Nottingham. Once again the Constable of the Castle confirmed the date of your arrival but, when I asked him to describe Captain Melford, the appearance of the man he depicted hardly fitted that of your now dead servant. So, I concluded Melford went to Coldstream, waited for Irvine and, with the cooperation or connivance of that bitch of a prioress, cut the poor fellow's throat before riding to join you at Nottingham Castle. No one would pay particular attention to how many servants you had or which one accompanied you when you first arrived there.'

'A chilling story,' Catesby sarcastically replied.

'You are not so clever, Catesby!' I accused. 'You should really watch your tongue. On our return from France you actually pondered the possibility that Moodie might have killed Irvine. You claimed the priest might have gone to Coldstream, but how would you know that?'

Catesby stared back, genuinely perplexed. I leaned forward.

'No one told you,' I explained in a mock whisper, 'that Irvine had been killed *at* Coldstream. We suspected it but the only person who would know for sure would be the murderer himself!'

'So many deaths,' Benjamin murmured. 'Such terrible murders. There were others, weren't there, Sir Robert? Like the man we met in Nottingham, Oswald the moss-trooper? Whom did you send after us there? Was it Melford or one of these hired killers?' Benjamin nodded at the two Highlanders. Catesby gnawed at his lip, his face a white mask of fury.

[Now in my travels, I have talked to several learned physicians – a rarity indeed! Nevertheless, these were wise men who had studied Avicenna, Hippocrates and Galen. I discussed with them the mind of the true murderer and all the physicians agreed some people have a fatal sickness, an evil humour in the mind which makes them kill. Indeed, such men rejoice in the murder of others and relish the death throes of their victim. They plot their crimes with great cunning, showing no remorse afterward, only a terrible anger at being discovered. In public life they act normal, appearing sane, well-educated people, but in reality they are devils incarnate. Catesby was one of these.]

He seemed to have forgotten why he was there but saw our conversation only as a game of wits which he was about to lose.

'You forget one thing,' he snapped, 'the White Rose, the conspiracy of *Les Blancs Sangliers*!'

'Nonsense!' Benjamin retorted. 'When Ruthven and

Selkirk died it would have been easy for you or Melford to drop a white rose in their chamber. Who would notice it amidst all the confusion? You may even have placed them there before your victim died.' Benjamin stared at his would-be killer. 'Oh, I concede,' he continued, 'there are secret Yorkist covens, deluded men and women who pine for past glories, but you used their cause to mask your own evil intentions. Don't you remember our journey to Leicester?'

Catesby glared at him.

'Well, Sir Robert,' Benjamin mocked, 'you really should have read your history.' He turned to me. 'Shouldn't he, Roger?'

I studied my master's face and felt the first stirrings of despair. Despite his bantering tone, I saw the fear in Benjamin's eyes and the beads of sweat rolling down the now marble-white face. I understood his glance. He was begging for more time, though God knew for what reason.

'Yes, yes, Sir Robert,' I spoke up. 'If you had read Fabyan's *Chronicles* you would know that after the Battle of Bosworth, Richard III's body was tossed into the horse trough outside the Blue Boar in Leicester and left there for public viewing and taunts. Later it was buried in the Lady Chapel at Greyfriars Church. Now a true Yorkist, any member of *Les Blancs Sangliers*, would have treated both places as shrines yet all members of the Queen's household allowed their horses to drink from that trough. Moreover, during our short stay in Leicester not one member of Queen Margaret's retinue visited Richard's tomb in Greyfriars Church. So,' I concluded, 'we began to suspect that the White Rose murders were only pawns to cover a more subtle, evil design.'

Catesby's mood changed: he stamped his spurred boot on the floor until it jingled and clapped his hands as if we had staged some enjoyable masque or a recitation of a favourite poem. He wiped his eyes on the back of his hand.

'Dear Benjamin, dear Roger,' he leaned forward, 'I thought you such fools – my only mistake. I will not make it again.'

'But we have not finished,' Benjamin spoke up. 'We have told you how these men died but not why.'

Catesby's face stiffened. 'What do you mean?'

' "Three less than twelve should it be," ' I chanted. 'Don't you want to know, Sir Robert? Surely the Queen, your mistress, will demand a report.'

'Her Grace has nothing to do with this!' Catesby retorted.

Benjamin smiled and shook his head. 'In these murders, Master Catesby, there were the victims, and these we have now described. There was the murderer, and we are now looking at the man responsible.'

'And what else?' Catesby snapped.

'There were those who cooperated with the murderer or provided the very reason the murders took place.'

Catesby sprang up and, bringing back his hand, slapped Benjamin across the face. My master gazed back at him.

'If I have told a lie,' Benjamin retorted, 'then prove it is a lie. But if I have spoken the truth, why did you hit me?'

'You insult the Queen!' Catesby mumbled. As he went back to his seat, the two Highlanders relaxed, their hands going away from the long stabbing knives stuck in their belts. I watched Catesby's face and knew the truth: Queen Margaret was as guilty as he. Benjamin, the left side of his face smarting red from Catesby's blow, leaned forward. I gazed around that darkened church. I felt stiff and the freezing night air was beginning to penetrate my clothes with a chill damp which made me shiver. I wondered how long this travesty could continue.

'Surely, Sir Robert,' I spoke up, 'you want to know the truth?'

Catesby's humour changed again and he smiled.

'Of course!' He picked up a wineskin from the ground beside him and offered it to Benjamin who shook his head. 'Oh, it's not poisoned!' the murderer quipped and, unstopping the neck, lifted it until the red wine poured into his mouth, spilling thin red rivers down his chin. He resealed it and tossed it to me. I needed no second bidding. A little wine can comfort the stomach; I half-emptied it in one gulp as my master began to decipher the riddle of Selkirk's poem.

Chapter 12

'The roots of this tragedy,' Benjamin began, 'go back ten years when Queen Margaret, a lusty young princess, was first married to James IV of Scotland – a prince who loved the joys of the bed chamber and had a string of mistresses to prove it; indeed, he had bastard children by at least two of his paramours.'

Catesby nodded, a faraway look in his eyes.

'Now, Margaret,' Benjamin continued, 'was joined in Scotland by yourself, the young squire Robert Catesby. You were devoted to your Queen and watched with her as James moved from one amorous exploit to another. A deep hatred was kindled in Margaret's heart, made all the more rancorous by James's open support for the Yorkist Pretenders. Margaret retaliated, or so my uncle the Lord Cardinal told me privily, by sending information to James's main rival and opponent, King Henry of England.'

'You speak the truth, Master Daunbey!'

'He does, Sir Robert!' I said, taking up the story. 'Matters came to a head when King James planned his invasion of England which culminated in the tragedy at Flodden Field. Queen Margaret and, I suspect, yourself played upon King James's fertile imagination. You plotted a number of stratagems to create unease in him and his principal commanders: the famous vision of St John where James was rebuked for his love of harlotry; the death-bearing voice, prophesying at Edinburgh Market Cross on the stroke of midnight that James and all his commanders would go down to Hades. These were planned by you, weren't they?'

Catesby smiled and stroked the side of his cheek with his hand.

'You succeeded brilliantly,' Benjamin spoke up. 'James became uneasy, indeed he may have begun to suspect that malcontents in his kingdom might use the Flodden campaign to stage his murder. Accordingly, during the campaign as well as the actual battle, James dressed a number of soldiers in royal livery so as to deflect any assassination attempt. Now, the battle was a disaster. A number of the royal look-alikes were killed – I suspect a few by assassins as well as by the English. Surrey found one of these corpses, proclaimed it was James's body and sent it south to his master, King Henry.'

Catesby glowered at Benjamin.

'That is why,' I added, 'the corpse did not have the penitential chain James wore round his waist. Or why Margaret never asked for the corpse to be returned for burial. Was she frightened,' I jibed, 'that someone in Scotland might discover it was not the King's body?'

Catesby beat his hand upon his thigh. 'And I suppose,' he guffawed, 'you will tell me that King James himself escaped?'

'You know he did!' Benjamin snapped. 'He was dressed in ordinary armour. He and a knight of the royal household, Sir John Harrington, together with Selkirk, fled to Kelso Abbey. There, King James dictated a short letter which he sealed with his signet ring and despatched via Selkirk to his wife, begging for aid and sustenance. The physician took this message to the Queen sheltering at Linlithgow but, instead of sending help, she sent assassins to kill her husband and Harrington.'

Catesby's face now assumed a haunted, gaunt look.

'The perfect murder,' Benjamin whispered. 'How can you be accused of killing a prince whom the world already reckons is dead? God knows what happened to the body but, when Selkirk returned to Kelso, his master was gone and the monks were too frightened to speak. Selkirk escaped from your clutches to France where his mind, tortured by the horror of these events, slipped into madness. Of course, you searched him out but it was too late — the Lord Cardinal's men had already found him. Naturally, you were relieved to discover that Selkirk, due to the passage of time and his own insanity, jabbered his secrets only in obscure verse.'

'James was an adulterer,' Catesby muttered as if to himself. 'He was like Ahab of Israel, not fit to rule, and so God struck him down!'

Benjamin shook his head. 'If James was Ahab,' he replied, 'then Margaret was Jezebel. She murdered James, not because she hated him but because she, too, had been a faithless spouse. She had to hide her own infidelities with Gavin Douglas, Earl of Angus.'

'That's a lie!' Catesby rasped.

'Oh, no, it isn't!' I answered. 'Margaret's second son, Alexander, Duke of Ross, was born on the thirtieth of April 1514. He was born, so I have discovered, two months early, in which case it should have been June 1514. If we go back nine months, or the thirty-eight weeks of a natural pregnancy, that would place the time of conception at the end of September, no less than a fortnight after James was killed.'

I licked my lips, watching the two clansmen who were becoming restless, as if bored by this chatter of strange tongues.

'Oh,' I murmured, 'we can play with the dates. James left Edinburgh with his army in August. The records of the household will prove the last time he and Margaret were together as man and wife was in the previous July. I am correct?'

Catesby just glared.

'Indeed,' I continued, 'we know Margaret was playing the two-backed beast with Gavin Douglas some time before Flodden.'

'You insult the Queen!' Catesby raged. He glared at us and I realised that Catesby loved Margaret and couldn't accept his golden Princess being proved a lecherous adultress.

'We have proof,' I sang out, my voice ringing clear as a bell through that ghostly church. 'Selkirk claimed that after Flodden he, together with James and Harrington, discussed what they should do. In his confession Selkirk mentioned the King being uneasy about the malicious gossip which had reached his ears concerning Margaret. No wonder James lost his army at Flodden: visions, voices of doom, rumours about his wife, possible threats against his life!'

'I wonder,' Benjamin interrupted, 'if the King ever put the two things together: the rumours about an assassin on the loose and the gossip about his wife?'

'Mere fancies!' Catesby snapped.

'No, they're not,' I replied. 'Selkirk rode through the night to Linlithgow yet, as soon as he met the Queen, he became uneasy. Your mistress was hardly the grieving widow. Selkirk became suspicious and hurried back to Kelso but the King and Harrington were gone.'

'And I suppose this Harrington,' Catesby queried, 'just allowed his King to be murdered?'

I glanced at Benjamin and noticed his eyes flicker, always an indication that my master, an honest man, was about to tell some half-truth.

'Harrington,' he replied, 'was only one man, exhausted after the battle. He would be little protection for James. Harrington, too, was probably murdered. Do you know,' he continued, 'when I was in Scotland I saw a Book of the Dead in the royal chapel of St Margaret's in Edinburgh, a list of those who had fallen at Flodden. I can't recollect seeing the name Harrington.' My master looked quickly at me and I knew he was lying. He didn't find out about Harrington until after we had met in Paris.

'So,' I taunted quickly, 'Margaret and Douglas were lovers before Flodden.'

'That's why they married so hastily,' Benjamin added. 'To provide Ross with some legitimacy. Who knows, even the present Scottish heir may be a Douglas! Is this, together with King James's murder, the bond which still binds Margaret to the Earl?'

Catesby leaned forward, his face white and skull-like as if quietly relishing the death he planned for us.

'So,' Benjamin continued, trying to distract his attention, 'Selkirk's verses are now explained: the lamb is Angus, who rested in the falcon's nest, namely James's bed. The Scottish King is also the Lion who cried even though he died, and the phrase "Three less than twelve should it be", together with Selkirk's mutterings about how he could "count the days", is a reference to the secret and adulterous conception of Alexander, Duke of Ross. Selkirk, a physician, suspected that Alexander was not King James's son.'

'What proof do you have of this?' Catesby jibed, standing up.

'Oh,' I replied, 'as it says in the last verses of Selkirk's poem: he wrote his confession in a secret cipher and left it with the monks at St Denis outside Paris.'

'Mere jabberings!' Catesby accused. 'Of a feckless fool!'

Benjamin shook his head. 'Ah, no, Selkirk left proof. He'd kept all the warrants issued to him by King James during his reign. At first, I thought they meant nothing, after all there were scores of them, but then I found one dated the twelfth of September 1513, dated and sealed three days *after* James was supposed to have died at Flodden!'

Catesby just stared, dumbstruck.

'Of course,' Benjamin continued quietly, 'after James's death Margaret soon tired of Angus. She quarrelled with him, tried to seize control of the children and, when baulked of that, fled south to her brother in England.'

Catesby pursed his lips. 'Lies!' he muttered as if talking to himself. 'All lies!'

'No, they're not,' I answered tartly. 'Margaret was frightened lest her secret be discovered. Who knows, perhaps she suspected King James might still be alive, lurking in some dark wood or lonely moor. She had to be sure that Angus, who had been party to her husband's death, would also keep silent, which is why we were sent to Nottingham. We found Angus sulky,' I glanced at the two Highlanders who glared back malevolently, and Lord d'Aubigny suspicious, but no hint of scandal. Queen Margaret,' I concluded bitterly, 'now knows she is safe and has planned her return to Scotland.'

Catesby cradled his hands in his lap. 'Do you know,' he observed as if we were a group of friends gathered in a cosy tavern, 'I considered you buffoons, two idiots who would blunder about in the dark and go before us to seek out any dangers. I was so wrong.'

'Yes, you were,' Benjamin answered. 'You grew alarmed when Selkirk began to talk to me, so he had to die, though you probably planned his death before Roger and I joined this murderous dance. Nevertheless, Selkirk did talk and Ruthven began to reflect on his own suspicions so he, too, had to die.'

One of the clansmen suddenly stepped forward, like a hunting dog sensing danger. Catesby snapped his fingers. The fellow drew his dagger while his master stood peering into the darkness.

Catesby listened for a moment. 'Nothing,' he murmured. 'Only the dark.' He looked down and smiled. 'And the soft brush of Death's dark dream.'

'You are going to kill us?' I spoke up, desperately looking around for some route of escape.

'Of course,' he whispered. 'I cannot let you live. Now everything will end well. The Queen will return to Scotland, and I shall look after her whilst young James grows to manhood.'

'You forget Selkirk's manuscripts.'

'They can disappear!' Catesby snarled.

'And us?'

Catesby nodded to the wild heathland outside the church. 'Such thick copses and deep marshes; other bodies lie buried there, why not yours?' He looked down at

Benjamin. 'Goodbye,' he whispered, and turned to the clansmen. 'Yes, yes, you had better kill them now!'

I stood up but Corin knocked me to the floor. I glimpsed Alleyn grasp my master by the shoulder as he drew his hand back for the killing blow. Suddenly a voice called out: 'Catesby, stop!'

The murderer ran down the steps, gazing into the darkness.

'Catesby, on the orders of the King, desist!'

I looked up, the Highlander grinned, and the long, pointed dagger began its descent. I heard the rasp of something through the air. I opened my eyes. The clansman was still standing but his face was now crushed into a bloody pulp by the crossbow bolt buried there. I flung myself to one side. The other clansman was still standing above Benjamin but his back was arched, his hands out as he stared down in disbelief at the crossbow quarrel embedded deeply in his chest. He opened his mouth, whimpered like a child and crashed to the sanctuary floor.

Both Benjamin and I turned; Catesby was about to draw his own sword but Doctor Agrippa and soldiers wearing the Cardinal's livery were already sweeping up the darkened nave. The doctor threw us a glance, snapped his fingers and, before Catesby could proceed any further, both sword and dagger were plucked from his belt.

The Cardinal's men examined the two corpses of the clansmen and kicked them as you would dead dogs. Another soldier ran down the steps and came back shouting that two more bodies were down in the crypt. Agrippa drew back the hood of his cloak and smiled benevolently at us.

'We should have come sooner,' he observed quietly. 'Perhaps intervened earlier, but what you were saying was so interesting.'

He picked up Catesby's sword, gave it to Benjamin and gestured at the prisoner, who stood sullen-faced between two guardsmen.

'Kill him!' Agrippa ordered. 'Let's make things neat

and orderly.' He thrust the sword into Benjamin's hand. 'Kill him,' he repeated. 'He deserves to die.'

My master let the sword fall to the ground with a clang.

'No,' he murmured. 'He deserves a trial then to be hanged like the murderer he is.'

Agrippa pursed his lips. 'No,' he whispered. 'Nothing like that.' He picked up the fallen sword and thrust it at me. 'You, Shallot, kill him.'

'Let the sword fall,' Benjamin warned. 'Roger, you may be many things but not this.'

I let the sword clatter on to the flagstoned floor.

'He is not to die,' Benjamin repeated.

Doctor Agrippa shrugged and turned to the captain of the guard. 'Take Catesby to the Tower,' he ordered. 'Into its deepest and darkest dungeon. Queen Margaret is not to be told.'

The fellow nodded, seized Catesby by the arm. The arch murderer smiled at us as he allowed himself to be led away.

Agrippa issued more orders and the soldiers hurried down into the crypt, dragging up Melford's and Scawsby's corpses which they laid next to the bodies of the two Highlanders. Agrippa examined each, making strange signs above them in the air.

'Catesby was right in one thing,' he murmured, 'the heathland outside makes a good cemetery. Let them be buried there.'

After that Agrippa hardly spoke to us but took us back to the Tower where we were lodged in comfortable imprisonment. Benjamin was silent; for at least two hours he could hardly stop shivering. I had my own remedies. I demanded a jug of wine and hours later slumped down on the pallet-bed blind drunk.

The next morning a still taciturn Agrippa took us along Billingsgate, Thames Street, through Bowyers Row on to Fleet Street and down to Westminster. We were followed by a heavily armed, mounted escort who screened us as we were pushed through a maze of corridors at the palace and into a small comfortable chamber next to St Stephen's Chapel where the Lord Cardinal was waiting for us.

I remember it was a fine day. The sun had broken through a thick layer of clouds and a touch of spring freshened the air.

Wolsey greeted us warmly. No insults now but rather 'Dearest Nephew' and 'My redoubtable Shallot'. The Cardinal cleared the chamber of clerks and minions, only Agrippa remaining, then made Benjamin relate the previous evening's encounter with Catesby. Now and again Wolsey would nod or ask a question of Benjamin or me. Once my master was finished, the Lord Cardinal, a half-smile on his face, shook his head in wonderment.

'So much evil!' he whispered. 'So many murders. Such a great secret.'

'But you suspected as much, dear Uncle, did you not?'

Wolsey stretched his great bulk and yawned. 'Yes, yes, dearest Nephew, I did. Didn't we, good doctor?'

Agrippa murmured his assent.

'You used us!' Benjamin accused. 'Catesby was right about that. We were hired,' he continued, 'to blunder about like fools and open doors for others to enter!'

Agrippa looked embarrassed. The Cardinal gazed fondly at his nephew.

'Yes, I used you, dearest Nephew,' he replied. 'But only because you were the best person for the task.' He smiled thinly. 'And, of course, the ever trusty Shallot.' He placed his elbows on the arms of the chair and steepled his fingers. 'You saw what good actors they were, Benjamin? Catesby with his open, trusting face and air of anxious concern, whilst Queen Margaret can simulate rage better than her brother.'

'My Lord Cardinal,' Agrippa intervened, 'must not be judged too harshly. Catesby had a hand in your appointment for My Lord Cardinal described your exploits at a banquet held at Greenwich. Catesby made his own enquiries and the rest followed as naturally as night follows day.'

227

'Was Scawsby part of the plan?' I asked.

'Yes,' Agrippa murmured. 'Catesby undoubtedly heard of young Shallot's strokes against the Scawsby family and realised their enmity would only add spice to the game. Moreover, if murder was planned, Catesby did not want some physician with a keen eye and sharp brain. Scawsby was a quack, a pedlar, a man who would do as he was told.'

'Was he party to Catesby's plot?' I repeated.

'No!' The Lord Cardinal gazed down at me like a hawk. 'Scawsby certainly knew there was a mystery but he saw the appointment as royal preferment. Of course, he hated you and rejoiced in your discomfiture. His death, Master Shallot,' he added meaningfully, 'was, according to the law, an unlawful slaying.'

'Roger did not kill Scawsby!' Benjamin interrupted. 'The physician allowed his greed to get the better of him. Moreover,' he concluded slyly, 'Scawsby is best out of the way. He never could keep a still tongue in his head.'

The Cardinal nodded. 'True, true,' he murmured. 'Scawsby is dead and Roger shall have a pardon issued under the Great Seal for his part in the slaying.'

'You suspected me, did you not?' Agrippa abruptly accused.

'At one time I did. Catesby was so convincing, he could have caught spiders in the web he wove.'

'But why?' I interrupted. 'Why all this charade?'

Agrippa looked at Wolsey and the Cardinal nodded.

'No!' I exclaimed before the doctor could speak. 'There are other matters. How did Catesby know about the Church of St Theodore? And your arrival, Agrippa, was so opportune.'

'That was my fault,' Benjamin muttered. 'I really did think Agrippa could be the murderer or, at least, his associate. You said it was a gamble, Roger, and so it was – before we left the Tower I informed the good doctor here of where we were going. There could have only been one logical outcome: if he was the murderer, he would have arrived first, and Catesby would be innocent.'

'Of course,' Agrippa interrupted, 'if I was innocent but suspected the game being plotted, I would ensure Catesby knew of your trap at St Theodore's and ensure I arrived when everyone had laid their cards on the table.' He shrugged. 'Scawsby was acting suspiciously, he kept to himself and left the Tower early. I, of course, hurried to Queen Margaret and spun some tale about how young Benjamin had solved the riddles and had their solution at St Theodore's. The rest,' he spread his hands, 'happened as you know it did.'

'You could have been late!' I accused.

Agrippa shook his head. 'All life is a gamble, Roger. The Cardinal's men were ready. We arrived to arrest Catesby and rescue you from his clutches.'

'And if you had been too late?'

'We would have arrested Catesby and made sure your bodies were given honourable burial.'

I glared back furiously. Benjamin just shook his head.

'You see,' Agrippa rose and paced restlessly round the room, 'we live in stirring times. Across the Channel, France is united under a powerful King whose hungry eyes are on Italy. To the south lies Spain, building massive fleets and searching out new lands. Further east is the Holy Roman Empire with its tentacles in every merchant's pie. And England?' Agrippa paused for a moment. 'England is balanced on a tightrope above these clashing powers and dare not make a mistake. These islands should be united − England, Ireland, Scotland and Wales − under the one King, and who better than our noble Henry?' Agrippa paused, looked at me sardonically, and I remembered his words on the lonely wastelands outside Royston. 'Our King needs such a challenge,' he continued. 'He has the energy to achieve it. He must have a vision or he will turn in on himself and God knows what will happen then.'

'So he must control Scotland,' my master intervened quickly.

'Yes,' Wolsey answered. 'Scotland must be controlled. King Henry thought he could do this through the marriage of his sister to James IV but that came to naught. Indeed, the marriage was a disaster and worse followed: James began negotiations with France, which threatened to crush England between the teeth of two pincers, Scotland in the north, France in the south. Henry begged his sister to intervene and Margaret did what she could.' He paused and stared at the jewels sparkling on his purple-gloved fingers. 'Old Surrey saved the day,' he murmured, 'that and Margaret's intense hatred for her own husband.' He glanced up at Benjamin. 'Oh, you were right, dear Nephew,' he continued in a half-whisper, 'the Queen played upon James's mind and undoubtedly had a hand in his murder. Now,' he smiled thinly, 'Scotland has no King, the country is divided and poses no threat to our security.'

'But how did you suspect James was not killed at Flodden?'

'Hell's teeth, Shallot!' Agrippa remarked, quoting my favourite oath. 'You were there. Surrey did comb the battlefield. He found at least six royal corpses, none with a penitential chain around its waist. Our suspicions began then.'

'And Irvine?' I asked.

The cunning Cardinal made a face. 'We already knew that Irvine had discovered rumours of James being seen at Kelso. He probably learnt them from Oswald the moss trooper.'

'But you brought him south and informed Catesby of his arrival?'

'Irvine was a lure,' Agrippa snapped, 'to panic Margaret and Catesby. They rose to the bait.'

Oh, I stored that away. In Wolsey's and Agrippa's eyes, everyone was expendable.

'What will happen now?' Benjamin asked.

'Oh, the King will have a quiet word with his sister Margaret. She will return to Scotland where she will do exactly what we say or face the consequences. The Careys can go with her.'

'And Catesby?' I asked.

'In the Tower,' Agrippa replied, echoing the words of the soldier I had met there, 'are dungeons which just disappear.' He toyed with the silver pentangle which hung round his neck. 'Even now,' he concluded flatly, 'a trusted mason is bricking up the entrance to his cell. We will hear no more of Catesby.'

'There are others!' the Cardinal rasped. 'The lady prioress at Coldstream will answer for her crimes, and the Earl of Angus will receive a sharp rap across the knuckles.'

'Now that puzzles me, dear Uncle.'

'What, Nephew?'

'Why did the Earl of Angus and Queen Margaret become so intimately involved, marry so hastily after Flodden, and so bitterly repent of their impetuous passion?'

Wolsey smiled. 'My noble master, the good King Henry,' he murmured, 'has the Earl of Angus in his pocket.' He pursed his lips. 'No, you deserve to know the full truth. King Henry bought Angus long before Flodden: he was a handsome, charming coxcomb whom Henry paid to seduce his sister.' The Cardinal made a moue. 'After Flodden and Angus's marriage to Margaret, the King could see no point in wasting more good silver.'

Now I just stared dumbstruck. I am a wicked man but here was a Cardinal coolly telling us that a king had paid a nobleman to seduce his own sister, blinding her with passion so that he could control the kingdom she ruled! I suddenly saw the terrible beauty of King Henry's evil design, one repeated by succeeding English monarchs. Even without Flodden, James would have been brought low. Sooner or later Margaret's adulterous liaison would have been discovered. James would have gone to war. Scotland would have been divided as he and the Douglas clan fought to the bitter end.

Do you know something? I once told young Elizabeth about her father's crafty plot and what did she do? Exactly the same! She arranged for that nincompoop Darnley to marry Mary, Queen of Scots. Mary fell in love with Bothwell, there was murder, civil war, and the rest is history. Oh, Lord, the subtle devices of Princes!

Nonetheless, on reflection, Henry wasn't as cunning as he thought. He spent his reign going from one spouse to the next in order to produce lusty male heirs. And what did he get? Poor, mewling Edward. Once he was born Henry tried to get his puny son married to a Scottish princess in the hopes of uniting England and Scotland under one crown. What really warms the cockles of my heart and makes me giggle is that his sister Margaret's escapades turned the whole thing topsy-turvy. Can't you see? (My chaplain shakes his head.) If the young boy, James, was the product of Queen Margaret's adulterous liaison with Douglas, then James's grandson, the present King of Scotland, is also of bastard issue yet, when old Elizabeth dies, he will inherit the crowns of both England and Scotland. Isn't it funny? England and Scotland being ruled by a bastard who is a descendant of bastards! Bluff King Hal must be spinning like a top in Hell!

'You did well, Master Benjamin,' the Cardinal trumpeted. 'You and your friend, Shallot, shall not be forgotten.'

Beside Wolsey, Agrippa grinned like a small, black cat at the Cardinal's pun on my name.

'There will be other matters,' the Cardinal continued airily, 'but for the time being, dearest Nephew, accept this as a token of our appreciation.' He opened a small coffer beside him and tossed a fat, clinking purse to Benjamin. I caught it deftly and hid it beneath my robe.

'You have certain papers?' Agrippa interrupted silkily. 'Master Selkirk's secrets from Paris?'

'You have them now,' my master snapped. 'When you came to collect us this morning, you picked up the casket.'

Agrippa looked at the Cardinal. 'Oh, there's proof

enough in there,' he answered. 'James's warrants, your nephew's translation of Selkirk's secret confession. Though,' his eyes flickered towards Benjamin, 'only the copy, not the original.'

'I had that at St Theodore's,' Benjamin replied. 'Catesby seized it off me and destroyed it. You have everything else.'

Agrippa nodded benevolently. Wolsey extended one fat hand for us to kiss and we were dismissed with the Cardinal's praises ringing loudly in our ears.

'Keep walking, Roger!' Benjamin hissed as we strode quickly down the corridor. 'Don't stop, though be most prudent. Every so often make sure we are not being followed.'

Benjamin and I left Westminster as if we planned to take the road north to Holborn but then he suddenly changed his mind and we hurried back into the palace yard, pushing aside servants, clerks and scullions as we ran down to King's Steps on the riverside. Benjamin jumped into a boat, dragging me after him. He rapped out orders to the surprised boatman to pull away immediately and, for twice the fee, to row as fast as he could up river.

The oarsman pulled with a will. Soon we were out in mid-stream hidden by a light river mist.

'What's the matter, Master?' I asked.

'In a while, Roger, the last piece of the puzzle will slip into its rightful place.'

Once we were past the Fleet where the refuse of the city floated in a thick oozy mess on the surface of the river, Benjamin ordered the oarsman to pull in and we disembarked at Paul's Wharf. He tossed some coins at the boatman and we hurried up Thames Street. Now old Shallot thought the game was over. I wanted to stop and stare, drink in the sights, sounds and smells of the city, particularly the fat merchants and their silk-garbed wives and pretty buxom daughters hiding their lovely and lusting faces under caps of gold. Benjamin, however, hurried me on, past beautifully carved, half-timbered houses, their plaster brightly painted and gilded, some a washed cream, others snow white, a few even pink. We ran down stinking alleyways and through the gardens of the rich with their elegant fountains, trimmed hedges and sweet-smelling herb gardens. We continued up Bread Street, then turned right into Watling, cutting across a garden, ignoring the astonished cries of servants and children. We entered Budge Row near the Chancellor's inn. Only then did Benjamin stop at the mouth of an alleyway to see if anyone was pursuing us.

'No,' he murmured. 'We are safe!'

He smiled, wiped the sweat from his brow and, linking his arm through mine, walked me into the musty but warm embrace of the Kirtle tavern.

'You have Uncle's gold, Roger?'

I nodded.

'Then, Master Innkeeper,' Benjamin called across, 'we wish to hire a chamber for the day and the best meal your kitchens can offer.'

Oh, believe me, we ate well. Even now, staring at the green, neatly clipped privet hedge of my maze, I can picture that chamber, warmed by chafing dishes and small glowing braziers. We dined on fish soup, a haunch of beef cooked in a sauce of wine and spices, and thin white wafers soaked in garlic. Benjamin matched me cup for cup of robust claret, sweet malmsey and the chilled wine of Alsace. I supposed we were celebrating the end of the business, the solution to the mystery, our escape from Catesby, as well as relishing the fulsome praises of the Cardinal.

'So, you think the game is over, Roger?'

I leaned back and considered what had happened in the Cardinal's chambers. 'Yes, though of course you told one lie — Catesby never destroyed that manuscript. And why should anyone follow us now?'

Benjamin pulled off one of his boots and from the lining drew out three neatly folded pieces of parchment.

One was yellow with age but the other two were still fresh and cream-coloured. He tossed the battered parchment to me.

'You recognise that?'

I unfolded and studied it.

'Of course. It's Selkirk's secret confession. The one we found in Paris. Why didn't you give it to Agrippa?'

Benjamin picked up the other two pieces and unfolded them.

'Ah, yes,' he murmured, handing one over. 'Now read this.'

I studied the neat, careful hand-writing.

'Master, you're playing games. This is your translation of Selkirk's confession.'

Benjamin lifted up his hand. 'Then read it, Roger, one more time. Read it aloud!'

' "I, Andrew Selkirk, royal physician," ' I intoned, ' "courtier as well as friend of James IV of Scotland, do now make my confession to God and the world in this secret code about the events which followed our disastrous defeat at Flodden in September 1513. Be it known to all that as dusk fell and the Scottish Army broke, King James and I fled from the field of slaughter. The King had fought all day dressed as a mere knight. He confided in me that he feared assassination by some unknown hand. Certain of his household knights as well as squires of the body had been dressed in the royal armour and tabard, not out of fear or cowardice in the face of the enemy, but as protection against stealthy murder.

' "Know you that on that same night we reached Kelso Abbey, we were joined by Sir John Harrington, knight banneret and one of those the King had chosen to wear his colours during the battle. Now the King, Harrington and I took secret lodgings in the abbot's house and planned counsel on what we should do next. His Grace and Harrington decided that they should stay whilst I would take a letter from the King to his wife, Queen Margaret, at Linlithgow, asking for her help. His Grace, however, seemed most reluctant. Indeed, he confessed that before the battle his mind had been turned by the phantasms he had seen as well as secret and malicious gossip regarding his Queen." '

I stopped and looked at Benjamin. 'Master, we have read this before.'

'Roger, please keep reading. You may jump a few lines.'

I hurriedly scanned the page. ' "I arrived at Linlithgow," ' I continued, echoing the dead Scotsman's words, ' "and delivered His Grace's message. The Queen was closeted with the Earl of Angus and I was surprised for the Queen had already received news from the battle field about her husband's death. I was ordered to take refreshment in the hall. An hour later the Earl of Angus came down and said riders had been despatched to collect the King and bring him to the Queen. I must confess I was ill at ease. The Queen's demeanour had surprised me: she was not a distressed widow who had lost her husband or a Queen who had seen the flower of her army massacred. Sick at heart, I hurried back to Kelso. I arrived early in the morning and, after diligent enquiries, learnt that Harrington had fled whilst men from the Hume and Chattan clans, common soldiers, had taken the King away." '

I looked up in astonishment.

'But, Master, in the confession you showed me in the tower, Selkirk claimed Harrington was also taken by the soldiers.' I snatched up the second piece of cream-coloured parchment and scanned it quickly. 'Yes, look, it's written here!' I threw it back. 'So, what is the truth?'

Benjamin grinned and picked up Selkirk's secret confession.

'The truth is in this: Selkirk confessed that Harrington had fled. I translated it but then began to wonder. So I copied it out again, only this time changing it slightly to make it appear that Harrington, too, was captured.' Benjamin tossed Selkirk's confession on to the charcoal brazier. I watched the flames lick the corners of the paper and turn it to smouldering black ash.

'Why?' I asked. 'What's so important about Harrington?'

'Well,' Benjamin leaned back in his chair and looked up at the ceiling, 'when I was studying Selkirk's original poem, I remembered certain letters in particular had been capitalised. Now,' he continued, 'when I talked to Selkirk in the Tower, he said that he was a good poet, and so was the King. He also mentioned a court troubadour called Willie Dunbar.' Benjamin stared across at me. 'Have you ever read any of Dunbar's poetry?'

I shook my head.

'I did,' Benjamin answered, 'when I was in Scotland. Now Dunbar is one of these crafty fellows who likes to garnish his verse with subtle devices and secret codes which hold special meanings to the chosen few. Selkirk's poem borrowed such a device.' Benjamin picked it up. 'I have looked at this again,' he continued. 'I find it strange that the following letters in certain words were capitalised: the "L" in lion; the "N" in Now, the "S" in Stands, as well as the first letters of "In Sacred Hands". Put all these words together and you get "The Lion Now Stands In Sacred Hands." '

'That's not possible!' I whispered.

'Oh, yes, it is.' Benjamin tossed the poem across and I perceived the cunning subtlety of Selkirk's verse.

'But Selkirk said men from the Hume and Chattan clans took James away?'

Benjamin rose and clapped his hands. 'No, he doesn't. All he repeats is what he was told at the abbey. This confession was to demonstrate James survived the battle as well as the evil intentions of Queen Margaret and the Earl of Angus. However, the message left in code in the poem is for the close friends of James who would realise that the King had fled abroad.'

'In other words,' I interrupted, 'Margaret's soldiers, mere commoners who would keep their mouths shut, took from Kelso Abbey a man dressed in royal armour. Of course,' I murmured, 'Sir John Harrington!'

Benjamin nodded. 'Who knows? James may have given him the chain round his waist as well as other royal insignia. Harrington sacrificed himself for James!'

'And the King?' I interrupted. 'What did happen to him?'

Benjamin made a face. 'What could he do? Announce that he had survived the battle? Who would believe him? The royal corpse was supposedly in England. James had been rejected by his wife and, even if he did come forward, he would have only been arrested as an imposter and secretly executed in some dungeon. Don't forget, Roger, James had just suffered one of the most disastrous defeats in Scottish history. He would not be popular.'

'But where is he?' I asked. 'What are these "Sacred Hands"?'

'When I was in Scotland,' Benjamin replied, 'I heard stories about James's romantic dreams of being a crusader. God knows, he may have gone to Outremer and joined one of the crusading orders.'

'So you changed the confession to protect him?'

'Of course. Uncle is very cunning. He may have begun to speculate on who actually did escape from Kelso. Our noble Henry had a passionate hatred for the Scottish King. If he even half-suspected James had survived and might still be alive, his agents would hunt him down.'

'I wonder if Queen Margaret really knows the truth?'

Benjamin shrugged. 'Perhaps she suspects it. The soldiers she sent would have killed the man they took from Kelso. Perhaps her exiled husband sent her a secret message.' He stirred excitedly in his chair. 'That's why,' he whispered, 'she was frightened: the reason she fled Scotland — not because she murdered her husband, but because she has a suspicion he may still be alive!' Benjamin refilled his cup. 'Do you remember when we left the Tower for St Theodore's? I said I had been to see the Queen about Sir John Harrington — I acted the hypocrite, the dumb fool. I claimed that the Regent had asked me if I knew of Harrington's whereabouts. Had he fled to England? I put this to the Queen. My God, you should have seen her pale!' Benjamin beat the top of the table excitedly. 'The bitch may think it's safe now to return to Scotland but the fear will never leave her.'

'Why didn't you tell Catesby this?'

'For the same reason I never told Uncle — something may have gone wrong. Murder is still murder, Roger. What difference does it make if it was Harrington or James?' Benjamin picked up the pieces of manuscript from the table before him.

'Don't burn them, Master!' I shouted. 'Let me have them!'

Benjamin paused and pushed them across the table.

'Take them, Roger,' he whispered, 'but hide them well. They could be your death warrant.'

We spent the rest of the day carousing. We had fought the good fight, finished the race, kept faith with our masters and, though he did not know it, with King James of Scotland. Oh, we became the Cardinal's friends, swore to be his servants in peace and war but we also secretly pledged each other to watch 'Dear Uncle' most closely. We were committed to his service and the White Rose murders were only the first of a succession of mysteries.

Epilogue

So, this story is finished, yet there's more to come: conspiracies at court, treason in both high and low places and, of course, bloody affray and secret assassination. They've dogged my steps like bloodhounds down the years. If I have time you will meet them all — subtle, crafty men and women with fire in their eyes and the devil in their hearts.

Now there goes my chaplain again, jumping up and down on his stool. 'You think every woman's a wench!' the hypocrite exclaims. 'Every girl a whore!'

He's a bloody liar! Will he mention the poor girls I feed in the village? Or that I've made many women laugh and none of them cry? No woman has received discourtesy at my hands. Nor have I broken any hearts or laughed at their tears, even though love has shattered my heart too many times to remember. He's never met Katerina. Oh, sweet Lord, there was witchcraft in her lips. I still weep at the very thought of her . . .

And why do I write my memoirs? To exorcise the spectres which still haunt my soul. Tonight, when the sun sets and the moon hides furtively behind the clouds, the ghosts will return, led by Murder on his death-pale horse. They will sweep up the causeway and gather once more under the casement window of my chamber.

I also tell my story as an edification for the young. To correct the laxity in morals, and as a warning against the dangers of hard drink and soft women. Oh, I wish Benjamin could tell his story. I wish I could see him just once more. He would understand. He would deplore the

241

depravity of our times, the allure of the flesh, the brave, empty promises of the world. Oh, the times! Oh, the festering lies! Oh, the lack of morals! Oh, for Fat Margot and a deep-bowled cup of sack!

Author's Note

We must remember Shallot is, by his own confession, a great teller of tall tales, but he may not be a liar. Indeed, many of his claims can be corroborated by historical fact. James IV of Scotland was a lusty man who had a string of paramours, and his extra-marital affairs did alienate his wife Margaret Tudor. James was warned by visions before the Flodden campaign and many historians think these visions were the work of his wife. We also know James dressed a number of royal look-alikes in his own coat of arms. A few historians mention that as many as a dozen 'fake Jameses' fought at Flodden. Surrey did find a body without the customary penitential chain around its waist: the corpse was restored by embalmers and sent south for Henry to view.

The body was never returned to Scotland. In Elizabeth's reign certain builders found it in a room in a palace and played football with the mummified head until a compassionate vicar took the remains and had them buried in the crypt of St Andrew's Undershaft. According to Walter Scott, when the moat of Hume Castle was drained in the eighteenth century, a skeleton was found with a chain wrapped round its waist. The Humes were close allies of Queen Margaret. Some historians maintain they were the actual assassins who killed James after Flodden and dumped his corpse in the castle moat. For years there were rumours and gossip that James had not died at Flodden.

Shallot is correct − Margaret Tudor was 'trouble in petticoats'. The facts of her passionate liaison with Gavin

Douglas are as described in these memoirs, as is his version of the events surrounding the birth of Alexander, Duke of Ross. Margaret did return to Scotland where she enjoyed many happy years, causing as much trouble as possible under the fraternal eye of Bluff King Hal. She fought for and gained a divorce from Angus and then promptly chose the Earl of Lennox as her third husband. She caused more confusion in Scotland than the combined armies of her brother!

Bluff King Hal and Cardinal Thomas Wolsey are accurately described in Shallot's memoirs. For a while, the Cardinal wielded total power in England and many alleged he used the black arts of a famed witch, Mabel Brigge, to control King Henry. Nevertheless, as Carolyn Seymour points out in her excellent biography of King Henry VIII, the prophecies about his being the Mouldwarp proved to be correct. At least fifty thousand people were executed in Henry's thirty-six-year reign. The pretensions of the House of York were also viewed as a major threat to the Tudor crown and, before he died, King Henry VIII had almost succeeded in wiping out every noble family with Yorkist blood in its veins.

King Francis I of France was as lascivious as Shallot describes. However, Shallot's remarks about his own close association with Anne Boleyn, his amorous liaisons with Queen Elizabeth and Catherine de Medici of France, not to mention his theft of the great diamond of Canterbury are, as he says, the stuff of other stories.